Homicide Related

— A Ryan Dooley Mystery —

Norah McClintock

Red Deer P R E S S

Homicide Related: A Ryan Dooley Mystery
Copyright © 2009 Norah McClintock

5 4 3 2 1

Published by
Red Deer Press
A Fitzhenry & Whiteside Company
www.reddeerpress.com

Edited for the Press by Peter Carver
Cover design by Jacquie Morris and Delta Embree,
Liverpool, Nova Scotia
Text design by Tanya Montini
Printed and bound in Canada for Red Deer Press

Financial support provided by the Canada Council, and the Government of
Canada through the Book Publishing Industry Development Program (BPIDP).

Canada Council   Conseil des Arts
for the Arts   du Canada

Library and Archives Canada Cataloguing in Publication
McClintock, Norah
Homicide related / Norah McClintock.
(A Ryan Dooley mystery)
ISBN 978-0-88995-431-1
I. Title. II. Series: McClintock, Norah . Ryan Dooley mystery.
PS8575.C62H64 2009   jC813'.54   C2008-908114-5

United States Cataloging-in-Publication Data
McClintock, Norah.
Homicide related : a Ryan Dooley mystery / Norah McClintock.
[256] p. : cm.
Summary: Ryan Dooley continues to struggle against circumstances
that would defeat most teenagers. Somehow, though, Dooley is able
to work his way through the immense hazards in his life and emerge,
not unscathed, but with his integrity intact.
ISBN: 978-0-8899-5431-1 (pbk.)
1. Mystery and detective stories. I. Title.
[Fic] dc22   PZ7.M33Hom 2009

Acknowledgments

To the girls,
more precious than they know.

One

It was Monday, another soul-sucking, numbness-inducing day exactly like every other day, except for a single moment that ambushed Dooley like a pop quiz. Dooley didn't like pop quizzes. He didn't like surprises. This particular moment was like a pop quiz in his favorite subject, the kind of quiz where you think, hey, no problem. All you have to do is circle the right answer: A, B, C, or D. You whiz through it so fast and with so much confidence that you're out of there before anyone else, convinced you aced it, until sometime in the space between when you downed your pencil and when you have that class again, it hits you: They were trick questions.

The day started like this:

He got up at seven after going to bed a mere six hours earlier because Kevin, the shit manager—*shift* manager—at the video store where he worked insisted that everyone—*and that includes you, Dooley*—close at least one weeknight every week. Closing meant nudging all the lingering customers out the door as soon as possible after midnight (Dooley still hadn't figured out just how bored or desperate or just plain disorganized a person had to be to show up at a video store at five minutes to twelve in the first place) and then straightening the shelves and mopping the floors while the shift manager—usually, unfortunately, Kevin—counted the cash and prepped the bank deposit, which, in turn, meant not getting out of the store until twelve-thirty at the earliest—most nights it was more like a quarter to one—and that meant not getting home until sometime after one and having to unwind without being able to indulge in any of the fun unwinding activities that he used to enjoy. Big whoop.

After dragging himself out of bed, he went downstairs for breakfast. On a Monday morning, it was usually just Dooley and his uncle in the kitchen, unless Jeannie, his uncle's friend—which is how Dooley's uncle had introduced her to Dooley: friend, not girlfriend—had stayed over. If she had, then either Dooley had the kitchen to himself because his uncle was still upstairs with Jeannie, or he'd find her in the kitchen reading the business section of the newspaper (she owned and managed two ladies' wear stores), her perfume mixing with the smell of coffee, while Dooley's uncle tackled the local news, which consisted almost exclusively of crime stories (he was a retired cop). This morning, it had been just Dooley and his uncle, and his uncle had been in the same crappy mood he'd been in for the past couple of days. Dooley kept waiting for him to explain what he was so pissed off about, but so far he'd kept that to himself while he carped about everything and anything. Like: "When the hell are you going to return those library books? I thought you finished that assignment."

Which was true. Dooley had finished it. And what a fun exercise it had been—one thousand riveting words about the causes of one of the dullest wars in history, the first *big one*.

"I'll get to it," Dooley said.

"When?" His uncle snapped the word at him. The guy should have been a reporter—his favorite words were who, what, when, where, and why (as in, Why the hell did you [fill in the blank with some dumb-ass thing Dooley had allegedly done]?).

"When I get a chance," Dooley said.

"I saw the slip. They're due tomorrow."

"So I'll take them back tomorrow."

"Why don't you take them back today? You're done with them, aren't you?"

"I said I'd take care of it," Dooley said.

"You should have taken care of it yesterday. That's when you handed in your assignment, correct?"

Jesus, it was like he was living with a cantankerous, semi-senile old granny instead of a supposedly on-the-ball uncle.

"I was working yesterday," Dooley said. In fact, he'd done a double shift, taking one from Linelle because she'd asked him and because he owed her—which his uncle knew because he was worse than a probation officer the way he kept tabs on Dooley.

"Always with the excuses," his uncle muttered.

Dooley looked across the table at him. His uncle was forty-nine years old, retired four years. He was a little shorter than Dooley and had more weight on him, but all of it was one hundred percent muscle. He wasn't a cop anymore. He was a small-businessman, but that didn't mean he'd let himself go. No, he ate right (except on poker night), worked out regularly—weights and cardio—and didn't take shit from anyone, ever. He could be one scary dude. He could also, like now, be a major pain in the ass. Dooley could have explained to his uncle—again—that he wasn't making excuses. He could have said, what's the problem; the books aren't even due yet. He could have told him, even if they were due, the fine is only thirty cents a day, and he could handle that easily; he had a job; that's where he had been for six-and-a-half hours yesterday. He could have said, back the fuck off. But that wouldn't have ended it. On the contrary, it would have been like trying to put out a smoldering fire with a can of kerosene. Besides, this wasn't about a couple of library books. It wasn't even about Dooley. It was about something that, so far, his uncle didn't want to talk about. As Dooley's therapist would have put it, it wasn't Dooley's monkey. So Dooley got up, rinsed his cereal bowl and put it into the dishwasher, and moved on to the next thrill of the day, which was:

School.

He hated school. He always had, even back when it consisted of finger painting and counting. He couldn't figure out what use he would ever have for geometry or trigonometry or even, let's be honest, French. He liked to read— when he was locked up that time, his uncle had brought him a book every time he came to visit, and Dooley had read them all. But he hated the reading they were assigned in school, always stuff they were supposed to learn a lesson from, the teacher always asking what the theme was, like that's what people's lives were about, instead of chance and mischance and good intentions gone all to hell. He only stuck with school because it was a condition they'd put on him when he was released, along with holding down a job, staying away from drugs, alcohol, weapons, and baseball bats, and attending regular counseling—all of which he did, finding, to his surprise, that going to school was the hardest to comply with. The school administration hadn't been exactly delighted when his uncle had enrolled him. Mr. Rektor, the A-to-L vice-principal, did everything he could to encourage Dooley to pack it in. He probably would have liked nothing better than to see Dooley in trouble again. His teachers all knew about his past, even though they probably shouldn't. One of them, a new female teacher who lived in the suburbs, had yet to make eye contact with him; a couple of times when he'd gone up to her desk to turn in an assignment, she had visibly cringed, as if she were afraid he was going to attack her. His history teacher was openly hostile to him. Dooley had lost count of the number of times the guy had been writing on the chalkboard, his back to the class, and someone had acted up, maybe stage-whispered some remark that made everyone laugh, and who did the teacher's eyes go to when he whirled around to locate the troublemaker? Yup. Dooley. The only class he even remotely liked was phys. ed., and that was mostly because he could work off some of what he was feeling. The gym teacher was a tough old guy who looked like he might have been a drill sergeant. He yelled at all the guys, not just Dooley. It was like being back inside.

Worse than school was homework, and he was looking at a gigantic heap of it when he stepped outside again at three-twenty that afternoon. At least, that's what he was looking at, at first. And then there it was—that pop-quiz moment. It wasn't even multiple choice. It came down to A or B—pay attention to this or pay attention to that. It seemed dead easy.

He had just left school through one of the side doors when he saw a car pull up half a block away—a midnight blue Jag convertible with the top down, because it was an astonishingly warm day for early November and the sun was brilliant in the clear blue sky overhead. Dooley stopped short on the school steps, surprising the kid behind him, who rammed into him and swore at him: Why the fuck didn't he watch where he was going? Dooley turned and, okay, there was no point in denying it, he got a kick out of way the snarl and bluster died on the kid's face when he saw who he'd rammed into. He got even more of a kick out of the kid's muttered apology. He turned from the kid to stare again at the Jag. Even at this distance he could see that the guy behind the wheel had more going for him than just the vehicle he was driving. He also had a haircut that looked like it was windproof. He'd probably paid a bundle for it so that it would lie down where it was supposed to, when it was supposed to, no matter what. His teeth were so white that they gleamed like a porcelain gash across the middle of his face when he flashed a smile at his passenger. The fact that he was driving a Jag meant that he was probably

loaded—or, more likely, Daddy and Mommy were. Also—
and this was where Dooley's stomach did a backward dou-
ble-gainer—he had the prettiest girl Dooley had ever seen
sitting right up there beside him.

Beth.

Her head was turned to the driver, but Dooley would
have recognized her even if she'd had her back to him and
she was a full block away. He continued down the steps and
onto the sidewalk. The driver of the car was saying something, and Beth was laughing. Dooley stepped back a pace
so that he was out of sight while he tried to figure out what
it all meant. What was Beth doing with that guy? Who the
hell was he? What were they doing *here*?

Then, behind him, someone—a woman—said, "Excuse
me" in a soft voice.

Dooley tore his eyes away from Beth and the guy with the
porcelain mouth and turned toward the sound of the voice.

And there it was—suddenly he had two females claiming
his attention, and all he had to do was pick one and let the
other one go.

It was a no-brainer. He turned back to see what Beth was
doing. He was aware of the soft voice behind him, but the
blood was pounding so loudly in his ears that he couldn't
make out the words. He could barely feel his feet on the
sidewalk, either. He was looking at the Jag but, from where
he was standing now, all he could see was the front bumper
and the hood. Beth hadn't appeared yet. She must still be in
the car with that guy. What was she doing?

He started toward the car, but found himself tugged backward and felt something—a slip of paper—being pressed into his hand. He glanced over his shoulder, annoyed. The voice speeded up, the words coming at him in a breathless rush, like the woman who was talking was afraid he was going to walk away before she finished whatever it was she had to say.

He heard a car door slam.

Beth stepped into sight down the block. Dooley caught his breath as he waited to read the expression on her face. She smiled. She seemed glad to see him. And, boy, he was always glad to see her. She had lively brown eyes, and hair the same color, only glossy. She had creamy white skin and full pink lips, and she was nice and slim.

He crumpled the slip of paper, let it fall to the ground, and started to walk away. Something closed on his arm again, and again he felt himself being hooked backward. The crumpled paper was pressed into his hand again. Jesus, what was the matter with her; why didn't she leave him alone? He jerked his hand away and strode toward Beth, jamming the piece of paper into his pocket this time, thinking he would toss it later. His heart pounded. His eyes and thoughts were on Beth and only her. He wanted to throw his arms open and see if she would walk into them, but at the last minute he was afraid to, because what if she didn't? She came straight to him and slipped her arms around his waist. He inhaled the familiar scent of her hair, her skin, the soap she used, the shampoo, and then, he couldn't have stopped himself even if he'd wanted to, he kissed her and slid his arms around her and marveled, not for the first time, at how soft she was and how firm, too, underneath the long sweater she was wearing.

"Surprised to see me?" she said.

"Yeah," Dooley said, and that was the truth. "You skipping school?" Beth went to a private school, girls only. She actually seemed to like it. She took school seriously, too. But her classes ended twenty-five minutes later than his, so there was no way she could be all the way down here so early, even if someone—Mr. Midnight Blue Jag—had given her a lift.

"There was a faculty meeting," she said. "They let us out early, so I decided to surprise you." She glanced around him. "Who were you were talking to?"

Dooley turned and saw that the woman was standing exactly where he had left her. He gave her a sharp look. Her eyes met his and a little smile played across her lips. She nodded almost imperceptibly before turning and walking away.

"Just some woman," Dooley said.

"What did she want?"

"She was lost. She wanted directions," Dooley said. He glanced at her again. She was a block away now, looking small and getting smaller with every step she took. "Who's the guy in the Jag?"

Beth's cheeks turned pink, like she'd been caught out.

"That's Nevin," she said.

"Nevin?" Who the hell was Nevin? Dooley had never heard the name before. And what kind of name was Nevin anyway? "Who's he?"

"A guy I know. From school."

"From school? I thought your school was girls only."

"I don't mean he *goes* to my school," Beth said. "He's on the debating team at his school." Beth was on her school's debating team. Dooley didn't understand why. He didn't understand why anyone would want to be on a debating team. But Beth said it gave her experience in public speaking and in thinking on her feet. She said they were important life skills, and it would be good for her to know how to do both things. "We debate all kinds of schools, Dooley, not just other girls' schools. We debate boys' schools, co-ed private schools, even public schools."

"So, what, you know him pretty well?" Dooley said.

"I guess. His parents are friends of my parents—well, of my mom's." So she didn't know him just from school. "You should see him in action." Dooley bet he was really something, especially with that Jag. "He's amazing. He wins almost every debate he enters. We get together sometimes and take each other on."

"Take each other on?"

"We put a bunch of be-it-resolveds into a hat—you know, be it resolved that history is the academic branch of propaganda, or be it resolved that citizens should be required by law to vote—and then we debate them raw."

"Raw?" He didn't like the sound of that.

"That's what Nevin calls it. It means without any preparation. I've learned a lot from him."

He wondered why she'd never mentioned that before. She'd never mentioned Nevin, either.

"This getting together and taking each other on," he said. "When does that happen?"

She shrugged. "Just whenever."

"Do you do it at school?"

"Sometimes. Sometimes we do it at his place. Or my place."

"Your place?"

She pulled away from him a little, and the warmth that her body had imprinted on him cooled almost instantly.

"You're not jealous, are you, Dooley?" she said, frowning up at him. "He's just someone I know. He gave me a lift, that's all. I came over here to see *you*. I thought we could go to the library and do our homework together. How about it?"

Dooley's chest, which had been so tight that he could hardly breathe when he'd seen Beth sitting in the Jag, slowly relaxed. He pulled Beth close and noticed right away that, as usual, she didn't resist. Sometimes they held each other for what seemed like forever. It was the best feeling in the world, better even than being high. If there was something between her and Nevin, she would have been pulling away from him, wouldn't she? He would have been able to feel it—wouldn't he?

Then she did it. She wriggled free of him.

"So," she said. "Are we on?"

Dooley reached into his pocket, feeling like a pathetic loser because now he had to do something that he bet Nevin never had to do. He had to call his uncle to ask—*ask,* for Christ's sake—if he could go to the library because, as his uncle never tired of telling him, they had a deal. The deal was: Dooley went to school and then, unless he was scheduled to work, he went straight home. Any deviation from the deal required a phone call and the third degree.

He pulled out the cell phone that his uncle had finally agreed to let him have to replace the stupid pager that was all his uncle had allowed at first.

"Yeah," Dooley said when his uncle asked him if he couldn't just as easily do his homework at home, meaning where his uncle could call him on the home phone and know, when Dooley answered it, exactly where he was, whereas with a cell phone, well, who really knew where anyone was? "Yeah, I could do it at home. But I'm with Beth."

Beth took the phone from him and, with a smile in her voice that outdid the one on her face, said, "Hi, Mr. McCormack." She chatted with Dooley's uncle for a minute and laughed and said, yes, she bet it was hard to get used to, before finally handing the phone back to Dooley. "He wants to talk to you again," she said.

Dooley put the phone to his ear.

"You gonna at least return those books?" his uncle said.

Jesus. Dooley said goodbye and dropped his phone into his pocket.

"You just bet what's hard to get used to?" he said to Beth.

"The thought of you in a library."

Dooley started to say he didn't know what was so hard about that. His uncle knew he went to the library; where did he think he'd gotten those library books he kept nagging Dooley to return? But he was interrupted when his cell phone rang again. He checked the display. J. Eccles.

Jeffie.

What the—?

Jeffie was never good news. But Dooley took the call

anyway because Jeffie was one of those people, if you ignored him, he'd keep calling and calling until you finally found yourself answering just so you could tell him to leave you the fuck alone. The first thing he said to Jeffie was, "How did you get this number?"

"I heard where you were working," Jeffie said. "There's this girl there." Dooley bet he was referring to Linelle. "I told her how long I've known you and some of the shit we did together—nothing you probably wouldn't tell her yourself." Uh-huh, Dooley thought. "Hey, is she with someone, because she sounds—"

"What do you want?" Dooley said.

He listened to what Jeffie had to say and then thought about his request while Jeffie moaned about how important it was and about the shit he'd be in, clear up to his mouth, maybe even over his head; he'd be drowning in it, if Dooley didn't help him out.

"You owe me, Dooley," Jeffie said. "If it hadn't been for me, you would have ended up just like Tyler."

Just like Tyler? No way, Dooley thought. But, yeah, he owed Jeffie. He owed him big-time.

"Okay," he said. "Okay, I get the picture. I'll see if I can get away." Jeffie didn't like the *if* part. Well, too bad for him. "I'll do my best, but I can't guarantee it," Dooley said and then held the phone away from his ear—when it came to bitching and moaning, Jeffie was a champion.

"Can't guarantee what?" Beth said when Dooley dropped his cell phone back into his pocket. "Who was that?"

"No one," Dooley said. When she gave him a look—

13

where had she heard that before?—he said, "Really, it's nothing." There were some things that it was better she didn't know, especially if she was learning stuff from a guy named Nevin who drove a Jag.

"Oh," she said. "Before I forget—I finally got my own cell phone." She'd had a cell phone before, but her mother had paid for it and had got into the habit of borrowing it from time to time, which had led to a major screwup one time before Dooley realized what was going on. He'd punched in Beth's number, had assumed the hello was hers, and had started in being cute—he thought. It turned out the hello had come from Beth's mother, and she was not amused. "Here's the number." She wrote it down on a scrap of paper she tore from her school agenda. He put it in his pocket.

■ ■ ■

Five hours later, Dooley was dancing from foot to foot and wishing he was still with Beth, partly because there was nothing better than being with her, partly because, if he was with her, he wouldn't be freezing his ass off down in this godforsaken ravine, and mostly (he hated to admit it) because if he was with her, it meant that Nevin couldn't be. His hands were buried in the pockets of his jean jacket and he was thinking he should have put on something warmer. It had been bright and sunny after school, but then the air had started to change. A sheet of cloud had rolled across the sky like a tarp across stadium turf, signaling fun over. In the past couple of hours, it had turned bitingly cold. The wind whipped away the protective layer of warmth that came off Dooley's body, leaving the dampness in the air to close in until he felt like he was encased in a film of ice. He looked around. Where the hell was Jeffie? On the phone, he'd told Dooley ten o'clock. It was twenty after already and Dooley was still waiting. And why had Jeffie insisted on this place? Why outdoors? Why not a nice, warm restaurant? Even a not-so-nice restaurant would have been fine, just so long as it was heated.

Dooley caught movement out of the corner of his eye and turned toward it. He tensed up immediately. There, fifteen or twenty meters away up the path, was an animal of some kind. A raccoon, maybe? No, a dog. Jesus, a big one, too, and it was coming Dooley's way. He scanned the ravine for human life, specifically, a dog owner dangling a leash from one hand, but he didn't see anyone. In Dooley's experience, dogs in dark, out-of-the-way places were like people in dark, out-of-the-way places. You never knew what they were doing there or what they might do. But a dog with an owner and a leash— that was a different story. It was almost comforting. Well, most of the time it was. There was a guy who used to live in Dooley's old neighborhood. He strutted around with a pair of fight-hungry pit bulls at the end of a couple of chains. There was nothing comforting about that.

Dooley averted his eyes from the dog and hoped it would change direction or walk on by. It didn't. It stopped. Dooley ventured a quick peek. The dog was standing maybe ten meters up the path now, its eyes focused on Dooley, its body rigid. Dooley looked away quickly and forced himself to breathe in and out at regular intervals. He tried to make like a tree or a rock, something immobile and uninteresting to a dog. Okay, so maybe a tree wasn't the best idea.

The dog didn't move. It didn't come down the path toward Dooley, which was good, but it didn't retreat either. It seemed to be studying Dooley. Goddamn Jeffie. Dooley would give him five more minutes, less if the dog so much as twitched in Dooley's direction, and that was it. It had been a major pain in the ass to get here in the first place. His uncle had wanted to know where the hell he was going at nine-thirty on a school night. Yeah, well, Dooley had been prepared for that one.

"I'm going to drop off those library books you've been nagging me about."

"The library's closed."

"They have a drop box. The books are due tomorrow. I don't want to forget."

"You told me you'd take care of it," his uncle said.

"And I'm going to. Right now. What's the matter? You don't trust me?"

His uncle fixed him with that used-to-be-a-cop look of his that was supposed to tell Dooley that, no, as a matter of fact, he didn't.

"Give me a break," Dooley said. "I'm holding down a job. I'm going to school, and so far I'm passing everything. You gonna give me a hard time for the rest of my life?"

His uncle stuck with his cop look, but Dooley had been around him long enough by now to know that he wasn't the one-hundred-percent tyrant that he worked hard at making himself out to be.

"I spent two-and-a-half hours in the library this afternoon writing an essay for English," Dooley said.

"You couldn't have returned the books then?"

"We were at the reference library. You can't borrow books from there and you can't return them there. Besides, my brain feels like it's gonna explode. I thought I'd take a walk, clear my head, return the books. That's all."

"At nine-thirty at night?" his uncle said.

Boy, once a cop …

"You want to come with me, hold my hand?" Dooley said.

"Yeah, and maybe keep you out of trouble?"

"Jesus," Dooley said, starting to pull off his jacket. "Forget it, okay? I'll do it after school tomorrow, *if* I remember." He wrestled free of the jacket, tossed it onto the back of a chair, and turned to leave the room.

Worst case: Jeffie would have to wait a day.

"Where were you planning to walk?" his uncle said pretty much on schedule, which is to say, when Dooley was halfway down the hall on his way to the stairs. One thing (but probably not the main thing) that Dooley had learned over the past few months was that a little credibility goes a long way. When he had first come to live with his uncle, he'd had none. He'd been, in the eyes of his uncle, a fuck-up—someone who had screwed up so much and sunk so low that he was going to have to both eat and shovel shit for an eternity, and smile while he was doing it, just to prove that he could take whatever the straight-and-narrow world chose to dish out to him. Well, he'd done that. He'd paid those almighty dues. He'd abided by each and every

17

condition dictated by his uncle and the court. And he had not, repeat not, fallen into that major sinkhole a while back. He'd left that to the rich kid.

Dooley didn't turn when his uncle asked him where he was planning to walk. He just glanced over his shoulder, like, what difference did it make now?

"I was going to go to the library and then walk around and get some air. If I'm not at school, I'm at work. If I'm not at work, I'm here." Well, most of the time. Sometimes he got sprung. Sometimes he got to be with Beth.

And then there it was, that heavy sigh, the sweet sound of his uncle caving.

"Be back by eleven at the latest," his uncle said, laying out terms so that it was clear who was in charge.

"Forget it," Dooley said. "It's not important."

"Jesus, Ryan," his uncle said, exasperated. That was one thing Dooley could always count on: The pinched look on his uncle's face and the impatient snap in his voice every time Dooley didn't do whatever his uncle had it in mind that he should do. "You want to take a walk and return those damned books, then do it. All I'm saying is, be back by eleven."

"Well ..." Dooley said, thinking it over. "Okay."

Down in the ravine now, books safely deposited into the library's drop box, Dooley eased his arm out slowly—he wasn't making any sudden moves as long as that dog was still there—and glanced at his watch. The only way he was going to be home by eleven was if he started back no later than twenty to. But what was the point in waiting that long?

Jeffie had said ten. It was twenty-five after now—no, make that twenty-six-and-counting after. Fuck it.

"Dooley. Hey, Dooley!"

Dooley turned and saw a familiar figure scrambling down the path toward him. Jeffie, looking thinner and smaller than Dooley remembered, his baggy jeans so low on his hips that they looked like they were going to slide right off, his jacket—leather, Dooley noticed—unzipped, its cuffs half covering Jeffie's hands. The dog saw him, too. It barked and growled. Jeffie stopped, bent down, picked up something— a rock?—and whipped it at the animal. He must have hit the mark, too, because the dog yelped and ran off in the other direction. Dooley shook his head.

"What if you'd pissed it off and it attacked you?" he said when Jeffie was close enough to hear him.

"Then I would have blasted it," Jeffie said.

Whoa.

"You have a gun?" Dooley said. No way did he want to be around anyone who was armed. Not now. Not ever again.

"Relax," Jeffie said. "It's a figure of speech." Dooley wasn't sure that his English teacher would agree, but that was another difference between Dooley and Jeffie: Dooley had an English teacher. "You think I'd take a chance like that?"

Dooley didn't know what to think. Except for a brief chance meeting on the street at the beginning of the summer, he hadn't seen or spoken to Jeffie in a long time.

"Besides," Jeffie said, "I showed him who's boss, didn't I?"

Right.

"What took you so long to get here?" Dooley said. "You

19

said ten. It's nearly ten-thirty." His voice echoed a little down under the bridge where he was standing, and he was startled to hear how much he sounded like his uncle. Was that where he was headed?

"You know how Teresa can be," Jeffie said.

"You still with her?" Dooley said, surprised. Teresa was small and dark and, when she was out in public with Jeffie, she came across as kind of cute and helpless. But Dooley had seen them alone together. Then she was always at Jeffie for something: Why hadn't he remembered this, why hadn't he done that, always sounding like she was mad at him for something, which made Dooley wonder why she stayed with Jeffie. She sure didn't seem to like him much. More important, he couldn't figure out why Jeffie put up with her and her constant carping.

"Yeah," Jeffie said. "It's okay, I guess. She keeps saying we've been together long enough, we should make it legal. And she's been hinting around about a kid." Dooley couldn't figure how any of that fell into the category of okay. "She keeps telling me what a great father I'd be."

Dooley tried to picture Jeffie soothing a baby who was teething or giving it a bottle, but couldn't. For one thing, Jeffie was in the wrong line of work. Also, he was too impulsive. He'd get an idea to do something and, boom, off he'd go and do it without thinking about the stuff he was supposed to be doing in the first place. He wasn't that bright, either. Mostly it was because he had a learning disability—Dooley knew a lot of guys like that. He'd heard somewhere that a high percentage of guys who got into trouble had either a learning disability or some kind of mental problem. Jeffie couldn't spell for shit. He was a disaster at math. And his memory? Tell him a phone number or an address, and chances were he'd forget it within five minutes. Plus, he had no reference point, no idea what a father was, let alone a great one.

"You gonna do it?" Dooley said. "You gonna have a kid with her?"

"Are you crazy? I'm nineteen. Who wants a kid at nineteen?"

Dooley couldn't think of a single person.

"What about you?" Jeffie said.

"What about me?"

"You with someone?"

Dooley didn't answer. Jeffie was past tense. Beth was the present and, he hoped, the future. Jeffie didn't push it. He had other things on his mind.

"I really appreciate it, Dooley," he said. "You know I wouldn't have asked, but—"

"What's it for, Jeffie?"

Most of the time, Jeffie had a goofy-sweet expression on his face, like he was only catching about eighty percent of what was going on. But what you saw with Jeffie wasn't always what you got. Jeffie was no genius, but he was no fool, either. Nor was he a pushover. Anger flashed in his eyes.

"What difference does it make?" he said.

"I want it back, that's what," Dooley said. "If you're just gonna piss it away on some game—"

Jeffie bristled. When he was wearing his normal, befuddled expression, he looked harmless. Make him angry though, and you'd better watch out. But he didn't scare

21

Dooley, who had worked out exactly how many hours he'd put in at the video store to earn what he was about to hand over to Jeffie.

"You're good for it, right, Jeffie?" he said.

"I said I was, didn't I?" Jeffie was trying to make himself as tall as Dooley. They locked eyes for a few seconds, Jeffie breathing hard at first and then, gradually, slowing it down, maybe figuring he'd better back off a little if he wanted Dooley to deliver. "One week, that's all I'm asking," he said. "There's this guy, Dooley. He's one of those downtown guys, you know, in one of those big towers. He has more money than he knows what to do with. He was looking for a connection. The guy could be a gold mine. He likes to party. Hey, and you know what? He reminds me of you."

Right. Ryan Dooley, party animal. He wanted to tell Jeffie, I don't do that anymore; I've cleaned up my life. But what were the chances that Jeffie would believe him?

"This guy," Jeffie said. "If I deliver, I'm set."

"So why do you need me?" Dooley said.

Jeffie shrugged, as if it was no big deal, but Dooley caught the shadow of fear in his eyes. "There's this guy I owe. He's insistent, you know? He doesn't want to wait. If I tell him he's got nothing to worry about, all he needs is to give me another couple of days, he's gonna—"

"Okay, whatever," Dooley said, cutting it short. He didn't want to know what Jeffie was into. He just wanted to know that he wasn't flushing hard-earned money down the toilet. "I need it back, that's all I'm saying. Some people work for a living, Jeffie."

22

"I hear some people even live with ex-cops and go to school regular," Jeffie said, grinning at Dooley now, like, are you for real? "When are you up, Dooley? When are you gonna cut loose?" Meaning, when could Dooley go back to being Dooley? There were times—plenty of times—when Dooley thought about exactly that—when he would have the authorities off his case, when he could party again, when he could do all the things he used to do that made him forget all the crap in his life, that made him float, that took the sharp edges off, that made all the bullshit go away. If he wanted it, Jeffie could fix him up with something. It would be so easy.

"I'm out of that now," Dooley said.

"Right," Jeffie said, still grinning—see?—not believing him. Well, why would he? Why would anyone who had known Dooley then believe that he was different now? It irked him, though, to have put in all that time, to have done everything that he had these past few months, and then to come face-to-face with someone like Jeffie and realize that Jeffie didn't see the difference. What was the point?

Dooley dug into his jeans pocket and pulled out the money he had withdrawn from the bank. It was a good thing—good for Jeffie—that he had called when he did because what he wanted was more than the daily limit that Dooley was allowed to withdraw from an ATM. Twenty minutes later, the bank would have been closed and Jeffie would have been out of luck. But because he'd called when he had, Dooley still had time. He'd told Beth he wouldn't be long; he had to do an errand and he would meet her at the library. Then he'd gone and stood in a long line to get the money from one of two tellers working at a counter that had six teller stations. He held the money out to Jeffie now. Jeffie snatched it out of his hand, like he was afraid if he didn't, Dooley would change his mind. He started to count it.

"Hey, fuck you," Dooley said. Didn't anyone trust anyone anymore?

"You have any idea what kind of shit storm I'll be in if I'm short?" Jeffie said. He continued thumbing the bills. When he finished, he jammed the money into his pocket.

"You're *sure* you're good for it?" Dooley said.

"One hundred percent."

"Because I can find you if I have to, Jeffie. You don't want to mess me up over this, you really don't. You got that?"

Jeffie grinned, but even in the darkness Dooley caught the uncertainty in his eyes as Jeffie remembered the Dooley he used to know. Maybe that was a good thing. Maybe it would give Jeffie the right incentive to pay him back.

"Don't worry," Jeffie said. "You'll get your money. If you want, I'll deliver it to your house."

That was the last thing Dooley wanted.

"There's a restaurant across the street from where I work," he said. He told Jeffie where it was. "Meet me there on Monday, nine o'clock. That's when I get my break." He ignored Jeffie's amused smirk and checked his watch. Unless he wanted to have to come up with excuses, which he knew his uncle would never buy, he had to get moving. "Monday night, Jeffie. Nine o'clock. Be there, okay?"

"Yeah, sure," Jeffie said. "Don't sweat it."

"Jesus H. Murphy," Dooley's uncle said as he came into the kitchen the next morning. "Just because I own a dry-cleaning store"—in fact, he owned two—"that doesn't make me head laundress around here. The hamper is overflowing. When was the last time the thought of laundry crossed your mind, Ryan?"

"I'll get to it," Dooley said.

"Yeah? Like you're going to get to picking up the clothes all over your floor? There's a closet in your room, in case you didn't notice. A chest of drawers, too."

Dooley gulped down the last of his orange juice and stood up.

"You still want me to come by the store after school?"

"What for?"

What for? Dooley shook his head. "You told me a hundred times last week you're getting the offices painted." There were three offices at the back of his uncle's original store—his uncle's, the store manager's, and the bookkeeper's—all dingy and windowless. "You said you wanted me to move furniture for you."

"I have to go downtown today."

"How come?"

"I have a meeting with Larry." Larry Quayle, his uncle's financial advisor.

"I thought you met with him last week." In fact, Dooley was sure of it. He had come down to breakfast one morning and found his uncle sitting at the kitchen table with a bunch of documents spread out in front of him. He'd been grousing about interest rates and the stock market.

His uncle gave him a sharp look. "*You're* keeping tabs on *me* now?" he said.

Dooley rinsed his juice glass and set it in the dishwasher. Whatever had flown up his uncle's nose, Dooley wished he'd snort it out soon.

"I gotta go," he said. "I'm gonna be late. I'll go by the store after school and move the furniture, okay?"

His uncle grunted.

Two

The next night at supper Dooley said, "If you want me for anything later, you're going to have to get me on my cell phone."

His uncle looked up from his plate. "Why?" he said. "Is the phone here busted and no one bothered to tell me?"

"I have to go out," Dooley said. "And it's poker night, right?" Dooley knew for a fact it was, because it was written on the calendar on his uncle's fridge. His uncle and a bunch of his cop and ex-cop friends played whenever they could pull a game together. When that happened and Dooley's uncle left Dooley alone at home, he always called to check on him. He insisted on calling him on a regular phone line, never on his cell phone, his way of making sure Dooley was where he was supposed to be.

"Where were you planning to go?" his uncle said, his choice of tenses making it clear that it wasn't a done deal.

"To the library. I'm going to see if Beth can come with me."

"You two have been spending a lot of time at the library lately."

There was no pleasing some people. When he'd first met his uncle, it was always, "Read a book, for Christ's sake," as if lack of reading had landed Dooley in trouble in the first place. Now it was, "You spend a lot of time at the library," like that was the road to disaster.

"You know Beth," he said. "She's into school."

"She's a smart girl." His uncle liked Beth. He particularly liked that Beth wasn't the least bit intimidated by him. "Library closes at ten, correct?"

Dooley nodded.

"So be back at ten-thirty. Call me on my cell when you get in." The idea being that his uncle would be able to see from the readout on his phone that Dooley was actually home.

"Make it eleven," Dooley said. "Give me time to take Beth home."

His uncle gave Dooley a look that Dooley couldn't decide about. Either he was surprised that Dooley was so careful with Beth or he was suspicious, maybe wondering if Beth's mother was going to be out and that's why Dooley wanted to take Beth home, if maybe he'd take her home early—thinking that over and then probably wondering if Dooley would even make it to the library. Finally he nodded and said, "Eleven. I'm going to be expecting that call."

As soon as Dooley's uncle left for his poker game, Dooley phoned Beth.

"I have to go to the library to work on something for school," he said. "You want to come?"

"Again?" she said. "You were there last night—and the day before yesterday."

"I ended up not going last night," he said. "You know, on account of you couldn't make it because … what was the reason again?"

"I had an essay due today," she said. "And when I go to the library with you, I end up not getting a lot of work done."

Normally Dooley would have smiled at that—but not tonight.

"So how'd it go?" he said.

"The essay?"

"Yeah."

"I handed it in on time. What a relief."

Right, Dooley thought.

"You worked hard on it, huh?" he said. What he was remembering: He'd started for the library but had lost interest when Beth said she couldn't go. Instead, he'd drifted over to her building, thinking he'd maybe call her when he got there and see if her mother was out. If she was, maybe Beth would let him come up for a while. Or maybe she'd come down. It turned out that was a big mistake because while he was standing across the street so that he could look up at what he knew was her apartment, he saw a midnight blue Jag pull into the visitor parking area and a guy with perfect hair get out. Nevin. He went in through the main door and still hadn't come out again forty minutes later when Dooley's cell phone rang. It was his uncle, telling him, "Pick up some tonic water on your way home, would you? Jeannie's coming over."

"I always work hard on my essays," Beth said now.

"Come to the library with me," Dooley said. "I'll let you

29

work. I promise." He would let her do whatever she wanted, just so long as she was with him and not Nevin.

"I can't." There was a slight pause—what was that about?—before she said, "My history team is coming over."

"Your history team?"

"We got divided into teams for a class project. My team is meeting tonight."

"You didn't mention that," Dooley said, meaning, when he had talked to her last night. And, just like that, he was thinking about Nevin again. He wondered how long Nevin had been there last night and what he and Beth had been doing up there in Beth's place. He couldn't believe it was debating. If Dooley had been alone with her in her apartment, the absolute last thing he would ever be interested in was debating. He wouldn't even be interested in talking.

"We just got assigned today," Beth said. "Believe me, I'd rather go with you. But I can't."

History teams. What kind of dumb idea was that, especially when, from what Beth had told him, there was no team spirit at her school when it came to academics? The way Beth had described it, getting the best grades was practically a blood sport.

"There aren't any boys on your history team, are there?" he said. He tried to say it like he was kidding around.

"It's a girls' school, Dooley."

"A girls' school that debates *boys'* schools."

"The history teams are all girls," Beth said. She dropped her voice, and Dooley wondered if her mother was listening in. "Come on, Dooley. If I could go with you, I would. But—"

30

"If you can't, you can't," Dooley said. "It's no big deal." Well, it wasn't, was it? "I'll talk to you tomorrow."

He cleaned up the kitchen and then went up to his room to grab a sweatshirt. He ground to a halt when he passed the bathroom.

What the hell …?

The hamper had been overflowing this morning. Now it wasn't. He lifted the lid. It was empty. Shit. He'd promised his uncle but …

He went into his room. Double shit.

Not only had all the clothes been picked up off his floor, but there were two fresh piles of laundry on his bed. And, triple shit, there was a little heap of stuff on his dresser that hadn't been there this morning—a half-gone pack of gum, some coins, a couple of crumpled pieces of paper, damn, and a couple of rubbers. His uncle had emptied Dooley's pockets before doing his laundry. The thing Dooley couldn't figure out: Why his uncle hadn't rubbed his nose in it over supper. He picked up one of the pieces of paper, smoothed it out, and stared at it for a moment before folding it and tucking it into his jeans pocket. He grabbed the sweatshirt he had come upstairs to get, pulled it on, and went back downstairs. He locked the house and walked to the bus stop, where he got on the bus and rode it to within one block of the central library. He went straight to the information desk and asked one of the women behind it half a dozen questions about where he could find information for a project on global warming. The library was full of people—students and older people, plus a lot of people from different countries. A lot of *them* were using the rows and rows of computers on the main floor. Dooley thanked the woman behind the information desk and went upstairs. Half an hour later, he couldn't stand it anymore. He couldn't handle the library when he wasn't with Beth. She always worked hard, which made it easier for him to concentrate. Plus he could look at her. But when she wasn't there … He wondered about her history team. It had to be all girls, right? She went to an all-girls school.

He went back down to the main floor and got in line to leave. The library had an electronic security system, but it obviously left a lot to be desired because it also had guards posted at the exits to search briefcases, purses, backpacks, whatever you were carrying. One of the guards must have been on a break or something because the line-up for the only other guard was long. Everyone in it was speaking a foreign language. Dooley thought it was Chinese or maybe Korean, he wasn't sure which. Finally he got to the head of the line and opened his backpack for inspection. The guard barely glanced into it. Dooley left the library—which was still crowded—without saying a word to anyone. He stood outside for a moment, trying to decide what to do. He kept thinking about that slip of paper in his pocket. Should he call? What would he say? What would she say? Maybe he should just drop by and check things out. Jesus, every thing had been going so well. At least, that's what he'd thought. Why did it have to go and get all complicated?

Fuck it.

He walked to the bus stop and got on the first bus that

came along. It wasn't long before he was standing in front of an apartment building. He hesitated. Should he or shouldn't he? Do the right thing, Dooley. Don't screw things up.

He crossed the street and marched up the concrete-slab walk. A man was coming out just as Dooley reached the security door. Dooley turned away quickly, as if he had forgotten something. The man strode past him without looking back, which made it easy for Dooley to grab the security door before it clicked shut.

■ ■ ■

It was two minutes past eleven according to the clock on the stove by the time Dooley flicked on the kitchen light, picked up the phone, and punched in his uncle's cell phone number. His uncle answered on the third ring. Dooley heard music in the background. What was that—a radio? A sound system?

"Are you playing poker or having a party?" Dooley said.

"Go to bed," his uncle said, pissed off about something—again.

"Good luck with the cards," Dooley said. He hung up and then stood there for another minute, staring at the phone. He reached for the receiver again but pulled back at the last minute. Some things it was better not to know. Hell, a *lot* of things it was better not to know, even if trying not to think about them drove you crazy.

"How'd you make out at the game?" Dooley asked the next morning when his uncle came into the kitchen.

"I'm the one who does the checking up, not you," his

uncle said. He glanced at the coffeemaker. "So, how about it? You make it to the library?"

"What?" Dooley looked at his uncle, whose sharp gray eyes were drilling into him. What kind of question was that? "Yeah. Of course."

"How was it? You get any work done?" There was a hook in his voice, like he was trying to catch Dooley out.

"I got done what I set out to do," Dooley said. He was relieved when his uncle stopped staring at him and turned his attention to pouring himself a mug of coffee. "So, who all was there?"

His uncle, who was opening the fridge to get out the milk, glanced at him. "Where?"

"At the poker game."

"Why?"

"Just making conversation," Dooley said.

"Who wants conversation? I haven't had my coffee yet, for Christ's sake." He slammed the fridge door. "Don't you have school?"

Jesus, not only was he still in *that* mood, but he was in it to the power of ten. Dooley gulped down the last of his own coffee and put his mug in the dishwasher.

"I'm working tonight," he said. "I'll grab something to eat on my break. I'm off at eleven."

But his uncle was seated now and had the paper open to the metro section, to the crime stories, and was sipping his coffee as he read. Thank God for that.

■ ■ ■

At nine o'clock, Kevin came up to the cash where Dooley was working, slid the "Sorry, this cash is closed" sign onto the counter, and stood there watching while Dooley finished with a customer who was renting a couple of new releases. The other two customers in Dooley's line shuffled over to Linelle's cash. After Dooley had bagged the customer's movies and handed him the receipt, he turned to Kevin.

"What?" he said, thinking Kevin was going to ride him for a couple of freebies he'd given to a woman who had come in twenty minutes earlier itching for a fight. Seems she had rented some Disney piece of crap for her kid and had got *all the way home,* as she put it, making it sound like she'd trekked across a couple of continents instead of driving her SUV a total of four blocks (Dooley had checked her address in the computer) only to find that the case contained the director's cut of *Basic Instinct,* which fact she had discovered only when she went into the TV room to check on her kid (a twelve-year-old boy who, if you asked Dooley, had outgrown Disney a minimum of five years ago) and caught him replaying the scene where Sharon Stone uncrosses and crosses her legs. Not only was the woman *incensed* at the *incompetence* of whoever had put the wrong disk in the case (from the way she looked at Dooley, Dooley believed she had decided on him as the prime suspect) and the *slack attitude* of whoever had *neglected* to check that the case contained the correct disk (Dooley hadn't even been working the first time the woman was in the store), but she was also *appalled* that her son had been *exposed* to such *inappropriate* material. She had pointed dramatically to the kid, whom she'd dragged back to the store with her and who didn't look nearly as *appalled* as his mother. In fact, when Dooley winked at him, the kid had grinned, but boy, he'd wiped that look off his face when he sensed his mother turning in his direction. Well, whatever. Dooley apologized, even though he hadn't been at fault, and let her have two Disney movies, no charge. When she demanded that he double-check the disks, he not only managed to say "Sure, no problem," without a hint of sarcasm, but he'd showed her the disks so that she could reassure herself that her son wouldn't be subjected to any more *inappropriate material*. He'd even thrown in a free candy bar for the kid, mostly because he felt sorry for him.

But, no, that wasn't what Kevin wanted to talk to him about.

"Your uncle called," Kevin said, something in his tone telling Dooley that he was relieved his uncle hadn't showed up in person. Dooley's uncle scared the pants off Kevin. He had ever since that night Kevin had been up at cash, calling customers who had items out past the return date and telling them that they had exactly twenty-four hours to drop the items back into the store's drop box before a charge for the full replacement value would be applied to their credit cards. Dooley hadn't been paying attention other than to note that Kevin was talking to these particular customers like they were deadbeats who needed to be taught a lesson. Less than fifteen minutes later, the electronic buzzer above the door sounded and Dooley's uncle appeared in a T-shirt, pajama bottoms, and slippers, his hair wild, suggesting to Dooley that he had leapt into his car out of a sound sleep.

Dooley's first thought: I screwed up somehow and he's here to yell at me. But Dooley's uncle didn't even seem to notice Dooley. That's when Dooley saw that he had a DVD case in his hand—something he must have rented for Jeannie. He marched straight to the counter and waved it under Kevin's nose. "Did you just call me?" he demanded. Jesus, he was pissed off. "Because if you did, I'm here to tell you, you take that tone with me again, and I personally am going to take this *item*"—he waved the DVD case at Kevin—"and insert it into *your* drop box." Kevin looked like he was going to piss his pants. He opened his mouth and reached for the phone beside the cash. Dooley's uncle dropped a hand onto Kevin's arm. "And don't try to intimidate me by threatening to call the cops. I *am* a cop, you knucklehead." His uncle slapped the DVD case onto the counter and marched out of the store. Kevin, white-faced, glanced over at Dooley and for the next couple of days—Dooley was pretty sure it wasn't his imagination—he treated Dooley a little nicer.

"Did he say what he wanted?" Dooley asked.

"He said he wants you to go home. *Immediately*." The last word came out sounding exactly like Dooley's uncle.

"What for?"

"He didn't say." Sub-text: *And I sure as hell didn't ask.*

"He didn't want to talk to me?"

"He just said, 'Tell Ryan to come home immediately.' He asked me if I thought I could handle that. He's never going to get over that phone call, is he?"

"Probably not," Dooley said. He ducked out from behind the counter.

"I'm not paying you for missed time," Kevin said.

Right.

■ ■ ■

As soon as Dooley got out of the store, he took out his cell phone and speed-dialed home.

"Is everything okay?" he said.

"You got my message?" his uncle said.

"Yeah."

"So get home."

"I'm on my way, but—"

"Just get here, Ryan."

Something was wrong, but what? His uncle's voice didn't have that edge of annoyance to it that signaled to Dooley that he had done something his uncle disapproved of or was pissed off about. But it didn't sound right, either. It sounded flat. Tired.

here was a car parked outside Dooley's uncle's house, blocking the driveway. Dooley's first thought: No matter how tired or preoccupied or annoyed his uncle was, if (when) he saw that car, he'd be on the phone to one of his cop buddies. Pretty soon after that, the owner of the car would have to shell out big bucks for a fine and towing fees at some inconveniently located police impound lot, and Dooley would have to listen to his uncle bitch about it for days ("What kind of numb-nuts parks his car right across the mouth of someone's driveway, for Christ's sake?"). As Dooley passed the car on his way into the house, he took a closer look at it. Scratch that scenario. His uncle didn't have to call one of his cop buddies. The boys in blue were already here—in fact, they had just come out of the house and were on the porch—which was enough to make Dooley wish he was back at the store. Dooley's uncle was one thing. Yeah, he was a hard-ass. But his cop days were in the past. He ran a dry-cleaning business now. He could (and did) give Dooley a hard time, but he couldn't lock him up and throw away the key. Dooley's uncle's friends were something else, especially the ones who were still on the job. Sometimes, like on poker night, Dooley would walk into the house, come up against a wall of true blue, and have to fight the reflex to plant his hands and spread 'em. But what were cops doing here tonight? Dooley's stomach clenched as he made his way up the front walk.

The cops, two of them, both in plainclothes, were coming down the porch steps. They looked at Dooley as they passed but didn't say anything, which told Dooley that they weren't here to see him. But the somber expressions on their faces also told him that they weren't old pals of his uncle who had been here on a social visit. Dooley heard two car doors open and then close again. He glanced at the cop car. The two cops were in it, but so far the one behind the wheel hadn't started the engine.

The front door was unlocked. Dooley pushed it open. Yeah, something was definitely wrong. His uncle was sitting on the couch, his head in his hands. He looked up when Dooley appeared in the doorway.

"Sit down, Ryan," he said, still in that flat, tired tone.

Dooley stayed where he was.

"What's wrong?" he said. "What were *they* doing here?"

"It's Lorraine."

Well, that figured. Lorraine had always had a knack for taking a good day and turning it into crap.

"What about her?"

His uncle stared at him for a moment before finally saying, "She's dead."

Dead?

"What happened?" Dooley said.

"They're not saying much, but it looks like it's drug-related."

Something else that figured.

"Overdose?"

It took a moment for his uncle to answer.

"Could be. Or bad drugs. You never know what's out there."

Dooley stood in the doorway between the front hall and the living room for a few moments, absorbing the news.

Lorraine was dead. That was it. It was over.

He crossed from the hall into the living room and sank into an armchair opposite his uncle. Bad drugs he could understand. His uncle was right—you never knew what was out there. But an overdose—well, that raised a big question: accidental or intentional? Knowing Lorraine, it was probably the former. But what if it wasn't that? What if—?

"When?"

"Last night."

"*Last night?* How come they're just telling you now?" As soon as Dooley asked, he realized what a stupid question it was. "She didn't have you listed as next-of-kin, huh?"

"Actually, she did." His uncle sounded surprised. "But they only found her this morning, and it took them a while to ID her. She didn't have a purse or wallet on her."

"Where?"

"Downtown." His uncle stood up. It seemed to be an effort. "They want me to go and identify her." That explained why the cops hadn't taken off. They were waiting for Dooley's uncle. "You want to come?"

Was his uncle expecting him to say yes? Should he say yes? If he was some other guy with some other mother, he probably would have.

"No."

His uncle nodded. Dooley detected no disappointment, no disapproval, no surprise.

"I could have left it," he said. "I could have let you finish your shift."

But he hadn't. He'd called and told Kevin to send Dooley home because that's what you were supposed to do. And now here Dooley was, refusing to play his part.

"If you want me to come ..." he began.

His uncle shook his head. "I'll take care of it." He hesitated. "You think you'll be okay here by yourself?"

"Yeah, sure," Dooley said. He couldn't believe it. She was dead.

He stayed in the chair for a full ten minutes after his uncle left. Jesus, what he wouldn't do for a drink or a joint, anything to chase away that jangly feeling inside him. He got up and went into the kitchen. His uncle kept his booze in a cupboard above the counter. When he passed it, his hand shook. It would be so easy to reach up and take down a bottle of Jack. His eyes shifted lower, to a bulletin board, everything on it—a calendar, a shopping list, emergency phone numbers, a couple of business cards—all lined up neatly and, beside that, the phone. He grabbed the receiver and punched in Beth's cell phone number. It had started to ring by the time he realized that he'd punched in her old number, not her new one. He hung up before Beth's mother could answer, dug in his pocket for the slip of paper she had written the new one on, and tried again.

He was relieved when Beth answered on the second ring. Then he thought about why his uncle preferred it when Dooley called from a landline. The thing about cell phones was that you could take them anywhere and when you answered them, you could *be* anywhere. If he wanted to be sure where she was, he should have called her on her home phone, except that nine times out of ten when he did that her mother picked up. He could always hear the frost in her voice when she realized who was calling. Most of the time she said Beth wasn't home. Most of the time it turned out she was lying.

"Hey," Beth said. "What's up?" Hearing her voice eased some of the tightness in his chest.

"Where are you?" Dooley said.

"Where do you think I am? I'm at home. And so are you." She must have seen his uncle's number on her readout. "I thought you were closing tonight."

"I got off early," Dooley said. "What are you doing?"

"Homework."

"Alone?"

"Of course, alone," she said. But he couldn't help wondering: Why *of course?* She hadn't been alone last night. She'd been with her history team. Nor, as far as he could tell, had she been alone the night before. "You sound funny. Is everything okay?"

"Yeah. How'd you make out with that team thing?"

"Same old." She sighed and Dooley pictured her leaning back in her chair, maybe even moving to her bed. He

43

pictured her in what she usually wore to bed, which was mainly little tank tops and drawstring pants. Boy, he loved those drawstrings. He wondered if Nevin had ever pulled them. "What about you? What's up with you?" she said.

"Nothing much," Dooley said. Well, except that his uncle was down at the morgue identifying a body. But he didn't want to get into that. It would just open up doors that he had already told Beth were closed. "I'm off tomorrow night." He hesitated. He didn't want it to sound like that was the only reason he had called because it wasn't. For once, it wasn't even close. "I don't suppose your mom has plans?"

"Why?" Beth said. "Did you want to come over?"

He did, but not if Beth's mother was going to be there. Beth said she didn't care what her mother thought. She said her mother couldn't tell her who she could see and who she couldn't, and Dooley bet that was true. But all the same, he hated going over there when her mother was there because, on top of everything else, she never let them have any privacy. No way would she let them go into Beth's room. That meant they were stuck in the dining room, maybe doing homework together, or they were in the living room watching TV or a movie, with Beth's mother more annoying than all those commercials, the way she kept interrupting, checking up on them. She didn't even try to be subtle. She would appear in the doorway and stare at Dooley, letting him know that she had his number, she knew exactly what kind of guy he was, and if he valued his life, he had better keep his hands off her daughter.

"I want to see you," he said.

"I don't know," Beth said, slowly, drawing the words out, rattling him a little because he still couldn't believe he was going with a girl like her, and he wondered sometimes— okay, *a lot*—exactly what she saw in him, especially when there were guys like Nevin around, guys she could debate with, if that's what she wanted to do, while she was riding around in a midnight blue Jag. "She has her book club tomorrow night."

Oh. Possibly the one thing worse than a bunch of cops and retired cops playing poker was a bunch of middle-aged women earnestly discussing some book that had recently been on Oprah's bedside table.

"And it's at your place, huh?"

Beth laughed. Was that a good sign?

"They're going to see the movie version of the book they read last month. They do that sometimes. After that, they're going out for drinks. We'll have the place to ourselves until at least midnight."

We?

"Come over at six," she said. "I'll make dinner."

And there it was in that grave-dark night—one bright little light, something to look forward to.

■ ■ ■

Dooley was watching TV when his uncle got home. He notched down the volume and waited. His uncle went straight through to the kitchen. Dooley got up and followed him. His uncle poured himself a scotch, straight up. He

45

downed it in one swallow and poured himself another, this one more generous. He took a sip before brushing wordlessly past Dooley on his way back into the living room, where he dropped down into an armchair.

Dooley sat down again and waited, but his uncle didn't say anything. He just worked on his scotch. He made pretty good progress, too, in pretty good time. Dooley had never seen his uncle drink like that. It made him wonder.

"So," he said after another moment. "Was it her?"

His uncle gave him a sharp look, like what kind of bone-headed question was that?

Okay, then.

"Now what?" Dooley said, mainly because he felt he had to say something, and he sure couldn't say what was really on his mind.

"Now they do an autopsy. When they finish that, they release the body and we do something about a funeral," his uncle said, sounding a whole lot more annoyed than Dooley imagined he himself would if his sister had just died, assuming he had a sister, which he didn't. "I'll make some calls in the morning."

Dooley watched him for a moment, wondering if this was a good time. Probably not. Where Lorraine was concerned, there was no such thing as a good time, which meant he might as well come right out and ask the question he'd been wondering about.

"You said they found her downtown," he said.

"Yeah. So?" He sounded pissed off. Or maybe that was just his way of showing grief.

"So, did the cops tell you anything? Do they know how long she'd been in town or what she was doing here?"

His uncle met Dooley's eyes for a split second, and Dooley was rattled by the change he saw in them, as if he'd been looking into a brightly lit window only to have someone suddenly pull the curtains shut. It took a moment before he answered.

"She lived here."

"Lived here?" What did that mean?

"She had a place across town," his uncle said.

"For how long?"

"What difference does it make?"

What difference?

"For how long?" Dooley said again. He felt his chest tighten.

His uncle downed the last of the scotch and set his glass on a coaster on the side table. "A few years."

A *few?* That meant more than two. His eyes locked onto his uncle, who was staring at the empty glass, maybe doing what Dooley was doing, maybe wishing it was full and he could lift it to his lips and …

"I asked you that time what she was up to," Dooley said. "You said you had no idea."

His uncle glanced up at him, frowning slightly, like he'd been asked directions to a place he'd never heard of.

"I thought she'd taken off," Dooley said. He was breathing a little harder now. His fingers were tingling. He had to fight the urge to jump up out of his chair. "You know, because she was always talking about that, about going out west. I told you that, remember?"

"What's your point, Ryan?"

"I thought she was gone." That was his point. "And the whole time, she was living just across town?"

"So what if she was?" His uncle picked up his glass, saw that it was empty, and put it back down again. "You telling me that if you'd known where she was living, you'd have gone over there every week for Sunday dinner, something like that?"

No, nothing like that. Dooley couldn't imagine going over there any more than he could imagine Lorraine cooking Sunday dinner.

His uncle heaved himself up out of the chair and stood there a moment, studying the empty glass. Finally he picked it up and carried it into the kitchen. Dooley heard him unscrew the top off the bottle of scotch. He heard the *glug-glug-glug* of a generous measure being poured. His uncle reappeared, glass in hand. As he walked back through the living room, he paused and said, "I'm sorry." He walked carefully through the living room, clutching the glass, and made his way unsteadily up the stairs.

Dooley stayed where he was. The TV was playing a rerun of a sitcom that was on a hundred times a day. The characters were all young and had great apartments filled with all kinds of cool stuff, which didn't make sense to Dooley because most of them had crap jobs. But Dooley wasn't really watching. He was wondering what his uncle meant. Was he sorry Lorraine was dead? Or was there something more to it?

Four

I f anyone had asked him, *Hey, imagine if Lorraine suddenly stopped breathing, what do you think you'd be doing the very next day?*, he never would have come up with what he was actually doing, which was shoving books into his locker that he didn't need for the morning and pulling out others that he did need. He paused as his hand closed around his math textbook. What the hell was he even doing here? His mother had just died. You were supposed to do something when that happened, weren't you? Something besides the same-old same-old.

"Hey, Dooley," someone said behind him.

He turned to look at Warren's moon-shaped face and his nervous eyes blinking behind black-rimmed glasses that made him look like the picked-on brainiac that he was.

"Hey, Warren," Dooley said, even managing a smile so that maybe Warren would relax a little. Dooley wasn't sure why, but Warren approached him every time as if he wasn't quite sure if Dooley was going to shake his hand or rip off his head, and this after Dooley had saved his ass that one time and Warren had repaid the favor. "How you doing?"

"Good … I guess," Warren said. He shifted his weight from one foot to the other and glanced down to the end of the hall, like he was wishing he could be there instead of here at Dooley's locker.

"Everything okay?"

He looked miserable as he squared his shoulders and drew in a deep breath, looking to Dooley like a guy who was being forced at gunpoint to walk barefoot through a nest of rattlesnakes and was now thinking that a quick bullet in the head would be preferable to the sure but slower and more painful death by venom that lay in store.

"What's going on, Warren?"

Warren dug something out of the binder he was carrying—an envelope—and stared at it for a moment before thrusting it at Dooley.

"Alicia's birthday is coming up," he said. Alicia was Warren's sister. She had Down's syndrome. She came by the video store at least once a week. For a few months, she'd been renting the penguin movie. Now she was into the one with the little girl and the talking bear, the one in full-body armor. She could have bought a library of DVDs with the money she spent renting the same movie over and over again, always when Dooley was on shift, always coming to Dooley's cash or, if he was on the floor instead, waiting up at the counter until Linelle or whoever else was up there called him and stepped aside so that he could scan Alicia's choice and take her money. "She wants you to come," Warren mumbled, his eyes focused on his shoes. "You know, if you're not working or whatever."

Dooley opened the envelope and pulled out an invitation. "I'll check my schedule," he said.

"Right," Warren said, as if this were exactly the answer—the dodge—he'd been expecting.

"What I mean is, it's two weeks from now," Dooley said. "If I *am* scheduled to work, I'll have plenty of time to switch my shift. Tell Alicia I'll be there."

Warren perked up. "Really?" One thing you could say about him: He never took anything for granted.

"Yeah," Dooley said.

"You're going to come?" Warren said, leaning in to Dooley to make sure he heard the answer clearly this time.

"Yeah, I'm going to come."

Warren nodded slowly, as if he still wasn't sure he had it right. "She said to tell you she's having an ice-cream cake. Chocolate."

"All the more reason," Dooley said. And, bingo, Warren smiled. For the first time since Dooley had heard about Lorraine, he felt good. The feeling lasted until homeroom bell rang. He hated school.

■ ■ ■

At five that afternoon, he was fresh out of the shower and standing at the ironing board in the kitchen wearing nothing but a towel when his uncle walked through the door, surprising him. Fridays were busy dry-cleaning days. His uncle hardly ever came home this early on Fridays. He looked at what Dooley was doing and said, "You're not working tonight?"

51

Dooley shook his head.

His uncle zeroed in on the shirt Dooley was ironing. "Beth?"

"Yeah." Dooley finished the shirt and put the ironing board back into the kitchen closet where his uncle kept it along with all his cleaning supplies.

He picked up his shirt and was headed out of the kitchen when his uncle said, "We should talk about the arrangements. But if you're in a hurry, it can wait until tomorrow."

"No," Dooley said. "We might as well get it over with." The words came out with a hardness that surprised him. Well, why shouldn't they? Lorraine had never come to see him when they had him locked up. She'd never showed much concern before that, either. "What do you think we should do?" Dooley had never thought about funeral arrangements before.

For a moment his uncle looked lost, and Dooley thought he was waiting for Dooley to come up with a plan. Then he got that don't-even-think-about-giving-me-any-crap, cop-turned-dry-cleaner look of his on his face and sounded as hard as Dooley when he said, "I put a notice in the paper, in case she had any friends. I thought there should be a service of some kind. I was also thinking cremation."

"Cremation?"

"Unless you want her someplace where you can go and visit her."

Dooley thought about that for maybe two seconds. Lorraine had never visited him and all of a sudden he was going to—what?—make a pilgrimage once a week to some cemetery to talk to her headstone? Hell, past the age of twelve, he had hardly ever talked to *her*.

52

"I'm okay with cremation," he said. He'd be okay with just about anything if he could get the hell out of the kitchen, get dressed, and get over to Beth's.

That reminded him. He glanced at his uncle. Maybe this wasn't the best time to bring it up, but he couldn't think of any time that would be better.

"About Beth," he said slowly. "I don't want you to think she doesn't care or anything."

"Why would I think that?"

"You know, if she doesn't come to the funeral."

"She comes, she doesn't come; it's her choice. She didn't know Lorraine."

"Yeah," Dooley said. He could have left it at that, but it wouldn't have been fair to Beth. "The thing is, she sort of thinks Lorraine died a long time ago."

His uncle looked wordlessly at him, his eyes hard and disapproving.

"Come on," Dooley said. "It's not like I committed a crime." He wasn't proud of lying to Beth. He hadn't planned to do it. He hadn't planned to mention Lorraine to her at all. But she'd asked about his mother and he hadn't had the heart—the courage—to get into it. He was even more reluctant now, when a guy like Nevin was hanging around. Besides, at the time, he didn't think he'd ever see Lorraine again. He'd thought she was out of his life for good. And now, for sure, she was.

His uncle stared at Dooley's freshly ironed shirt for a few moments. "So, you taking her out somewhere?" he said at last. "Maybe to celebrate?"

Jesus. What kind of thing was that to say?

"Okay, look, I probably shouldn't have said Lorraine was dead," Dooley said.

"Probably?"

"It's complicated."

"No, it isn't," his uncle said. "You were ashamed of her so you lied about her. Is that about the size of it?"

"I *like* Beth."

"Oh, well then. All the more reason to tell her a whopper."

Dooley regretted that he'd broached the subject.

"I'm sorry," he said, even though he wasn't, not even remotely. He just wanted to go upstairs, get changed, and get over to Beth's. He would have done just that, too, except for one thing: Beth came over sometimes, and sometimes she talked to his uncle on the phone.

"What?" his uncle said, seeing how Dooley was eyeing him.

"I was wondering if you could maybe not mention it to her."

"Not mention that my sister, your mother, just died, you mean?" Like Dooley had asked him to cover for Jeffrey Dahmer or Paul Bernardo.

"It's bad enough I had to tell her about me," Dooley said. "And there's this other guy." He hadn't meant to say that, but if his uncle mentioned Lorraine to Beth now, when Nevin was sniffing around … "He drives a Jag."

"Yeah," his uncle said. "I could see how a mother dying of a drug overdose would handicap you in *that* race." He went to the fridge, pulled out a can of beer, popped it, and took a long, long, *long* swallow right in front of Dooley. "So what do you two have planned for tonight?"

Dooley didn't want to answer, not when his uncle was looking at him like that, ready to keep digging at him if he didn't answer. So okay, fine.

"She's making dinner."

His uncle considered this. Dooley knew that he liked Beth. He probably thought she was a good influence. He sounded less pissed off when he said, "Is she a good cook?"

"I dunno." She had never cooked for him before. "I gotta go. I don't want to be late."

He was almost through the door when his uncle said, "They did the post-mortem today."

"And?" Dooley said. "Was it an overdose?"

"She had pulmonary edema, so probably. But they won't be able to say until they've done toxicology. Even then they may not know. It's not like TV."

Dooley knew that from his own experience.

"If it *was* an overdose," he said, "will they be able to tell if it was accidental or, you know ... whatever?"

"They'll look into it."

"And they'll let you know?"

"Yeah." His uncle pulled out a chair and sat down. He looked exhausted. "Have a good time with Beth."

Dooley nodded and turned to go.

"You know about safe sex, right?" his uncle said.

"Yeah."

"You got rubbers? Because if you don't—"

Dooley felt the heat rise in his cheeks.

"I'm covered," he said. If there was one thing he did *not*

want to discuss with his uncle, it was sex. He had a hard enough time some nights trying not to picture his uncle and Jeannie going at it, and now that his uncle had brought the subject up, he couldn't help picturing his uncle picturing him and Beth going at it. "I really gotta go."

■ ■ ■

He was halfway to Beth's place before he thought, I should bring her something. If Nevin were going to her place for supper, he'd bring something.

But what?

Beth didn't drink—thank God, because that would have complicated everything. Dooley thought maybe dessert, maybe pastries, except that what if she had already bought something or made something—would she be offended? Then he thought, flowers. Girls like flowers, right?

He stopped at a small Italian supermarket and bought a colorful bouquet. The lady at the cash smiled approvingly at him as she wrapped the flowers in a paper cone.

Beth smiled, too, when he held them out to her. She went on tiptoes to kiss his cheek, but he couldn't shake the feeling that he should have brought something else. Something nicer. Something more personal. Trouble was, he didn't know what.

She had music on soft, like audio wallpaper. She'd set candles on the table, which she lit when he came into the apartment. She had made chicken in some kind of sauce with mushrooms, and rice, and salad. For dessert she'd made a pie—apple—which she served with ice cream. If his uncle asked again, he'd say, "Yeah, she's a terrific cook."

After they ate, he helped her clear the table because if there was one thing he'd learned from his uncle, it was that you don't just sit there while someone else does all the work, especially if the work involves putting food in your belly. He'd been planning to help her wash whatever wouldn't go in the dishwasher but, as soon as everything was off the table, she smiled and took his hand and led him down to the end of a hall that ran off the living room and into her bedroom, which was so white it was like stepping into a cloud. The walls were painted white and so was the floor. The curtains on her windows were white, the blinds were white, the furniture was all white. The sheets and the bedspread were white. When he'd asked her about it that first time he'd seen it, she had said, "It's clean, you know?" For sure it was that; it was clean.

She pulled him inside and wrapped her arms around his neck and pressed her lips to his, and, for the first time in almost a week, for the very first time, he didn't think about Nevin. He didn't think about Lorraine, either.

■ ■ ■

For once, Dooley's uncle wasn't waiting up for him. His bedroom door was open, a sure sign he was alone. Dooley peeked in. His uncle was asleep—passed out?—on the bed. He was fully clothed and he was snoring.

■ ■ ■

The weekend. Dooley went to work, where he emptied the drop box and scanned and re-shelved all the incoming items before heading up to the cash to start checking them out again, Saturday being the video store's busiest day. He wished he was working all weekend. It would pass the time. Beth had left with her mother first thing in the morning to visit some of her mother's friends at their cottage up north somewhere. They wouldn't be driving back until late Sunday night.

His uncle was cleaning up the kitchen when Dooley got home.

"Did you eat?" he said.

Dooley shook his head. His uncle began taking things out of the fridge—lemon chicken, rice, broccoli with some kind of sauce on it.

"A couple of detectives came by the store," he said as he slid a plate of food into the microwave.

"Cop detectives?"

His uncle nodded.

"What did they want?"

"They were asking about Lorraine."

"Asking what?"

"What she'd been up to."

"What do you mean?"

"Apparently someone told them she'd been clean for a while," his uncle said. "They asked me about that."

"Why?"

"They're taking a closer look at what happened. They may want to talk to you, Ryan."

"*Me?* What could I tell them?"

"You're her son." As if that answered his question. "You know your rights?"

"My *rights?*" What did his rights have to do with Lorraine?

"You're still a juvenile. You don't have to talk to them if you don't want to and, for sure, you don't have to talk to them alone."

Dooley stared at his uncle. "You told me they said it was a drug overdose."

"It was."

"So what are they looking at?"

"They're looking at why."

"Why what? Why an overdose?" They had to be kidding.

"Apparently there were some bruises."

"Bruises?"

"Apparently. Could be nothing related. Or could be that someone was holding her, maybe forcing her."

"Forcing her to what?"

"There were needle marks, but only one was recent."

"So?" Dooley said. When a person quit trying to stay straight, all it took was one.

"I don't read minds. I'm just telling you what they said."

The microwave beeped. Dooley's uncle opened it, took out the plate of food, and set it down in front of Dooley.

■ ■ ■

Dooley didn't get out of bed the next day until noon. What was the point? He didn't have to work, and Beth wasn't around. He had homework to do, but he couldn't get himself

59

even remotely excited about it. He thought about Lorraine. She was dead. That should have meant something to him. She was his mother, after all. But the only feeling he could identify was anger. She had never come to see him, even though it turned out she had been living just across town the whole time he'd been locked up. What kind of mother behaved like that? What business did she have even being a mother? The best thing he could do was forget about her. Move on. Move forward. Do what he'd been doing ever since they'd let him out—be something different. Be nothing at all like her. Not only did he think he *could* do it but he actually *wanted* to do it. He wanted something different. Something worthwhile.

So, yeah, forget about her.

His uncle was quiet all day. He spent most of his time up in his office, working on whatever it was he worked on when he was up there. His business, mostly. He reviewed his accounts. He fiddled with spreadsheets. He read dry-cleaning newsletters. He devoured the financial pages of the newspaper. He made plans. He'd been talking about a third store, if he could find the right location, maybe somewhere near a police station where he could offer specials to cops.

Supper was Chinese take-out. They ate in front of the TV, his uncle acting like he was riveted by *60 Minutes* before he finally went back upstairs. Dooley stayed down in the living room and surfed the channels. He got a real jolt when he saw Lorraine's picture on the eleven o'clock news—a thirty-second clip about "yet another drug death" that mentioned, but did not go into, an "ongoing police investigation"—and was glad Beth was in a car somewhere, driving back from wherever she'd been. He wondered who else might be watching the news and might be as surprised as he was by that picture. But the truth was that none of the people he knew now had met Lorraine. He never talked about her. She had a different last name than his. Most of the people he used to know had never met her, either. He'd never taken any of his friends back to his place. The whole deal back then had been to get away from wherever home happened to be and to stay away as long as possible.

■ ■ ■

The service for Lorraine was held on Monday morning. Dooley put on the suit he had worn only once, also to a funeral. When he went downstairs, his uncle, also in a suit, a black one that had cost him more than Dooley made in three or four months at the video store, was adjusting his tie. His eyes met Dooley's in the hall mirror.

"You still didn't tell her?" he said. He meant Beth.

Dooley shook his head. He thought his uncle might have something more to say on the subject, but he didn't. Instead, he studied his reflection, frowned, and adjusted his tie again. When he was finally satisfied, he said, "We might as well get this done."

Dooley was surprised to find maybe twenty people in the room at the funeral home. He knew his uncle was surprised, too, because he went back out and checked the name in the slot beside the door to make sure he hadn't stumbled in on the wrong service.

"I guess putting a notice in the newspaper worked, huh?" Dooley said.

His uncle didn't answer. He didn't circulate, either. But a couple of people—women—went up to him and introduced themselves. Dooley decided that they must have known Lorraine pretty well because they had no trouble picking him out as her brother.

"I can't believe she's really gone," one of them said.

Dooley's uncle didn't say anything.

Another woman, this one thin and hard, with a voice corroded by too much of something—cigarettes? booze? drugs?— approached Dooley and said, "You're her son." Dooley must have looked surprised, because then she said, "Lorraine showed me a picture. She was doing so well."

Dooley couldn't imagine it.

The guy who did the service—Dooley supposed he was some kind of clergyman—obviously didn't know Lorraine. Dooley wondered where his uncle had found him. Maybe he was part of some cut-rate cremation special deal. He called Lorraine the devoted (*devoted!*) mother of Ryan and beloved (uh-huh) younger sister of Gary. He talked about her struggle with drugs and alcohol (the drugs and alcohol part was right, but Dooley had never witnessed any struggle; what he'd seen had been more like a love affair) and said that she had recently made progress in that area. (Who had told him that? The same person who had told the cops?)

And that was it.

The clergyman (assuming that's what he was) finished

talking and left the front of the room. Dooley's uncle stood up and left the room altogether. By the time Dooley caught up with him, he was out in the parking lot, his overcoat on, loosening his tie and looking—Dooley had no trouble reading the expression on his face—like he needed a drink.

"Is that it?" Dooley said.

"Yeah, that's it," his uncle said.

Dooley wanted to shake him and say, "She was your sister. Didn't you want to say anything?" But he kept his mouth shut. If his uncle had had something to say, he would have said it. There would have been no stopping him.

"You should go to school," his uncle said, putting it to him as if that was what everyone was expected to do right after they'd paid their last respects to their mother.

"You're kidding, right?" Dooley said.

His uncle fixed him with his flinty cop eyes.

"You going to tell me you're too broken up to concentrate?"

Jesus. Dooley knew his uncle was a hard-ass, but this took it to a whole new level.

"What about you?" Dooley said. "Are you going to work?"

His uncle gave him a look, like, what else?

After his uncle left, Dooley went back into the funeral home. Most of the people who had been at the service were still there, clustered in small groups outside the room where the casket was. One of the groups, consisting of four women, turned and looked at him. Then three of the women glanced at the fourth—slender, with a tired but friendly face—who stepped away from them and came toward Dooley. She was better dressed than the others, like she belonged in an office and kept up on the fashion trends. She smelled good, too, like soap and shampoo and toothpaste. Clean.

"You must be Ryan," she said.

He nodded.

"Lorraine was very proud of you."

He stared at the woman. She looked normal, but it was almost impossible for Dooley to imagine a normal person saying that with a straight face.

"I'm Gloria Thomas," she said. "I was Lorraine's sponsor."

"Sponsor?" Did she mean what he thought she meant? "What group?"

"Narcotics Anonymous."

He almost laughed.

"Well, she died of a drug overdose, so ..."

"I know," Gloria Thomas said. "I'm sorry." She had blue-green eyes that never let go of his. "She called me the night she died."

"Yeah?" Dooley could just picture it: Lorraine crying on her sponsor's shoulder: *I'm so tempted; help me, stop me.* Or maybe she'd called after she was already fucked up: *I'm so bad. I said I would stop, and now look what I've done.* Looking for absolution. "What did she say?"

"I was out." That seemed to bother her. "It must have been important, though, because she tried both my home number and my cell, but it was turned off. I was at a movie." Yeah, it bothered her, all right. The look on her face told Dooley that she felt she had failed Lorraine. Dooley hoped she would get over that idea. She seemed like an okay person; she just didn't understand Lorraine. "She left a message. She said she'd try me again later."

"And?"

"She never called back. I wish I'd been home or that I'd had my cell phone on. Maybe if I'd talked to her ..."

If that was the way she felt: "You could have called her back," Dooley said.

"I tried. She wasn't at home, and she doesn't have a cell phone. I star sixty-nined her, just in case, and tried that number. But all I got was a recorded message that said that the phone I was calling wasn't equipped for incoming calls. The police told me it was a pay phone."

"You talked to the police about her?"

"I called them when I heard how she died. I couldn't believe it. She'd been really trying, you know?"

Dooley could honestly say that he didn't.

Gloria Thomas drew in a deep breath. "I have something that I know she would have wanted you to have. I would have brought it with me, but, to be honest, I wasn't sure you would be here."

She was right to wonder about that, but Dooley couldn't help being offended. The only way she could have known about his ambivalence—okay, maybe hostility was a better word, or resentment—was if Lorraine had said something to her, as if she had a right to talk about him at all. But what had she said? Had she confessed to her failings as a mother? Maybe. But it was just as easy—no, it was easier—to imagine that she had painted him as a difficult and ungrateful son: *He didn't understand what I was going through. He was*

65

never home. He was always getting into trouble. He was unmanageable. He almost killed a woman ... Dooley got that feeling again, the one that made him want to grab hold of whatever would promise the quickest and longest-lasting oblivion. And whose fault was *that?*

"I could drop it off for you," Gloria Thomas said.

Dooley shook his head. Whatever she had, he wasn't interested.

Gloria Thomas looked deep into his eyes, as if she thought she could read him the way she probably imagined that she could read Lorraine. Be my guest, Dooley thought.

"Here's my contact information," she said at last. She handed him a business card. Dooley glanced at it. It turned out Gloria Thomas was an executive secretary for the vice-president of marketing for a major chain of grocery stores, which told Dooley that anyone could fall and, based on the card, anyone could get up again, maybe even Lorraine, although—and there it was, that bitterness again—he doubted it. "In case you change your mind," she said. "Or if you ever want to talk."

Talk? About what?

■　■　■

The cops were waiting for Dooley when he came out of the funeral home for the second time. Maybe they'd been there before and he just hadn't noticed. They were the same two cops he'd seen coming down the porch steps the night he'd found out about Lorraine.

66

"Ryan Dooley?" the taller and younger of the two said.
Dooley nodded.

"Detective Randall," the cop said, flashing his ID. "We'd like to talk to you about your mother."

Just like Dooley's uncle had predicted.

"I have to get to school," Dooley said. He couldn't believe how glad he was of the excuse.

"We'll drive you there," Randall said. "After we talk." He glanced up the street. "How about we buy you a cup of coffee?"

Dooley knew he didn't have to talk to them. He knew he could walk away. He knew that was his right. He also knew how it would look if he didn't talk to them. He nodded and walked with the two cops to a coffee shop a couple of doors up from the funeral home. He let them pick the table and order—coffee all around. He watched while they opened their notebooks.

"What can you tell us about your mother, Ryan?" Randall said.

"Not much. We weren't close," Dooley said.

"Did she use drugs?"

"Yeah."

"Do you know what kind of drugs?"

"What have you got?" Dooley said, realizing too late that it sounded like he didn't care and, because of that, was probably setting the detectives' cop antennae all aquiver. Randall was looking directly at him, that flat cop expression on his face so Dooley couldn't tell what he was thinking.

"When was the last time you spoke to your mother, Ryan?"

Spoke to her, as in had a real honest-to-God conversation?

"It's been a couple of years."

"How many years?" Randall said, registering no surprise that Dooley could see. But then, in Dooley's experience, cops usually tried not to show surprise when they were dealing with civilians, even when they'd been bowled over by something that had never occurred to them. Besides, Dooley bet that Randall, a homicide cop, had a pretty grim view of human nature. He bet Randall thought that nothing could surprise him. He also bet that either Randall or his partner had already asked his uncle the same question.

"Two, maybe a little more than that," Dooley said.

"Your uncle tells us she was at the house a couple of weeks ago."

"Oh?" Dooley tried to be as expert as Randall at hiding his surprise.

"Two weeks ago Friday, in the evening." Randall glanced at his notes. "Nine o'clock. Did you see her then?" Another question that Dooley was pretty sure the detective had already asked his uncle. He probably had the answer written down right there in his notebook.

"I was working," Dooley said. "Four to midnight."

"Where do you work?"

Dooley told him. He also told him, because Randall asked, the exact time he had walked through the front door that night. He was pretty sure his uncle remembered to the minute. He made it his business to keep on top of Dooley's whereabouts.

"So you didn't see her that night?"

"No," Dooley said, looking Randall right in the eye.

68

"What did your uncle tell you about her visit?"

"Nothing. He didn't mention it."

"He didn't tell you that she'd dropped by?"

"No." His uncle hadn't said a word about it.

"He didn't tell you what the two of them talked about, whether they argued, anything like that?"

Dooley shook his head. He wondered what his uncle had told the two cops.

"Does that strike you as unusual, Ryan?"

"What?"

"You say you hadn't spoken to your mother in two years. Then she shows up at your uncle's house and he doesn't even mention that to you. You don't think that's odd?"

"No," Dooley said. "Like I said, Lorraine and I weren't close. My uncle knows that."

"Right." Randall took a sip of his coffee. "You've had some trouble with the law, haven't you, Ryan?"

Here we go, Dooley thought.

"Yes."

"You want to tell us about that?"

No, he didn't. But he knew if he didn't, they would find out anyway and wonder why Dooley didn't just own up to it, seeing that they knew that Dooley knew they'd have no trouble checking him out, if they hadn't already, which they probably had. Dooley gave them the two-minute rundown.

"Didn't your mother visit you?" Randall said.

"No." What were they fishing for?

Randall stared at him for a few moments, probably to see

if he would squirm or say something to try to fill the silence. Dooley did neither.

"Where were you the night your mother died, Ryan?"

Dooley tried not to take the question personally. His uncle had warned him the cops would want to talk to him. This was a death investigation. There were procedures. Still: "I didn't have anything to do with what happened to her."

Randall glanced at his partner. They both stared at Dooley. Jesus, cops.

"I went to the library," Dooley said. "The one downtown."

Randall looked amused. "You like to go to the library, Ryan?"

"I'm in school. I have homework."

"You go with anyone?"

"No."

"How long were you there?"

"I don't know. A while. I was working on a homework assignment."

Randall grinned, as if he were picturing Dooley reading a picture book or taking notes in crayon.

"What about after you left the library? Where did you go?"

"Home."

"Yeah? What time did you get there?"

"Eleven. Look, why are you asking all these questions?"

"We're just trying to get a picture of what happened. Can anyone verify what time you got home?"

Finally, his chance to shake Randall loose.

"I called my uncle as soon as I got in. He keeps track of me. I'm on a supervision order. He's got call display on his cell. He can tell you when I called and where I called from."

"Did you go out again that night?"

"No." Jesus, why was he asking that?

"Can anyone back you up on that?"

"No, I guess not."

Randall didn't press the point. Instead, he said, "Where was your uncle that night?"

"Playing poker with some cop friends."

"When did he get home?"

"I don't know. It must have been late. I didn't hear him come in."

"So you have no idea when he got home?"

"No."

That seemed to be that. Both cops closed their notebooks. Randall's partner went to pay for the coffee. Dooley headed for the door.

"We can give you a lift," Randall said.

"No, thanks," Dooley said. No way was he going to arrive at school in a cop car, not even an unmarked one.

■ ■ ■

Dooley thought about school as he walked. He'd gone every single day since he'd moved in with his uncle. Well, almost every single day. He'd never been absent without a good excuse. But his mother had just died. If you couldn't be excused for skipping school then, when could you be?

The answer, of course, at least for Dooley, was never. Because if he skipped, Mr. Rektor would call his uncle. That was the deal. Dooley, apparently, was not to be trusted. Any and all absenteeism was to be immediately reported to his uncle. And then his uncle, who had more or less ordered Dooley to school and who was already in a pissy mood, would get even pissier, and Dooley would have to live with *that* on top of everything else. It wasn't worth it. So he went to school, and after that, he went to work. Besides, Jeffie was supposed to show up with his money. Dooley didn't want to give him any excuse to mess that up. The day had sucked enough. The very least he deserved was to get his money back.

"You okay?" Linelle said around six o'clock when there were just the two of them in the store and hardly any customers. Monday nights were always slow, and Kevin was on his supper break. "You look a little out of it."

Dooley liked Linelle. Nothing ever fazed her. She had been working part-time at the store for a couple of years now, all through high school. She'd graduated last spring and was now going to cosmetology school.

"Rough day," he said.

"Same as every other day, right?" She was perched on a stool behind the counter and was emptying the drop box, scanning the titles back into the computer, *blip, blip, blip,* and putting the cases on a cart for re-shelving. Dooley liked to watch her work. She was slow and efficient, both at the same time, and he could never figure out how she managed to handle the scanner, the DVD cases, the cash, and the change, all with two-inch acrylic nails glued over her own fingernails. But she did. She had agreed to cover for him dozens of times and had never asked why. How could he not like her? She was looking at him now, like for once she actually expected an answer, like it wasn't just one of those lame how-'ya-doin' questions.

"It is the same as every other day, right, Dooley?" She was frowning now. "God, don't tell me you broke up with Wonder Girl."

"No," Dooley said. Jesus, where had that come from? Did Linelle know something he didn't?

"The way you look, it's either that or someone died," Linelle said.

She looked at him again, like she actually cared, which must have been why Dooley said, "My mother."

Linelle stopped sweeping the scanner across the bar codes. "Your mother what?"

"She died. My mother died." Linelle was the first person he had told.

"I didn't even know you had a mother, Dooley."

He didn't say anything.

"Shit," she said. "That was a dumb thing to say. I'm sorry. It's just that you never mentioned her. What happened?"

"She just died. The funeral was today."

"Today?" She shook her head, like she couldn't believe it. "You should have called in. You should have taken the day off. Bereavement leave. You're entitled. It's in the manual." The employee manual, she meant. Dooley was surprised that she'd read it.

The electronic bell over the door sounded and they both turned. It was Kevin, back from his break and eyeballing the smattering of customers in the store, looking for furtive or

73

suspicious behavior, before checking on the employees to make sure they were doing something productive. Linelle stared directly at him as she passed the scanner over one DVD case, then another, then another, *blip, blip, blip.*

"I don't like to talk about her," Dooley said quietly. "Forget I said anything."

Linelle glanced at him, a question in her eyes, but she didn't say anything. She just kept waving the scanner over the DVD cases.

Twenty minutes later, Dooley's cell phone vibrated. He pulled it out of his pocket to read the display. From halfway down an aisle, Kevin noticed and looked pointedly from Dooley to his cell phone. The store had a rule: No personal calls during work hours. Dooley glanced at the phone's display—Jeffie—then shoved the phone back into his pocket. It vibrated again a minute later. Then again and again—a total of five calls in less than ten minutes—until Dooley started to feel like he had a vibrator in his pants. The next time it went off, Dooley clocked the aisles. Kevin was nowhere in sight. He pulled out the phone, checked the display, flipped it open and said, "You'd better not be calling to tell me you don't have the money. I'm expecting to see you at nine o'clock. You got that, Jeffie?" He ended the call, returned the phone to his pocket, and turned to find Kevin watching him again. Dooley retreated to the front of the store before Kevin could tell him off.

Forty-five minutes later, Dooley glanced up from the cash and saw Jeffie, an hour early and right there in the store instead of at the Greek place across the street. Dooley didn't like it. Kevin, at the back of the store, spun around at the sound of the electronic bell and frowned when he saw a scrawny brown guy in big pants, an extra-large T-shirt that hung down to his knees, a jacket over top—Jeffie aligning perfectly with Kevin's profile of a gangbanger out to liberate a little product. He started up the aisle toward Jeffie. Kevin's tactic with shoplifters: Get into their personal space immediately and stay there until they called it quits and left *his* personal space, which is to say, his store.

Jeffie veered left, making straight for Dooley's cash and greeting him by name, which did nothing to allay Kevin's suspicions. Terrific. On the basis of Jeffie's knowing Dooley, Kevin would probably start getting into Dooley's personal space.

"I'll be right back," he said to Linelle. He slipped out from behind the counter, grabbed Jeffie by the arm, and dragged him out of the store.

"I told you to meet me across the street," he said when they were out on the sidewalk. "I don't want you in there. I *work* in there."

"It's a *video* store," Jeffie said, as if that meant anything. What was it with people and video stores? They all copped an attitude about video store employees, like a person had to be practically brain-dead or at least down a few pints in ambition to work there, but they all came in regularly to rent stuff, and they all bitched and whined and expected miracles when they couldn't find what they wanted.

"Why'd you call me, Jeffie? And what are you doing here so early?" Dooley said. "You better not be going to stiff me on my money."

75

"Hey, no, nothing like that," Jeffie said. "You're going to get it, every cent, I promise. It's just—"

"It's just what?" Dooley said. He should have known. Jeffie was a screwup. He should never have given him the time of day, let alone a wad of money.

"One more day," Jeffie said. "That's all I need."

"You said you were going to pay me back today. That was the deal, Jeffie."

"That's why I came down here in person, you know, man to man," Jeffie said. Dooley crossed his arms over his chest and waited. "The thing is ... things didn't go the way I planned and—"

Dooley cut him off. "That's not my problem."

"No, you're right. It's not. And it's going to be all good. I got it covered. See, I was just coming out from a meeting the other night and I saw this guy back behind Jay-Zee's—you remember the guy I told you about, Dooley? I'm pretty sure he didn't see me. He was—"

"I don't care about any guy, Jeffie," Dooley said. "I just want my money."

"Right. I know that. And you're going to get it. It's just that I didn't get it at the time, but I saw the guy and he was with this—"

Jesus.

"You're not listening to me, Jeffie." Dooley stepped in close so that Jeffie had to back up a pace to get comfortable.

"I'm gonna pay you back," Jeffie said. "That's what I came here to tell you. I just need one more day. I'm about to score some serious money, Dooley. If I'd been thinking, I would have taken a picture. But, hey, he doesn't know I didn't—"

"Picture? What are you talking about, picture?"

Jeffie fumbled in his pocket for something—a pack of cigarettes. When he pulled it out, half a dozen scraps of paper fluttered to the ground. Dooley glanced at them as Jeffie ducked to pick them up. Phone numbers. Jeffie always had a pocketful of phone numbers because he could never keep them in his head. Dooley had told him one time that he could program them into his cell phone, but Jeffie hadn't liked that idea. Too risky, he said. Right. Like a pocketful of paper was top security.

"Jesus, Jeffie, I hope your downtown guy isn't one of those. What if the cops stop you?"

Jeffie grinned. "I don't need to write down his number. He's got one of those ones, you'd have to be a moron not to remember it." Dooley shook his head. Did Jeffie ever look in a mirror? "It's like a pizza number. It's only once I'm in that I need—"

"Never mind," Dooley said, impatient now. He didn't care about Jeffie's business. "Just make sure I get my money."

"You will. I swear. I'm going to make out on this one, Dooley. I mean, really make out. I've even been thinking, you know, I could get out of here, maybe go back home."

Jeffie had told him one time that he was from down east somewhere, but Dooley hadn't asked where. What difference did it make? All he knew was that when Jeffie was high or when he was hungry and cold or when he was jammed up, he'd talk about how one time when he was in foster care, he'd lived in a house that was right on the ocean. It wasn't a big house. In fact, he'd said, the place was cramped and kind of run-down. But you could look out the front window and see nothing but water forever and ever. You could smell it, too, that salty tang in the air all year round. And the best part, according to Jeffie, you could hear it and watch it, like a movie or TV. It was always changing. Big deal, Dooley thought. It was just water—salt water; you couldn't even drink it. But Jeffie would get this faraway look in his eyes and tell Dooley he didn't understand. He'd tell him, too, someday he was going to have his own place right on the ocean, and it wasn't going to be some crappy run-down place, either. It was going to be a nice place, and he was going to get himself a big chair and sit out there in his front yard and watch the water and listen to it and smell it.

Jeffie sighed. "Remember I told you Teresa was talking about a kid? It turns out she's pregnant. Nearly four months. Can you believe it?" He shook his head like he sure couldn't. Then he saw the annoyed look on Dooley's face. "Tomorrow," he said. "That's all I'm asking. Meet me tomorrow. I'll have your money; I'll be golden, you'll see."

Dooley grabbed Jeffie by the lapels of his jacket and pulled him close. "My money, Jeffie," he said, slow but loud, so Jeffie wouldn't miss what he was saying. "Get it or else."

That's when Dooley registered the electronic bong over the door. He glanced over his shoulder and saw Kevin standing there, arms crossed over his chest, waiting for Dooley to get back inside where he belonged.

Dooley told Jeffie where to meet him—a place across from his school.

"Three-thirty, Jeffie," he said. "Be there."

"Three-thirty," Jeffie said, squirming. "No problem."

Dooley released him and watched him scuttle away. Then he turned and brushed past Kevin on his way back into the store.

Five

A t four-thirty the next day, Dooley was sitting in a booth facing the door of the restaurant directly across from his school, working on his second cup of coffee. Big surprise, Jeffie was an hour late, which made Dooley think he wasn't coming at all, which, in turn, put Dooley in a bad mood because he'd given Jeffie a lot of money and he wanted it back. And that put him in an even worse mood because it underlined just how fucked up his life was. Lorraine had just died. If she'd been a normal mother—and if he'd been a normal kid—the absolute last thing on his mind right now would have been money, right? But there he was, his eyes glued to the door, his mind working on all the things he would do to Jeffie if Jeffie tried to stiff him. He had tried Jeffie on his cell phone half a dozen times already and had ended up in Jeffie's voice mail every time. The first time, he left a message: "It's me. Be here, Jeffie, or else." The second time: "Get your ass over here if you know what's good for you." The third time: "I told you, Jeffie. You fuck this up and you're gonna be sorry." The other times, he just ended the call. It didn't make any difference. Jeffie didn't walk through the door. Dooley swallowed what was left of his coffee, checked his watch and the clock above the counter one more time, and decided that if Jeffie wasn't here by now, he wasn't coming. He put some money on the table to pay for his coffee and left the restaurant.

■ ■ ■

When the doorbell rang just before supper the next night, Dooley looked through the glass in the door and saw the round florid face of Jerry Panelli, retired cop, friend of his uncle's, a cynical son of a bitch whose bitter-eyed world view extended to Dooley, as in, "You're gonna tell me a kid like that's ever gonna fly straight? That's like asking a dog to stop smelling shit." He knew Jerry had seen him, but Jerry pressed the doorbell again anyway, letting Dooley know exactly what he thought of him. Dooley swung the door open.

"Your uncle here?" Jerry said, already looking past Dooley.

And a good evening to you, too, Jerry.

"He's in the kitchen," Dooley said.

He stepped aside to let Jerry through, and then he went back into the dining room where he had his homework spread out. Jerry glanced at the textbooks and binders as he went by. He paused when he got to the kitchen door and stood there for a second until Dooley sat down and dug into a math assignment. Jerry looked at him a moment longer. When he went through into the kitchen, he closed the door behind him. Dooley heard the rumble of Jerry's voice, but he couldn't make out what he was saying. He sat there for a minute, staring at the table, then, what the hell, he crept to the door and held his breath as he listened.

"... relationship with Lorraine," Jerry was saying. "How you two hit it off, how often you saw each other, that kind of thing. He asked me a lot of weird shit, Gary."

Silence.

Then Jerry's voice again, Dooley's uncle not having said a word.

"I didn't get where they were going, but I didn't like the questions, you know what I mean? There was something behind them. It was like that prick Randall was insinuating something. I told him I didn't know anything. I told him if he had any questions, he should ask you."

More silence before his uncle finally said, "Thanks for coming by, Jerry."

Dooley slipped back to the table and was staring at his math text when Jerry and his uncle came out of the kitchen.

"If there's anything I can do—" Jerry said.

"I appreciate it," Dooley's uncle said. He didn't even look at Dooley as he walked Jerry through to the front door and saw him out. He stood in the front hall for a few moments after that, looking more tired than Dooley had ever seen him.

"Is everything okay?" Dooley said.

"Everything's just hunky-dory," his uncle said.

"It's just that he sounded concerned."

"He was expressing his sympathy."

His uncle went back into the kitchen. It wasn't long before the phone rang. Dooley heard his uncle talking but couldn't make out what it was about. After he hung up, his uncle called Dooley for supper. When they had finished eating and Dooley was clearing the table, his uncle said, "I have to go downtown tomorrow."

"Yeah?" Dooley said. He waited.

"The guys in Homicide want to talk to me."

Dooley paused on his way to the sink, a dirty dinner plate in each hand. "What about?"

"What do you think?" his uncle said. "Lorraine."

"I mean, why do they want to talk to *you?*"

"I told you, they're treating her death as suspicious."

"Yeah, and—?"

"And they want to talk to me." His uncle looked pointedly at the plates. Dooley rinsed them, set them in the dishwasher, and went back to the table to clear the cutlery.

"But everything's okay, right?" Dooley said. He picked up knives, forks, a couple of serving spoons.

"What do you mean?"

"I mean, Jerry will alibi you, you know, in case the cops think you had anything to do with it."

His uncle looked at him. "Why would they think I had anything to do with it?"

■ ■ ■

Dooley couldn't stand sitting around the house. He couldn't stand the buzz from the TV that he knew his uncle wasn't even watching. He called Beth. They talked for a while and Dooley thought she sounded different—distant, maybe distracted.

He had to work at filling the gaps in the conversation, which he'd never had to do before. Then, just when he was wondering what he'd done, or what Nevin had done, something in her voice changed and she said, "They're doing inventory at the store tonight."

Dooley perked up. "Yeah?"

Every couple of months the store where Beth's mother worked, did inventory. That always meant two, maybe three nights when Beth's mother didn't get home until past midnight.

"Yeah," Beth said. "You want to come over?"

She'd asked him—him, not Nevin. Maybe the things he'd seen didn't mean anything. Maybe it was like she said—maybe they were just debating. Maybe he had nothing to worry about.

"Well?" Beth said.

"I'll be right there."

His uncle didn't take his eyes off the TV when Dooley told him where he was going.

"Be home by eleven," he said.

■ ■ ■

When Dooley got to work the next day after school, Beth was at the front counter, talking to Linelle. At first he smiled. He still felt good from the night before. He wondered if she did, too. Maybe she wanted to tell him how great it had been. Maybe her mother was doing inventory again tonight.

She turned when she heard the electronic buzzer over the door, and the smile faded on Dooley's lips. He could see right away that something was wrong. He glanced at Linelle, who shrugged—wait a minute, was that an *apologetic* shrug? Before he could even begin to decipher what she might be apologizing for, Beth was in his face.

"You told me your mother was dead," she said.

Dooley shot Linelle another look. She raised her arms in a gesture of surrender: *So shoot me.* He looked back at Beth.

"She is."

"Very funny." But, boy, no way was she even remotely close to amused. "You lied to me, Dooley."

"Well, she's dead now," Dooley said. "And, anyway, what difference does it make?"

He knew as soon as the words were out of his mouth that he'd taken the worst possible approach. This was Beth he was talking to. Beth had lost her father *and* her brother. She'd cared a lot about both of them. She took family seriously. That's why she was staring at him like his skin had split open and she could finally see what lay under that Dooley face and what was hidden inside that Dooley body: Satan. Dooley took her by the arm to lead her outside where they could talk without Linelle and, now, Kevin, watching and hearing everything, but she shook off his hand. She hadn't been this angry in a long time.

"I can explain," Dooley said in a quiet voice.

She turned abruptly, her long dark hair flicking him in the face as it spun out around her, and did what he'd asked her to do in the first place—go outside—but marching out not because it was what he wanted but because it was what *she* wanted, which was to punish him. Dooley ran after her and caught her by the arm again.

"Come on," he said, begging her. She faced him, her arms crossed over her chest, her chin jutting out, her eyes filled with fury. "I'm sorry," he said. "I should have told you."

"You were *with* me," she said. "You were with me on Friday night and again last night, and you didn't tell me." Her eyes were hard on him. "But you told Linelle."

Yes, he had done that. And it had been a mistake. He regretted it. He should have kept his mouth shut. He shouldn't have told anyone.

"She was messed up," he said. "Seriously messed up. I hadn't seen her or talked to her in years."

"What happened?" Beth said. "How did she die?" Her tone told him that she was softening a little. She was concerned. She wanted to know. But he was pretty sure she would stiffen up again when he told her the truth.

"Drug overdose." The words had the effect of a cattle prod, sending a shock through her and making her retreat a pace.

"You mean, like sleeping pills?" she said.

He shook his head. She was dead, for Christ's sake, and she was still fucking him up.

"The kind of drugs she used aren't the kind you get from your neighborhood pharmacist. She had a problem, okay?"

She peered at him like a jeweler examining a suspect stone: Was he kidding? Of *course* he was kidding—wasn't he?

"That's why I didn't tell you," he said.

"What's why?"

"The way you're looking at me now. It's why I didn't tell you about her." What was the point? "Look, she wasn't part of my life. We never talked. She wasn't interested in me."

"But she was your mother."

"That doesn't mean the same thing to everyone."

She seemed to think about that. Or maybe she was thinking about what it might mean when you were going with a guy and his mother, who you thought was long dead, suddenly passed away from a drug overdose.

"Linelle said there was a funeral," she said at last. "She said she wasn't clear whether you'd gone or not. Did you?"

He nodded. He couldn't tell whether she was happy with his answer—at least he'd cared enough to do the right thing—or whether it made things worse—he had gone to his mother's funeral but hadn't asked her to come, hadn't even told her about it. He stepped toward her. She did not shrink back.

"I'm sorry," he said. "I should have told you. But I didn't know what to say. I didn't know what you'd think."

She tipped her head back so that she could look him in the eyes.

"Is there anything else you haven't told me?"

Boy, how could he even start to answer a question like that?

"I have to get back inside," he said. He glanced over his shoulder and saw Kevin's disapproving face on the other side of the glass. "I'll call you later, okay?"

"I have a history team meeting," she said. "I'll be late." There was something in her voice—a stiffness and a weariness—that jarred him.

"Okay, tomorrow then," he said.

"We're doing a field trip tomorrow night for English. We're going to a play. I won't be home until late."

"I have to work Friday night," he said. "Come on, Beth."

Kevin rapped on the glass. When Dooley turned, Kevin pointed to his watch.

"You'd better go," Beth said.

For the first time in a long time, she didn't go up on tip-toes and kiss him before she left.

Shit.

He called her cell phone on his break. She didn't answer. He left her a voice mail. He tried her cell again later, when he got off work. Voice mail again. He had already said what he had to say. He didn't leave another message.

■ ■ ■

Dooley's uncle was sitting in front of the TV, when Dooley got home.

"So, how did it go?" Dooley said.

"How did what go?"

"The cops. You went to talk to them, right?"

"Yeah, I talked to them."

"And?"

"And what?"

"What did they want? How come they wanted to talk to you?"

His uncle leaned forward toward the TV, trying to catch the weather report, like that was more important than answering Dooley's question, maybe even more important than going in to talk to the cops.

"What did they want?" Dooley said again, going for patience but not quite getting there.

His uncle kept his eyes on the TV screen. "They wanted to know where I was the night she died."

That was a no-brainer. They'd asked Dooley the same question. It was police investigation 101.

"You were at the poker game," Dooley said. "You already told them that, right?"

"Yeah," his uncle said.

Something was wrong. Dooley saw it in the dullness of his uncle's eyes, the slump of his shoulders.

"What else?" he said.

"They wanted to know where I was between eleven and eleven-thirty."

"Is that when she died?" Dooley said.

His uncle nodded.

No way, Dooley thought. There was no way they could have narrowed down the time of death to such a small time frame. Thanks to all those crime-scene shows, everyone knew they couldn't do that. The time frame was always longer.

"She was wearing a cheap watch," his uncle said. "They showed it to me. It was broken. Time said eleven-thirteen. I think they think that means something."

"But if you were at a poker game—"

"Seems I got there a little later than I intended."

A little later?

"How much later?"

"A couple of hours."

"Jesus," Dooley said. A lot could happen in a couple of hours. "Don't tell me you lied to the cops?"

His uncle's eyes flicked away from the TV screen to

Dooley. "I told them the truth."

"So," Dooley said, "when did you get there?"

"Get where?"

Where did he think?

"To the poker game."

"A little after twelve."

Twelve?

"So when I called you—" Dooley began slowly. He was having trouble processing this piece of news. He had called his uncle at eleven o'clock that night. He had heard music and had asked him if he was at the poker game or a party. He thought about their brief conversation. No way, he told himself. No way. Except that his uncle had given him a distinct impression. "You *lied* to me?"

His uncle muted the TV and turned his eyes on Dooley. His gaze was firm and steady. It felt forthright. But maybe it wasn't. Dooley couldn't shake the idea that his uncle was doing what Dooley himself did all the time—making a point of looking him straight in the eye because he knew if he didn't, Dooley would think he was trying to hide something.

"It wasn't intentional," his uncle said. "I just lost a couple of hours, that's all."

"What do you mean, you lost them?"

His uncle, whom Dooley had known for a grand total of two years and had lived with for a little over six months now, and who always came across as Mr. Straight-and-Narrow, said, without a trace of apology or regret, "I guess you could say I was kind of pissed by the time I got to Jerry's."

"Pissed?"

"I'd had a few drinks. Maybe more than a few. I wasn't keeping track. They talked to Jerry and some of the other guys. Then they wanted me to go down and talk to them again, so they could get everything straight."

"And they did, right?" Dooley said. "I mean, if you had a few drinks, someone must have seen you. You told them what bar you were in?"

"I wasn't in a bar," his uncle said. "I was in my car."

Alarm bells went off. "You were drinking in your *car?*" When did that ever happen?

"I had a bottle I was taking to the game."

"So you had a few drinks and then what? You got so pissed that you lost track of the time, and then you *drove* to Jerry's?"

"I think maybe I nodded off for a while first," his uncle said. "It's stupid, I know, especially considering the past six months." The past six months, during which he had been on Dooley's case to do the right thing, which, mostly, meant staying away from substances like alcohol. "But shit happens, right?"

Right. Except that his uncle wasn't a guy who got pissed on his way to a poker game. He didn't even get pissed when he was there unless the game was at his own house and he was either winning big or losing big. Getting pissed wasn't what his uncle was about—at least, it hadn't been up until the last couple of days. And getting pissed and then getting behind the wheel of a car? No way.

"What did the cops say?" Dooley said.

"They thanked me for coming down."

Dooley looked at his uncle, who was staring at the TV again. Something wasn't right. He looked around the house, feeling a void.

"Where's Jeannie?" he said. "I haven't seen her for a while." In fact, he hadn't seen her since before the cops had showed up with the news that Lorraine was dead.

"She's busy."

"Yeah, but I would have thought, you know, under the circumstances—"

His uncle's eyes flicked over him, the chill in them telling Dooley that his uncle didn't want to talk about that, either.

Oh.

"You didn't tell her, did you?" Dooley said. He couldn't believe it after the way his uncle had tried to make him feel about lying to Beth. "Does she even know about Lorraine?"

His uncle turned back to the TV and turned up the volume on some reality-TV bullshit that Dooley knew for a fact he wasn't really watching. No, that was just the excuse.

■ ■ ■

Dooley hated having to wait. He also hated not knowing, which was too bad because he was faced with a whole lot of both. He hated having to wait to see Beth and not knowing what was going on, what she was thinking, if she was even thinking about him at all. He hated having to wait to find out where the cops were going with their investigation into Lorraine's death and not knowing what they had talked to his uncle about and why they had asked Jerry Panelli all those "weird shit" questions. He hated not knowing what those weird shit questions were. He hated having to wait for his uncle to spit out whatever he seemed to be choking on and not knowing why he was acting the way he was, or even whether the way he was acting was in character or not because, when you came right down to it, he didn't know his uncle all that well. He'd met him for the first time two years ago, and what had come after that were once-a-week, sometimes once-every-two-weeks, visits, which really didn't tell him anything except what his uncle was like when he was doing his hard-ass, retired cop routine, visiting his newly discovered nephew who was up shit creek. Then came the past six months living in his uncle's house. Maybe those six months should have told him something, but, then again, maybe not. After all, his uncle had lived nearly three times longer than Dooley before Dooley had even made his acquaintance, and that made it hard for Dooley to tell if the way he had been the past six months was the way he always was or just the way he was now that Dooley was around. Finally—and, okay, it was a minor problem, all things considered—he hated having to wait for Jeffie to pay him back and not knowing whether he'd been stiffed or not. If he ever got his hands on Jeffie …

■ ■ ■

When Dooley turned up the front walk after school, a woman got out of a car that was parked at the curb. Gloria Thomas, Lorraine's sponsor. She had a package in her hand.

"You didn't get in touch," she said. "So I thought I should drop by." She held the package out to him.

Dooley looked at it. It was a squarish object in a big brown envelope.

"What is it?"

"Why don't you open it?"

He looked at her. She didn't know him, but he bet she thought she knew Lorraine.

She took one of his hands and folded it around the package.

"I don't want it," Dooley said.

Her hands were wrapped around his so that he couldn't let go even if he'd wanted to. He saw a steely determination in her.

"About two weeks after I met your mother, she went through a bad patch," she said. "I found her tearing her place apart, ripping things up, smashing things—she was on a real rampage. I managed to wrestle this away from her. I was sure she'd regret it if she destroyed it. When she pulled herself together, she asked me to keep it for her. It's yours now. What you do with it is up to you. It was very nice meeting you, Ryan."

She released his hand and started back to her car.

"Hey!" he called.

She turned.

"You said she called you the night she died."

She nodded.

"What time?"

He could tell she was wondering why he wanted to know, but she didn't ask.

"Ten," she said, "according to the read-out on my home phone."

The cops knew Lorraine had been alive at ten o'clock. They figured, by her watch, that she'd died a little more than an hour later. What they didn't know for sure yet—his uncle said they were treating her death as suspicious—were the circumstances. It made Dooley uneasy.

She walked to the curb and climbed back into her car. Dooley went around the side of the house where his uncle kept the garbage cans. He removed the lid from the nearest can and dropped the package inside. On his way back to the house, he realized that Gloria Thomas's car was still there. Their eyes met. Then she turned the key in the ignition and pulled out onto the street.

■ ■ ■

Jeannie came over that night—for the first time in a long time. She filled the house with her perfume, made his uncle smile a little, and, when she went upstairs with him later, made Dooley yearn for Beth. He tried Beth's cell. No answer. He prowled restlessly in his room. There was too much going on, too much to think about, and no way to make it all go away.

As soon as things quieted down in his uncle's bedroom, Dooley went outside and dug Gloria Thomas's package out of the garbage can. He held it in his hands. It felt like some kind of book. He thought about opening it but couldn't make himself do it. He wanted to tear it up, burn it, shred it, stomp it, hack it to pieces. His hands picked at the corner of the envelope. If he kept it, he'd destroy it for sure. He lifted the lid on the garbage can again. Then hesitated. Finally he took the package inside and slipped it into his backpack.

arren stopped short when he rounded the corner at school the next day and saw Dooley standing at his locker.

"You can't make it," he said, despondent but resigned.

"What?" Dooley said.

"Alicia's party. You can't make it." He shook his head. "I already told her you were coming. She was so excited—"

"I said I'd be there, and I will," Dooley said.

"Really?"

"Even if I have to call in sick."

Warren breathed a sigh of relief. "I really appreciate it, Dooley."

"I *like* your sister, Warren. She's a sweet kid."

Warren beamed at him. "She is," he said.

"Look, Warren, I need you to do something for me."

Warren didn't hesitate. "Sure."

Dooley pulled a bulky envelope out of his backpack and handed it to Warren.

"Hang onto this for me for a while."

"No problem."

"Just until I decide what I want to do with it."

"You got it."

"It's nothing that'll get you into trouble."

"I didn't think it was."

Dooley shook his head. There was such a thing as too much trust. He should probably tell Warren that some time.

■ ■ ■

The two homicide cops were waiting for Dooley when he got to work that afternoon.

"You remember us, right, Ryan?" Detective Randall said.

Dooley just looked at him—how stupid did he think Dooley was? But he couldn't remember Randall's partner's name. He couldn't even recall if Randall's partner had even mentioned his name.

"We'd like to talk to you," Randall said.

"I'm supposed to be working." Linelle was watching him through the window. Dooley wondered if she had made the two suits as cops.

"I'm sure your employer will understand," Randall said. "After all, it's about your mother. You want to help us get things straight, don't you, Ryan?"

"I guess."

"You don't sound sure."

"I told you, we weren't close."

"You did say that," Detective Randall agreed. "Still, we need

97

to ask you some questions."

"Are you arresting me?"

"Arresting you? Why would we do that? We just need you to help us clear up a few things." Randall glanced around. "Come on. Let's find a place where we can sit down for a few minutes."

Dooley glanced at Linelle again, but he couldn't read the expression on her face.

"Okay, whatever," he said.

He went with the two detectives to a restaurant two doors down from the video store. They sat in a booth. The cops ordered coffee. Dooley didn't want anything. Then Randall said, "Why don't you tell us again about last Wednesday night, Ryan."

"Last Wednesday?"

"The night your mother died."

"What for?"

"Like I said, we're just trying to get everything straight. You want to know what happened to your mother, don't you, Ryan?"

Dooley hated talking to cops. It unnerved him the way they always looked directly at you and didn't care that you knew that they thought everything you said was bullshit. Well, whatever. He'd already told them about that night. He'd tell them a hundred times more, if that's what they wanted. They couldn't touch him.

"I went to the library," he said. "I did some research for a school project. Then I went home. I was home by eleven. I called my uncle from the home phone. I know you can check that." They could get phone records that would verify what he was saying, or at least that someone had made a call from his uncle's house at eleven o'clock that night, and tell them the number that had been called.

"Did you talk to anyone at the library, Ryan?" Randall said.

"What? Why do you want to know that?"

Randall repeated his question.

What was going on? Were they trying to put him in it?

He thought for a moment. It had been over a week ago now. He hadn't memorized everything he had done that night, and even if he had, he wanted to come across like a normal person. Most normal people don't remember every detail of a routine evening a whole week ago.

"I went to the information desk," he said. He made a show of thinking it over. "Yeah. I was having trouble find-ing what I needed, so I went to the information desk and talked to a woman there."

"You mean, like an information clerk?"

"Yeah."

Randall pulled out a notebook. "An information clerk remembers talking to you," he said.

That brought Dooley up short. They'd already done some checking. He couldn't decide if that was good or bad.

"She recognized your picture," Randall said. His *picture?* They'd been showing his picture around? "She said you were very polite. Do you remember what time you talked to her, Ryan?"

"I'm not sure," Dooley said. But he had a feeling that wasn't going to cut it. If the woman remembered talking to him, maybe she also remembered when they had spoken. "I think it was pretty soon after I arrived."

"She helped you, didn't she?" Randall said. "She said she pointed you to some resources on the environment, is that right?"

Not only did the woman remember but it also sounded like she had a total-recall memory.

Dooley nodded.

"If you had to estimate what time you talked to the information clerk, what would be your best guess?" Detective Randall said.

"I guess maybe eight, eight-fifteen."

"Then what did you do?"

"I found the material I needed. I worked on my assignment. Then I left."

"Do you remember what time it was when you left?"

"No."

"If you had to estimate what time you left, what would be your best guess?"

Why was Randall pushing on where he'd been that night? What was he after? He couldn't possibly think—

"Ryan? What time did you leave the library?"

"I'm not sure," Dooley said. The place had been jammed with people, but he hadn't spoken to anyone except the woman at the information desk, so maybe he was okay. "But the place closes at ten, right?"

Randall shook his head, as if he were disappointed in Dooley.

"Are you saying you stayed at the library until it closed?"

"No," Dooley said. Not now he wasn't, not when Randall had that look on his face. "I don't remember when I left. I'm just saying it must have been sometime before ten because that's when it closes."

Randall glanced at his partner, whose name Dooley wished he had asked. Then he turned back to Dooley.

"One of the security guards remembers you, Ryan," he said. "He says you left the library at about ten minutes to nine."

"Yeah?" Dooley tried to look doubtful. "I'm pretty sure I was there longer than that. Maybe he made a mistake."

"He's pretty sure," Randall said. "You know how he remembers?"

Dooley was thinking, how could the guy possibly remember? There had been hundreds of people in the library that night, coming and going.

"Seems you picked a busy time to leave," Randall said. "Seems an entire class of Korean English-as-a-second-language students was leaving at the same time you were. Seems you stuck out like a sore thumb. What do you have to say to that?"

"I don't know," Dooley said. "Is he sure it was me? Maybe it was some guy who looked like me. You know what they say about eyewitness identification."

"As a matter of fact, I do," Detective Randall said. "People make mistakes all the time." Dooley waited. "But this particular security guard"—here it comes—"is a retired cop, Ryan. And you know what? He was a pretty good cop in his day. And he says he's positive it was you who left at the same time as those Korean students. The Korean students left at ten to nine. They were on their way to a restaurant nearby

101

where they had a nine o'clock reservation."

Dooley concentrated on looking mystified.

"You have anything to say to that, Ryan?"

"I guess I must have lost track of the time," Dooley said, realizing when he heard the words that he sounded just like his uncle.

"You were seen leaving the library at ten minutes to nine. You told us you walked home. You said you got home at eleven o'clock. You said as soon as you got home, you called your uncle. Ryan, you could have crawled home from the library on your hands and knees and you would have been home in an hour, max. You want to tell us where you were between ten minutes to nine when you left the library and eleven o'clock when you called your uncle?"

Why were they asking that? Why were they pushing on him so hard? Did they think he had something to do with what had happened to Lorraine? How could he have? They knew she was alive at ten when she called Gloria Thomas. And, according to what his uncle had said, they figured she'd died a little after eleven. Had they checked what he'd said before? He'd been in his uncle's house at eleven. Phone records would prove it. He started to have some sympathy for his uncle. For sure, if he'd known the first time he'd talked to the cops that they were going to be back asking more questions, he would have played it differently. He bet his uncle would have, too. Now, no matter what he said, it was going to come back and bite him—hard.

"It's time to come clean, Ryan," Randall said. "You don't want us to think you're hiding anything from us, do you?"

Dooley tried not to panic. But, Jesus, it sounded like they were trying to nail him for something. He thought back to that night. He thought of anyone who might have seen him after he left the library—who might *remember* him. He had taken the bus. Maybe, if they asked, the bus driver would remember him. Or maybe it would turn out that one of the passengers was a regular on that route and would remember him. After he'd got off the bus, he had walked to the apartment building. Maybe, if they asked, there were some people on the street who would remember him. Then …

The man.

There had been a man coming out through the security door when Dooley got there. Dooley had turned away and pretended to fumble in his pocket for his key so that he could catch the door before it clicked shut. He was pretty sure the man hadn't seen his face. But what if he had? Or—knowing Randall—what if the cops had already asked around, based on what the security guard at the library had told them? What if someone had seen him waiting for the bus? What if someone had seen him get on? What if the driver had not only remembered Dooley but had also remembered where he had got off? What if they'd already nosed around there? Boy, when all he'd been trying to avoid was not coming off as a total screwup—*again*. He didn't believe that honesty was always the best policy, but it sure was less complicated than trying to work through all the permutations and ramifications of lying.

"Okay," he said. "So I made a stop before I went home."

Randall leaned back in his chair and waited.

Dooley hesitated. There was no way this wasn't going to come back at him somewhere down the road. But how could he possibly have known what was going to happen that night? He drew in a deep breath, wished he believed in prayer so that he could say one, and told the two detectives exactly what he had done after he'd left the library that night. Neither of them interrupted. After he had finished, Randall asked him a dozen questions, some of them the same question but asked in a different way, as if he were testing Dooley, which, Dooley knew, he was. They both wrote everything down, including the address of the apartment building. Finally Randall said, "Why didn't you tell us this when we talked to you the first time?"

"Because I didn't think it mattered. I had nothing to do with what happened to Lorraine." It wasn't the real reason, but Randall seemed to buy it. "Besides, my uncle said it was an overdose."

The two cops exchanged glances.

"How did your uncle and your mother get along?" Randall said.

"I don't know."

Randall looked into Dooley's eyes. "What do you mean, you don't know?"

"I told you." Cops and their stupid games. You could tell them something a million times and they'd still ask you to see if you'd screw yourself by telling it differently the million-and-first time. "I wasn't close to her. Neither was my uncle, as far as I know."

"As far as you know? What do you mean by that?"

"I mean, I haven't known my uncle that long."

"Exactly how long *have* you known him?"

"Two years."

"You've only known your uncle for two years?"

"Yeah." Jesus, wasn't he listening?

"And before that?"

"Before that, what?"

"You never met him before that?"

"No."

"Why's that?"

"I don't know. Like I said, he and Lorraine weren't close. I didn't even know I had an uncle. Lorraine never mentioned him. She never told him about me, either."

"Is that right?" Randall said. It was always Randall, never his partner, who limited himself to scowling at Dooley.

"Yeah, that's right."

"So your uncle and your mother weren't close," Randall said. "That happens in a lot of families, am I right, Bob?" He glanced at his partner, who merely grunted. "You have any idea why they weren't close, Ryan? Did your mother ever say anything to you about it?"

"I told you," Dooley said. Shithead, I *just* told you. "I didn't know I had an uncle." So figure it out yourself, Einstein. If I didn't know I had an uncle, how could I possibly know why my mother wasn't close to him?

"Right," Randall said. "So you have your mother, who had you ... how old was she when you were born, Ryan?" Acting like he didn't know, trying to get under Dooley's skin. Dooley just stared at him. "Math not your strong point, huh,

Ryan?" Randall said. "Seventeen. She was seventeen when you were born. And you never knew you had an uncle. Makes you wonder what happened, doesn't it—you know, why your mother never told you she had a brother? And, from what you say, why she never told her"—he paused for a fraction of a second—"*brother* that she had a son. Why do you think that is, Ryan?"

"How would I know?" Dooley said. "Like I said ..."

"Right. She never told you that you had an uncle. What about your father?"

His father? Boy, one of Dooley's least favorite subjects. "What about him?"

"Where is he?"

And there it was—the reason Dooley hated the subject.

"I don't know."

"When was the last time you saw him?"

"I don't remember."

"You don't remember the last time you saw your father?"

"I don't remember if I ever saw him. If I did, it was when I was a baby."

"He doesn't come around?"

Dooley shook his head. Why were they so interested in his father?

"Did he keep in touch with your mother?"

"Not that I know of."

"You know his name?"

"Dooley something," Dooley said. "Or something Dooley. I don't know." Lorraine had told him he was named after his father—the Dooley part, anyway.

"Did your mother ever talk about him?"

He shook his head, even though that wasn't quite true. Sometimes, when she was fucked up or weepy, she bawled about him. But Dooley had stopped listening years ago.

"You don't think that's strange?" Randall said.

Boy, what he didn't know about Lorraine.

Randall pulled something out of his jacket pocket and slid it onto the table in front of Dooley. "What do you know about this, Ryan?"

Dooley glanced at the photograph, determined not to be interested, then, despite himself, he stared at it. What the hell? What *was* that?

He picked it up and took a closer look.

Three stones.

Three names.

Three sets of dates.

He squinted at them, double-checking that he was seeing what he thought he was seeing. He looked up at Randall.

"What are those?" he said.

"What do they look like? They're headstones, Ryan."

Dooley looked at them again. "Where are they?"

"Where do you usually find headstones?"

In a cemetery. But: "Which one?"

"You know that big one uptown, right near where the subway goes? They're in there."

Dooley couldn't take his eyes off the picture.

"I don't get it," he said.

"Have you ever been to that cemetery, Ryan?"

"No."

"Have you ever seen these stones before?"

"No."

"Your uncle never took you there?"

"No."

"Your mother?"

"No."

"Did either of them ever mention those stones?"

"No."

Randall looked across the table at him.

"It's a family plot," he said. "But your uncle didn't see to it that your mother was laid to rest there."

Dooley looked at the stones again, at the names and dates.

"Why do you think that is, Ryan?"

"How would I know?"

Randall gazed at the photo for a moment. "Makes you wonder, doesn't it?" he said.

If it wasn't cops sitting across the table from him, Dooley would have agreed.

"Maybe you should talk to your uncle," Randall said. "Maybe he can clarify things for you." He threw some money onto the table to pay for the coffees. He left the photo. He and his partner slid out of the booth. They were sitting in their car outside of the video store when Dooley went in to work but were gone when he looked out the window half an hour later.

■ ■ ■

Dooley closed the store with Kevin, impatient with how

108

long Kevin was taking, cursing under his breath as Kevin fumbled to lock the door. Then he was off, striding home. He let himself in the front door. Jeannie's purse was on the little table in the front hall. Dooley didn't care. He took the stairs two at a time and hammered on his uncle's bedroom door. Inside, his uncle yelled: "Jesus Christ!" Dooley heard his bare feet thump down onto the floor. A pause. The sound of a zipper—his uncle doing up his pants. The bedroom door flew open and his uncle's angry face appeared. He came out into the hall, closed the door softly behind him, and hissed, "What the hell do you think you're doing?"

Dooley thrust the photograph at him.

It took his uncle a moment to stop glowering at him and to focus on the photo.

"Where'd you get that?" he said.

"What is it?" Dooley said.

His uncle glanced over his shoulder at the closed door. He went back into the bedroom, shutting the door behind him. Dooley heard his voice, soft, talking to Jeannie. Then he was back again, brushing past Dooley and padding down the stairs. Dooley followed him.

His uncle went into the kitchen, heading for the scotch again, Dooley thought. But, no, he opened the fridge and pulled out some soda water, which he offered to Dooley. Dooley shook his head. His uncle poured a glass for himself and carried it to the kitchen table. He dropped heavily onto a chair. Dooley sat opposite him and slapped the photo onto the table between them.

"What is it?" he said again.

"Where'd you get this?" his uncle said again.

"The cops."

"When did you see them?"

"This afternoon. They were waiting for me when I got to work. A cop named Randall and his partner." He nudged the photo across the table to his uncle and watched him look at it again. "That's my grandfather, right?" he said, pointing to the first stone, the first name, the first set of dates. The second date on the stone matched when his uncle had said Dooley's grandfather had died. "And that one," he said, pointing at the second stone. "That's my grandmother, right?" She had died earlier than his grandfather, before Dooley was born.

His uncle nodded.

"What about this one?" He pointed to the third stone.

Dooley's uncle ran a finger lightly over the name on the stone.

"My sister," he said.

"Your sister Lorraine," Dooley said. That was the name on the stone.

"Yes," his uncle said, but it seemed to Dooley that he didn't want to talk about it.

"Your sister Lorraine who died"—Dooley tapped the second date on the stone—"thirty-five years ago."

"Yes," his uncle said.

"Not your sister Lorraine who died last week," Dooley said.

"No."

"So you had two sisters named Lorraine?" What kind of sense did that make?

"Yes." Pause. "No." Pause. "Sort of, I guess."

110

"Sort of?" Dooley said. "You guess?"

"I had an older sister."

"Older?" Lorraine—Dooley's mother, Lorraine—had been almost fifteen years younger than Dooley's uncle.

"A couple of years older. She died. It was an accident. My mother, your grandmother, took it hard." He looked at the glass of soda water on the table. "She took it really hard. By then she couldn't have any more kids. So they adopted a baby girl."

Adopted.

Dooley thought that one over, conscious of his uncle's eyes on him.

His uncle.

He thought that one over, too.

"Your parents adopted a baby that just happened to be named Lorraine?" he said finally. What kind of weird coincidence was that?

"I don't know what the original name was. My mother named her Lorraine."

"You're kidding," Dooley said. How fucked up was that?

"She was grieving," his uncle said. "If you ask me, she was clinically depressed. She didn't get out of bed for eight, nine months. Back then, they didn't have the kind of drugs they do now. My father thought ..." His uncle looked him in the eye. "Look, I know it sounds ..." He groped for a word, came up empty, and shook his head. "But that's what happened. They adopted a baby. It gave her a reason to get up in the morning."

If that's what it took, Dooley thought, it didn't say much

111

about his grandmother's feelings for the rest of the family. Maybe that was part of it.

"How did Lorraine"—this was going to get confusing— "how did the new Lorraine take it when she found out?"

There was a long pause before his uncle said, "To the best of my knowledge, they never told her."

That didn't make sense. "How could she not know? Someone must have said something. There must have been pictures, *something*."

His uncle shook his head.

"You have no idea what it did to my mother when Lorraine died. No idea."

"So ... what? You all just pretended the first one never existed?"

His uncle's eyes flashed.

"It wasn't like that. We just ... we just tried to make it easy on her. I never forgot my sister. And I've never pretended she didn't exist."

"But no one told Lorraine—*my* Lorraine? No one told her she was the second one?" The replacement.

"Not that I'm aware of."

Dooley couldn't decide if that was a good thing or a bad thing.

"Is that why you didn't like her, because she was adopted, because she made your mother happy when you couldn't?"

"I never said I didn't like her."

Technically, Dooley had to admit, that was true. But: "You never said anything good about her. You always told me how screwed up she was and that I was better off with her out of my life."

His uncle straightened up in his chair, bristling again. "You going to tell me you don't think that's true?"

"*You* going to tell me you liked her?"

His uncle looked at him for a few moments. "No," he said. "No, I'm not."

"Were you jealous of her? Is that it?"

His uncle snorted. "No. I didn't *like* her because she killed my mother."

"*What?* What are you talking about?"

"She was one of those girls, they're fine when they're little, then they hit puberty and all hell breaks loose," his uncle said. "She was wild—crazy wild. She ditched school more than she attended. Got kicked out regularly, too. She lied—about everything. If she didn't like someone, she made trouble for them—other kids, teachers, you name it. She was into partying—booze, drugs, whatever. She came home in the middle of the night when she bothered to come home at all. She'd disappear for days, sometimes weeks, and never call, and there would be my mother, frantic with worry, crying, not sleeping, sending me out there to look for her." By then, Dooley guessed, his uncle had been a cop for a while.

"Then when Lorraine would walk through the door, what would my mother do? Would she yell at her, tell her she'd better smarten up? No. She'd hug her and cry when she saw she was safe, she wasn't lying in a ditch somewhere. Did Lorraine care? No. She only ever came home to pick up some clothes, grab some food, steal some money or something she could sell to get money. She'd be home maybe a couple of days, sometimes just a couple of hours. Then she would pick a fight with my mother"—*my* mother, not *our* mother—"and off she'd go again. She didn't care. She was fifteen, sixteen years old and she just flat out didn't give a damn about anyone."

Dooley wasn't sure he wanted to hear this, but: "You said she killed your mother."

Dooley's uncle was sitting right there in the kitchen with Dooley, but he was staring at something that had happened a long time ago. Something he still felt. Something that was sharp enough that it still hurt.

"Lorraine hadn't been home in weeks. We had no idea where she was. Then she calls my mother, crying. She's sick, she's broke, she's sorry; she wants to come home. My mother asks her, where are you? Turns out she's up on some guy's farm north of the city and she's got no way to get back. My dad's not home. I'm working. So my mother takes the car and goes to get her. Lorraine's standing out on the side of the road waiting for her. They start back home. It's late. My mother is tired. She wasn't well, your grandmother. She had heart problems. She tired easily. She wanted to pull over for a few minutes, but Lorraine told her, no, she wanted to get back to the city; she said she would drive and my mother could rest. By then she had her license—one of the things my mother tried to get her to settle down. Let her get her driver's license, promise her if she's good we'll buy her a car. I don't need to tell you that never happened. Anyway, my mother let her drive and she closed her eyes to take a nap. Next thing you know, the car crossed the center line and hit another car head-on. Lorraine walked away with a couple of scratches. The other driver suffered non-life-threatening injuries. My mother died on the way to the hospital."

Jesus.

"It was an accident, right?" Dooley said.

"Both the cops and the ambulance attendants thought there was something not right about the way Lorraine was acting. They had her tested. She was high." He looked directly at Dooley. "She was high and she was driving. If she hadn't been high or she hadn't been driving, if she'd had even a sliver of common sense, it never would have happened." His uncle looked over at the cupboard where he kept the booze, but he didn't get up. Instead, he fiddled with his glass of soda water.

"You never told me," Dooley said. Not, to be honest, that his uncle had spent a lot of time talking about family. Lorraine hadn't told him, either. No wonder.

"It didn't seem relevant," his uncle said.

Right.

"Why do you think Randall showed me that picture?"

His uncle shrugged. "Like I said, they're treating Lorraine's death as suspicious. They think someone killed her, so they're starting with her nearest and dearest. That's where they always start because that's where it usually ends."

"You mean me?" Dooley said, startled.

"I mean me," his uncle said. He drank down the soda water in a couple of big gulps. "I'm going back to bed. You should get some sleep."

Dooley sat at the kitchen table for a few minutes, thinking about the picture and about what his uncle—his *uncle*—

had told him, especially that last part. He looked at the fridge and thought about the beer that was inside and about the cupboard near the phone where the scotch and vodka were. It had been a long time—a very long time—but he still felt the pull. It was like the most beautiful girl in the world was beckoning him and she would do anything for him if only he fell into her arms.

He stood up and left the kitchen.

■　■　■

Dooley was lying in bed, thinking again about the beer in the fridge and the scotch and vodka in the cupboard near the phone and wondered whether his uncle would hear him if he snuck back downstairs, when his cell phone, charging on his bed-side table, rang. He checked the readout but didn't recognize the number. He answered and heard a familiar, whiny female voice. "Dooley?"

"Teresa?" He glanced at the clock on his bedside table. It was nearly two in the morning.

"Did he say anything to you?" she said. "When he saw you, I mean?"

"Say anything? What are you talking about, Teresa?"

"Jeffie," she said, her voice shrill. Dooley imagined her with a cigarette in one hand, pacing while she talked. Teresa was one of those wire-thin chicks you'd make for a meth-head the way she was in perpetual motion. Really, she was just high-strung, nervous, always worried about something. Right now, it seemed, she was worried about Jeffie. "He told me he was going to meet you. He hasn't been home since. He hasn't called. He doesn't answer his phone. It's not like him. I'm worried. Did he say anything to you? Did he seem okay?"

"He was supposed to meet me, but he never showed up," Dooley said. "But that was three days ago, Teresa. You mean you haven't seen him since then?"

"I went to the cops, I was that worried," she said.

"And?"

"They ran him."

Dooley could picture their reaction. A guy with Jeffie's record goes missing, you figure he screwed up again and is hiding out somewhere. Or you figure he's screwing someone else. Or he's getting screwed. But you don't worry about him. You don't allocate manpower to finding him. You don't do anything, unless, of course, you catch him dead-to-rights committing a crime, either that or just plain dead.

"I'm sure he's fine," Dooley said. The most likely scenario—Jeffie was tired of being pressured into marriage. He was nervous, maybe even resentful, about Teresa's getting pregnant. Maybe he'd scored the money he was after and had done what he'd mentioned to Dooley—maybe he'd gone back home. Maybe he'd found someone else who didn't want as much from him as Teresa did. Or maybe he was just lying low for a while, trying to decide what he wanted.

"I'm sure he'll turn up."

"If you see him or hear from him, tell him to call me, okay, Dooley? Tell him I'm worried about him."

Dooley said he would.

Seven

Saturday morning, if he wasn't working, what Dooley liked to do was sleep in, until noon if he could get away with it, which, usually, he couldn't because it seemed to irritate his uncle if Dooley was still in bed while his uncle was up and pumped, usually from a ten kilometer run, and was cleaning the house or working in the yard or whatever.

But this Saturday, Dooley swung his legs out of bed as soon as he heard his uncle go out the back door for his run. He wasn't getting up early so much as he was carrying through the sleepless night that he'd spent thinking about Lorraine after not thinking about her at all for years. Okay, so maybe that wasn't quite true. Every now and then, her face would pop into his mind and he would wonder where she had got to. Wherever it was, he always hoped she was miserable. And now here she was, dead and in his head again. Dead and maybe murdered, and the thing was, if it turned out that was really what had happened, he wouldn't be surprised. He could imagine Lorraine out there partying—she loved to party. And, boy, the kind of people she hung out with—not that he was in a position to criticize. So, yeah, he could see her maybe shaking her ass and teasing some guy or maybe opening her mouth and saying something smart and pissing off some guy and, boom, she's dead.

Or maybe she'd been out there trying to amuse herself—Lorraine was always restless unless she was with people, unless something was happening, like she couldn't stand to be alone with herself, maybe couldn't stand herself, and Dooley could see why, no problem. So maybe she was out there and maybe—he'd give her the benefit of the doubt on this one—maybe she was trying to keep herself straight (Dooley knew what that was all about, how hard that was), but she was with some of her old friends who didn't respect that, hell, who didn't like the fact that she wasn't one of them anymore. He knew what that was about, too.

He could picture them saying, Come on, Lorraine, just one drink, or just one hit, come on, you want to feel good, don't you? People like that, sometimes they get mad when you say no. Sometimes they take it the wrong way that you're clean. Sometimes they think that *you* think that you're all of a sudden better than they are, which, of course, you aren't. But that's how they see it, mostly because they know they're messed up, even if they don't want to admit it. So first they tease you. Then they wheedle. Then, you can count on it, they force the issue. And when you still say no, maybe you sound self-righteous. Dooley could imagine Lorraine coming across that way; she always was extreme. Then these old friends of yours decide to make it their business to see to it

119

that you have fun. They need you to have fun. They need to drag you down. They need you to drink up or smoke up or shoot up. They'll even help you, whether you want them to or not. And maybe that's how Lorraine ended up dead with a needle in her arm.

He made his way down to the kitchen, noting on the way that his uncle's bedroom door was open, which meant that Jeannie was gone, which meant that she must have slipped out early, maybe in the middle of the night because Dooley hadn't heard her. Dooley wondered why. Usually when Jeannie ended up in his uncle's bed, she stayed there until morning, and usually his uncle brought her a cup of coffee to start her engines before she got up.

What went on between his uncle and Jeannie was none of his business, but Dooley liked Jeannie. He liked the way she never acted awkward about staying over. He liked the way she turned up in the kitchen in the morning wearing a silky robe and skimpy little slippers that let her toes, bright red with nail polish, stick out. He liked the way she wore lipstick to breakfast, and he liked the red lip marks her lipstick left on her coffee cup. He liked the little cloud of perfume that hung in the air wherever she'd been. And he liked her pancakes, especially when she threw a handful of blueberries into the batter. But she wasn't here this morning, so Dooley set up the coffeemaker and switched it on and got out a bowl and a box of cereal—the sweet kind that he had to buy himself and that his uncle glowered at every time he opened the cupboard and saw it and always made some crack about why didn't Dooley just fill his bowl with sugar and spoon that down, he'd get the same amount of nutrition, which was nil, and the same sugar shock, which was astronomical. He got the milk from the fridge. He was working on his second helping between swallows of his second cup of coffee when the phone rang. All Dooley managed to get out was, "Hello," before the caller—a man—launched into a rapid-fire delivery.

"Mr. McCormack, sorry to bother you so early in the A.M., but I wanted to catch you before you left the house."

"I'm not—" Dooley began, trying to head the guy off, tell him he wasn't Mr. McCormack. But the man raced on before he could get any further.

"It's about your sister's things—and, by the way, my condolences. You may be aware, Mr. McCormack, that the rental market is pretty tight, this end of it anyway, and I've already had some interest in the apartment. The police were here a couple of times, wouldn't even let me in the place, but they've released it now. I hate to rush you, Mr. McCormack, but if you wouldn't mind ... er ... that is to say, all of her things are still in the apartment and I'd really appreciate it if you could, you know, take care of them. Or, if you want, I could box everything up for you and you could pick it up. The furniture, well, I could take that off your hands, unless of course you'd like to look after that yourself ..."

Lorraine's things.

Dooley couldn't even begin to imagine what they might consist of. Clothes, for sure. Lorraine liked to look good—at least, she did when she wasn't so high she didn't give a shit about anything. She liked to be the one all the guys turned

121

to look at when she walked into the bar or the party or what-ever it was. Okay, so she was getting up there. She'd turned thirty-five the day Dooley came to live with his uncle, but from what he'd seen, she didn't look bad, all things consid-ered. Besides clothes, Dooley figured she just had regular household stuff—dishes and furniture and a whole bunch of other crap he had no use for. He wanted to pound his head against the wall and keep on pounding it until he'd driven her out of his head once and for all. She'd been so fucked up.

He was going to say, "I'll tell Mr. McCormack you called." He was going to let his uncle deal with it. His uncle, who did-n't like her any more than he did, but who had gone to the morgue to look at her. Who had arranged the funeral. Who had shouldered it while probably choking on his feelings. His uncle, who wasn't even related to her—unlike Dooley.

"Okay," he said instead. "I'll come over. I'll take care of it."

He finished his breakfast and looked at the clock on the stove. It was still early, but he tried Beth's cell phone anyway.

And got her voice mail.

She hadn't returned any of his calls, even the ones when he didn't leave a message, but he still knew that she knew it was him. She could tell by looking at her missed calls.

"It's me," he said. "It's Saturday morning. Call me."

He wrote a note for his uncle—*Out. Back soon*—and left the house.

■ ■ ■

122

When Dooley got to the building where Lorraine used to live, he scanned the tenant directory for the super's name and buzzed his apartment.

"I'm here about Lorraine McCormack's apartment," he said in response to the super's raspy, "Yeah?"

The super buzzed him into the lobby even though Dooley could easily have gotten in on his own. He'd tried the security door. The lock was broken. He waited inside on a grayish carpet that he suspected had once upon a time been a different color, although he couldn't begin to imagine which one, until the super, a stout man in work pants and a work shirt, appeared. He looked around, as if he were expecting to see someone else. But there wasn't anyone else. There was just Dooley.

"You're her *brother?*" the super said.

"Her son."

The super looked even more surprised, but Dooley couldn't tell why.

"She's up on seven," the super said. Then he caught himself. "That is to say, she was."

They rode the elevator together, both of them watching the numbers above the door light up one by one. When they got to Lorraine's floor, the super exited first and fumbled for a key on a ring that was so dense with keys that they stuck straight out like spokes on a wheel.

"She was okay, your mother," the super said as he opened the door to 713. "She mostly paid her rent on time. Never gave me a hard time about repairs. A lot of the tenants, they have no respect. It's not theirs, so they don't take care

123

of it. They break stuff and then they scream at me to fix it."
He sounded like every other super in every other rat-hole
building Dooley had ever lived in.

The super pushed the door open so that Dooley could go
in first. He wasn't surprised to see that the place was a
mess—the super had said that the cops had been there.
They had gone through the place. Dooley could see, too,
that they had dusted for prints. But he was surprised at how
much stuff she had.

"She didn't travel light, did she?" he said, mostly to himself.

"You know women," the super said. "They love to shop.
Love to buy shit. Am I right?"

Dooley stared at him.

The super looked down at the ground. "Sorry," he mumbled.
"Nearly three years she lived here, she never once
mentioned a kid. So, what do you want to do?"

Dooley turned around slowly to take in the combination
living room and dining room, the galley kitchen, one end
opening onto a dinette set, the other end facing the apartment door. Off the living room, a hallway with two doors
in it, one on either side, a bedroom and a bathroom,
Dooley guessed.

"I'll take a look around, see if there's anything I want to
keep, you know, for sentimental reasons." Like that was
going to happen. "Anything that's left after that, it's yours."

The super scanned the apartment with an assayer's eye.
"Yeah?" he said.

"Keep it. Burn it. Sell it. Give it away. I don't care,"
Dooley said. "Just give me some time to look around, okay?"

The super's eyes narrowed. "How do I know you're really her son?"

Well, finally, Dooley thought.

"As opposed to what?" Dooley said. "A burglar?" He crossed to a bookshelf that was filled with knickknacks, but that also contained—surprise!—books, and grabbed a framed photograph, which he thrust at the super: Lorraine, approximate age twenty-nine—Dooley remembered her bitching and whining about her next birthday being the *big* one—and Dooley, approximate age eleven, both of them glassy-eyed.

The super examined it and then examined Dooley. "You can't be too careful," he said.

Boy, he had that right. He handed the photo back to Dooley.

"The cops," Dooley said. "Did they take anything?"

"Fingerprints," the super said. "Some of her stuff—her address book, a few other things. They made a list and gave me a copy. You want it?"

Dooley shook his head.

"Close the door on your way out," the super said.

The minute Dooley was alone, he dropped the framed photograph into the nearest wastepaper basket. He went over to the bookshelf and examined the contents. Jesus, all those books. What was up with that? They were real books, too, not just chick lit and romances and Stephen King, the crap he remembered her reading sometimes when she was in a new relationship and wasn't completely fucked up. There was a book on psychology, a couple on home

125

décor—home *décor!*—another one on the history of salt, of all things. And what were those? Perfect. Self-help books. Twelve-step books. He pulled one off the shelf and flipped through it. It was well thumbed and highlighted throughout in yellow and gave off a scent that reminded him of Lorraine. He flipped to the front and checked the date. It had been published only last year, so whatever lame-ass attempt she had made to get herself right, it had been recent. Maybe it was really true. Maybe she had been trying. Maybe she'd even been ahead of the game. He didn't want to believe it—he was surprised at how bitter he felt—he didn't want to give her any credit, even though he knew anything was possible because, hey, look where he was now.

He sank down onto her sofa, opened the book again, and held it to his face. Boy, that scent took him back. It made him remember Lorraine, her hair thick and glossy, in tight jeans and a tighter T-shirt. Lorraine, checking her lipstick in the bathroom mirror before she set out to meet someone. Lorraine laughing as she raised a glass to her lips. Lorraine, standing unsteadily to uncork some more wine. Lorraine with her head in the toilet, puking. Lorraine passed out, spit caked on her cheek. Lorraine glassy-eyed. Lorraine enraged as she tore the apartment apart looking for a bottle, some pills, a needle. Lorraine spaced out, immobile. Lorraine shaking and scratching, needing something to make herself right. Lorraine screaming at whichever guy was at the apartment this week, whichever guy was slipping Dooley a ten and telling him to get lost, whichever guy was telling Dooley, stay in there—there being his room—or you'll be sorry.

Lorraine telling him, be a good boy, stay away from the apartment for a few days; you got someone you can crash with, right, pressing a couple of twenties into his hand, probably given to her by whatever guy was in the bedroom waiting for her. Lorraine prancing around in her bra and panties and some flimsy thing over top, trying to cook for some guy sitting at the dinette set, grilling a steak for the guy and sending Dooley to his room to watch TV with a couple of boiled hotdogs and a bag of chips.

She never said so, but Dooley was pretty sure he was an accident. Who *wants* to be pregnant at seventeen? And now he was supposed to believe that a twelve-step book, all marked up, had changed her? She had written comments in the margins, positive thoughts, encouragement—*You can do it. You can get through just one day. You have the courage. You have the strength*—exclamation points next to passages that, as far as Dooley could see, were platitudes written by some guy who had never been there. On one page, in the margin, a list of stuff she needed from the drugstore—that was more like Lorraine. A little further on, in an inside margin, written so small that he almost missed it, a phone number that she had drawn a heart around with a little lace pattern at the edges, like a valentine. He wondered if the cops had seen it and called the number and, if they had, what the voice on the other end of the line had told them about her. Not that he cared. He dropped the book into the same wastepaper basket as the framed photo and scanned the rest of the shelf. She had nothing that he wanted to read.

Someone knocked on the door. Before Dooley could get

up to see who it was, the door opened. It was one of the women from the funeral—the rough-looking one. She came in full of purpose, looking like she was ready to open fire with a barrage of words. But she stopped in her tracks when she saw it was Dooley.

"I thought it was the cops," she offered in a raspy voice.

Well, it wasn't. He wished she would go away. But she didn't, even though it was clear she'd been mistaken.

"Gloria lit a fire under them," she said, "and they started asking questions. I wanted to see if they turned up anything."

"What kind of questions?" Dooley said, interested now.

"Whether we'd seen her using lately."

We? She must have meant some of the other women at the funeral.

"And?"

"And no," the woman said, glaring at him. He wondered if she used the same attitude with the cops. He wondered, too, how reliable she was and what she really knew. People who tried to kick a habit could be pretty wily. They could hide things, at least for a while, until it got hard-core again.

"What else did they ask?" he said.

"Where she got her money, like that has anything to do with anything."

"Her money?" Lorraine used to waitress sometimes, but mostly she collected welfare benefits. Sometimes guys gave her money. "What'd you tell them?"

"What do you think I told them? She had a job."

"She did?" That was a surprise.

The woman looked at him as if he were crazy. "Thirty

hours a week in a store. But they were looking for something else. They kept asking if I knew about the money she'd been depositing in the bank every month. They didn't say how much it was, but I got the feeling it was enough to make them wonder."

Wonder about what?

"Used to make me wonder, too," the woman said. She eyed Dooley carefully, as if weighing his worth. "As long as I've known her, she always had cash—a lot of it—at the beginning of the month, even after she paid her rent and bought groceries. Even when she wasn't working. She'd party." Dooley imagined how Lorraine could come up with party money—she wasn't bad-looking and, as far as he knew, she was ready and willing to do whatever it took to come up with party fixings. "Until she decided to straighten up," the woman said. "I don't know if it's true or not, but about six months ago, she told me she'd opened up a savings account for the first time in her life." She was looking around the place as she talked. Her eyes came to rest on the small TV and the DVD player next to it.

"You want them?" Dooley said.

The woman looked hungrily at him.

"They were hers. I'm sure you're—"

"They're yours now," Dooley said. "Go ahead, take them."

The woman wasted no time. She piled the DVD player on top of the TV, unplugged them both, and picked them up.

"Did they ask about anything else?" Dooley said. The woman was studying Lorraine's tiny collection of DVDs. "The cops," Dooley prompted.

"Just about family stuff," the woman said, her eyes still on the DVDs. "Why she left home, what kind of relationship she had with her brother, whether she'd said anything about that or we'd heard any rumors about what went down between them when she was a kid."

"What kind of rumors?"

"They didn't say. But the way they said it, I got this weird vibe, you know?"

Weird. Jerry Panelli had used that word. He'd said the cops had been asking "weird shit" questions.

"And?" Dooley said.

"She never talked about her family—well, except you. She said she missed you."

Right. That was a good one.

"Go ahead," Dooley said. "Take the DVDs. Otherwise, I'll just throw them out."

The woman was already holding the TV and the DVD player, so Dooley got up and scooped up the DVDs and set them on top of the pile. He walked her across the hall and opened her apartment door for her. Then he went back to Lorraine's to finish up.

He went into the kitchen. Pots, pans, rancid food in the fridge, canned and boxed foods in the cupboards. On the counter, a coffeemaker, canisters of tea and coffee. Dishes, cutlery, kitchen stuff. All ordinary.

He opened her closet—shoes, clothes, handbags. Not a lot of stuff, but enough. The super could burn it, give it to charity, give it to his wife, if he had one, give it to his girl-friend. Dooley didn't care.

He crossed to her dresser, opened the top drawer, and immediately wished he hadn't—Jesus, thongs and skimpy little see-through bras. Second drawer: T-shirts, sweaters, tank tops. Third drawer: jeans, slacks, shorts. A bikini.

Her bedside table. The drawer, where he found condoms, which he had expected, and a vibrator, which he hadn't.

On to the bathroom, which contained toiletries, more condoms, birth control pills.

And that was it.

He paused on his way out and looked into the wastepaper basket where he had dropped the photograph and the twelve-step book. He stared into it, then bent and retrieved the book and the photo. He slid the photo out of the frame and between the pages of the book and then dropped the frame back into the garbage.

■ ■ ■

Dooley and his uncle, who, Dooley realized for the hundredth time, wasn't really his uncle at all, sat across from each other over pork chops, rice, and green peppers in a tomato sauce, both with a glass of soda water, both, Dooley bet, wishing they had something stronger.

"So," his uncle said, "you didn't work today?" It was the first non-supper-preparation words he had said to Dooley since he'd come home from checking up on his stores.

"No," Dooley said.

"You got plans for tonight?"

"I thought I'd hook up with Beth," Dooley said. *If* he

could get hold of her. "You? Jeannie coming over?"

"Maybe," his uncle said. "I don't know."

Dooley chewed a piece of pork chop and thought about Jeannie being gone so early that morning.

"Is everything okay between you two?" he said.

His uncle looked at him across the table. "What are you? Some kind of relationship counselor?"

Okay, so he was in that mood—again.

Dooley finished his supper.

"You want me to clean up?" he said.

"No," his uncle said. "You go ahead."

He left his uncle sitting at the kitchen table.

■ ■ ■

Dooley's experience with girls could be summed up in one word: Beth. Sometimes, when he was with her or when he was just thinking about her, he couldn't believe she was in his life. More than that, he couldn't believe that she wanted him in her life. Even more than that—he couldn't believe that she wanted him in her bed. Boy, and that was something else he could never believe, even when it was happening. It always went the same way—he'd go to see her when her mother was at work and they'd maybe do a little homework together or they'd start to watch a movie—just start; he didn't think they'd ever actually watched a movie all the way through from start to finish when they were alone in the apartment. Then he'd look at her across the table or next to him on the couch and he wouldn't be able to stop looking, she was that

132

beautiful, with coffee-colored eyes and coffee-colored hair, creamy-white skin and lush pink lips that, the minute he looked at them, all he wanted to do was kiss them. And that's what always ended up happening. At first, she'd been the one to start it, maybe because she saw how unsure he was. He had to be the only guy his age who had never really kissed a girl, not like that, anyway. The thing he liked about her—well, one of the maybe million things he liked about her—was that she seemed a little nervous about it at first, too. But she'd gone ahead and had come right up close to him and had looked up at him and smiled. She'd slipped her arms around him, so he had pulled her close, and he'd kissed her. Boy, he sure did like kissing her.

He liked touching her, too, and she seemed to enjoy it too. Her hands always slid under his shirt when he did. They worked their way down to his jeans. She'd been gentle and soft at first, and then not so gentle and soft. Then, one day, she took off all her clothes. Dooley couldn't get over it.

It always started off great, and it always got better. But if you asked him what the absolute best part was, he'd have to say it was after, when he was feeling good and she was smiling and was lying there in his arms, her head on his chest or on his shoulder, and they were both naked and he could run his hand down over the curve of her hip. He couldn't think of anything he liked to do more.

Right now, though, things weren't so good. Right now he had the opposite feeling, the one he'd been dragging around with him practically his whole life. An empty feeling. An uncertain feeling. He hadn't heard from her in three days. She hadn't returned any of his calls. He pulled on his jacket and left the house. He dug his cell phone out of his pocket. As soon as he was on the sidewalk, he punched in her number.

"Hi, you've reached Beth …"

He headed for the bus stop and stood for a few moments, shifting from foot to foot, waiting for the bus. When it didn't show up right away, he decided to walk. He looked up when he was finally across the street from her building and saw that someone was home. There were lights on in the living room, which had windows from floor to ceiling and a sliding door that opened onto a balcony. There was a light on a little farther down, too, in what he knew was Beth's mother's room. Shit.

A girl about Dooley's age was coming out the security door when Dooley got there. She smiled at him and held the door for him. Dooley thanked her and headed for the elevators. A couple of minutes later, he was knocking on Beth's apartment door.

Beth, not her mother, answered, but she didn't invite him inside. She looked more tired than angry.

"I'm sorry," Dooley said right away, before she could say anything.

She still didn't ask him in. Instead, she stood in the doorway, her arms wrapped around herself like she was trying to keep warm, and said, "Mr. Puklicz down the hall told my mother that the police were here this morning. He said they wanted to know if he'd seen you around here a week ago Wednesday."

Uh-oh. The cops had checked out what he'd told them.

On the one hand, that could be good news: If the guy had seen him and remembered him, it would get the cops off his case. But it also looked like it could be bad news—exactly what he'd been trying to avoid when he'd kept Beth out of it the first time he'd spoken to the cops. He hadn't wanted them talking to her, asking her if Dooley had been at her place that night, asking what she knew about his mother. But they'd been here. They'd talked to that man who, it turned out, knew her and her mother. What had the cops said to him? What had he said to Beth's mother?

"About that—" he began.

"You know what he told her?"

He'd been wrong about her not being angry. The tightness of her lips told him that she was furious. And the way she was telling it, with that look on her face, gave him a pretty good idea what this Puklicz guy had said.

"He told her he was leaving the building just as you were going in. He said you caught the security door so you didn't have to be buzzed in. He said he didn't try to stop you because he knows you're a friend of mine." Her eyes were burning into him.

"Look, Beth—"

"He said you looked furtive."

Furtive.

"He said you looked away from him, like maybe you were hoping he wouldn't recognize you. What were you doing here, Dooley?"

"I—" Should he tell the truth or would it be easier on both of them if he fudged it a little? "I wanted to see you, but—"

135

He made a choice. He went with the lie, a little white one. "I remembered you were with your history team."

"You *remembered?* I told you when you called that night that that was what I was doing. Didn't you believe me?"

"What? *Of course* I believed you!" This wasn't going at all the way he had hoped. "But I thought maybe I could see you anyway, maybe meet some of your friends." So far, she hadn't introduced him to any of them. "Then I thought maybe that wasn't such a good idea. I know how serious you are about school. So I didn't come up. I went home." That part was true. He'd been down there at the elevator, his hand out to push the button, determined to go up there, determined to check on her, to see if she was really doing what she told him she was going to be doing. And then something had happened: Common sense had kicked in. He'd imagined the look on her face when she opened the door and saw him there. He'd thought about what she would think of his explanation—*Hey, I know you're busy with your history team, but I—*. And that had stopped him, that *but*, and the lame excuse he would have had to follow it with, and the possibility—the probability—that she would see through it. That and the thought that he could well and truly blow it with her.

"I bet your mom freaked out when she heard the police were asking about me, huh?" he said, trying to keep it light, like it was no big deal.

She wasn't buying it.

"Why were the police even here?" she said. "Why were they asking about you?"

136

"I told you about that, Beth. I told you about how the cops are with me."

"Right," she said. "Right." The sarcasm in her voice rattled him. "Because when we started going out, you told me all about yourself."

Terrific. She was back to that again—back to Lorraine.

"That's why I came over tonight," he said. "To apologize."

"You said you'd told me *everything*."

He remembered that day. He'd sat down with her, his belly clenched like it was now, his head bowed in shame like it was now, feeling certain that the more he said, the greater his chances were of losing her, just like he felt now, but talking anyway because he felt he owed her that much. He wanted her and she deserved to know what kind of person he was. So he had swallowed hard and started talking. He'd told her every ugly, dirty thing he had ever done, every ugly, dirty thing he wished he could forget. He'd told her all about himself. Himself, not Lorraine. He couldn't remember if he'd even mentioned her.

"I'm sorry," he said again. "But she wasn't like your mother—not even remotely. Why do you think I live with my uncle?"

"You lied to me," she said.

"She's gone, Beth. She wasn't part of my life. She's never going to be part of my life. So it doesn't matter." Why couldn't she see that?

"I don't mean when you told me she was dead," she said. "I mean the other day, when I was at the store. You told me you hadn't seen her in years. That's what you said, isn't it?"

137

"Yeah," he said, cautiously. Now what?

She reached into her jeans pocket and pulled out a piece of paper. She unfolded it and thrust it at him. It was something she'd cut out of a newspaper, from the obituary page—a picture and a little write-up about Lorraine. He skimmed it. There was no way his uncle was responsible for this. It must have been some of Lorraine's friends, maybe the ones who had been at the funeral, the ones who had insisted that she had been doing so well.

"When I found out your mother had died, I looked in the paper to see if there was anything about it, and I found this. See, it even mentions you." She pointed out his name. "And that's your mother," she said, jabbing the picture. "Right?"

It was a photo of Lorraine from back a few years. She looked pretty good in it—smiling, her eyes with a real sparkle to them, although Dooley had no idea what had put it there—maybe a man, maybe a chemical—her hair falling in waves over her shoulders, her dark lashes—she never went anywhere without a couple of layers of mascara accentuating her pale blue eyes.

"That's her, right, Dooley?" Beth said again, her voice harsh now. "Your mother who you haven't seen in years, right?"

"Beth—"

"That's the woman you were talking to outside your school that day," she said. She shook the newspaper clipping under his nose. "You were talking to her, but when I asked you who she was, you said she was—"

Just some woman.

"—just some woman. That's what you said. You lied to

138

me, Dooley. You keep lying to me."

Which was his cue to say: "I'm sorry."

"I would never lie to you," she said.

She said it so easily, as if it were indisputable.

"I thought you were different," she said. "I respected you, Dooley." He couldn't think of a single other person who had ever said that to him, and it made it all the worse that she'd used the past tense. "I respected you because you told me about yourself, even though I knew you were afraid to. I thought, someone who would tell me all that about himself would never lie to me."

He could have said again that he was sorry. He could have said it over and over, a hundred times, a thousand times, a million times. But he had a sick feeling that it wouldn't make up for what he had already done.

"Come on, Beth. She was high almost all the time."

"That's not what it says here." She waved the clipping at him again.

"Her friends wrote that. A person's friends say nice things when a person dies. But she was my *mother*. I *know* what she was like."

A cell phone trilled. Hers, not his. She reached into her pocket, pulled it out, glanced at the display. Dooley saw it, too. *Nevin*. He looked at her.

"Are you seeing him?" Dooley said.

"I told you, he's on the debating team. We—"

"Take each other on," Dooley said. "Right. You going to take him on tonight?"

She stiffened. "What's that supposed to mean?"

"You tell me."

She flipped her phone open. "Nevin," she said, putting a smile into it. "Give me a minute." She held the phone to her chest. "Goodnight, Dooley," she said. She stepped back inside and closed the door.

ooley left his cell phone on that night, hoping that Beth would call. It rang at five AM. Dooley groped for it and stared groggily at the display. He held the phone to his ear.

Teresa. She was hysterical. Dooley felt himself go colder than ice as he listened to her pour out a stream of words, apologizing for waking him up, saying it was important, running on and on, faster and shriller, until Dooley told her, "Wait. Stop. Slow down, Teresa." He glanced at the clock radio on his bedside table. "Tell me again," he said. He repeated the address she gave him. "I'll be there as soon as I can," he said. He pressed the disconnect button and reached for his jeans, which were on the floor beside his bed. He jammed his legs into them and stood up.

Note, he thought as he crept down the stairs. He should leave his uncle a note.

He scrawled one on the back of a grocery receipt and stuck it to the front of the fridge: *Gone for a walk.*

A long one, it turned out, because the buses didn't run

often this early on a Sunday morning.

Teresa and Jeffie lived in an apartment above a storefront Greek bakery. Dooley craned his neck so he could look at the window on the second floor. He saw a face appear and then disappear. Teresa, watching for him.

The bottom door, wedged in between the Greek bakery and a knickknack store, was unlocked. Dooley pulled it open. Teresa, tears streaming down her face, was standing at the top of a set of dark, narrow stairs. He climbed them slowly, in no rush to get up there with her. As soon as he reached the top, she threw her arms around him. In no time, both his sweatshirt and his T-shirt were wet.

"Let's go inside," he said.

There were four doors leading off the gloomy hallway—two at the front and two at the rear, each one leading to a different apartment. The one to his right at the front was ajar. He steered her inside.

The place was small. Right inside the door was the kitchen—fridge, stove, microwave, sink, counter, small round table, four chairs, two of them jammed up against the wall under the window that looked out onto the street. He guided her through the kitchen into the living room. All the furniture was clean, but all of it was too big for the size of the room, as if it had been bought for someplace else, maybe some place Teresa wanted Jeffie to get where they could raise a baby. Poor Jeffie, Dooley thought, and then caught himself, remembering what had brought him here.

He looked at the rest of the place. Gigantic flat-screen TV. Beside it, a sound system. Beyond that, a hall to the bathroom and bedroom.

He made Teresa sit down on the couch and perched opposite her on a coffee table so big you could sleep on it. She was still crying. He hooked a tissue box with one finger and handed it to her. She looked blankly at it. He pulled out a couple of tissues and pressed them into her hand.

"What happened?" Dooley said. "What did the cops say?"

"He's dead," she said, the words liquid with tears. "Someone killed him."

"Killed him?" No way. "What happened?"

"I had to go with them," Teresa said. "I had to identify him." Dooley wasn't surprised. As far as he knew, Jeffie didn't have any family. He'd told Dooley he didn't know who his parents were. He'd been raised in foster care. "His head was all smashed in. His face—" She started to sob again. Dooley pressed some more tissues into her hand and waited. "He was wearing a ring I gave him. And he had those tattoos." A ship—big surprise—that looked to Dooley like a pirate ship, on his left upper arm, and a skull and crossbones on his right upper arm. "Even then—" More sobbing. More tears. "They said he's been dead for maybe four days, Dooley."

Jesus, no wonder she couldn't get it together. He couldn't begin to imagine what it must have been like to look at a body four days gone, especially the body of someone you cared about.

"Do you have any idea who did it, Teresa?"

She looked up at him, startled. "No."

"What did you tell the cops?"

"Just that I hadn't seen him since Tuesday morning. He

143

said he had to go out. He said he had some errands to do and then he was going to see you. He never came back. At first I was mad. I thought he'd run out on me. I'm pregnant. Jeffie was nice about it when I told him, but I think he was scared, you know? But he's a sweet guy, so after a couple of days, when he didn't even call me, I got worried. I called the cops. They didn't do anything. Then, last night, they came to the door and told me he's dead." More tears. Dooley handed her another couple of tissues. "They asked me the same thing you did. They asked me if I knew who would want to kill him."

"You sure you don't have any idea? Maybe he was in some kind of jam with someone?"

"Jam? What kind of jam?"

"You know him better than I do, Teresa."

She dabbed at her eyes. "Jeffie knows a lot of people, but he's always saying he doesn't know why he wastes his time with most of them. He says most of them aren't worth knowing—well, except for you, Dooley. Jeffie likes you. He said it was good you were back in school, even if you had to live with a cop. Is that true, Dooley? You live with a cop?"

"He's my uncle," Dooley said. "And he's not a cop anymore. He retired."

Teresa digested this.

"What did you tell the cops, Teresa?" he asked again.

"Only that the last time I saw him, he was going to meet you. That's all I could tell them. That's all I know."

Terrific. For sure the cops were going to want to talk to him—again.

144

"Did Jeffie say anything about owing money to anyone?" Dooley said.

"He owed money?" She looked like she was going to cry even harder now. "All he said was that he was going to meet you. He seemed really happy about it, too. He was going to meet you and when he came home we were going to celebrate."

"I was waiting for him, Teresa, but he never showed up. Remember? I told you when you called me the first time. Did you tell the cops that?"

"I told them that's what you said."

That's what you said—like there was some doubt about whether it was true or not.

"Did Jeffie say anything about some guy he was supplying? Some new guy?"

"Supplying?" Teresa said, frowning, as if she had no clue what he was talking about. "You mean a customer at the garage?"

"No, that's not what I mean."

"Then what?"

Was she serious? Yeah, Jeffie collected a paycheck from a garage where he worked a couple of days a week, supposedly doing bodywork. But what he earned there didn't begin to cover his expenses. There was no way Teresa could believe it did. There was no way she could be that stupid, even if Jeffie had lied to her and said that's where the money came from. Maybe she just didn't want to admit that she knew.

"He borrowed money from me, Teresa. That's why he was supposed to meet me. To pay me back."

"He owed you money?" she said. Clearly this was news to

her—unpleasant and unwelcome news. "A lot of money?"

"Enough," Dooley said. He was pretty sure she'd be upset if he told her how much. "You sure he didn't mention anything about a special customer? Maybe a new customer?"

Teresa shook her head. "What am I going to do?" she said. "What am I going to do about the baby?"

"You got someone you can call?" Dooley said. "Maybe someone who can come and stay with you for a while? Or someone you can go and stay with? You got family, Teresa?"

"My dad lives up north," she said, steel in her eyes now instead of tears. "I'd rather open a vein than see that piece of shit again."

Oh.

"You got anyone else? A sister maybe?"

She shook her head.

"Some girlfriends?"

She looked doubtful.

"Maybe Sienna," she said at last.

"Sienna?"

"She's a waitress at this place Jeffie likes. Jeffie says she's a good friend."

Friend? Dooley wondered what kind of friend. "You want me to call her?" he said. "Maybe she could stay with you a while."

"It's okay. I can do it." But she didn't make a move. Dooley looked around. There was a cordless phone on a bookcase that was filled with CDs and DVDs. He brought it to her. She stared down at it.

"You should call her," Dooley said. "You should ask her

to come over."

She punched in some numbers and started crying again as soon as whoever—Sienna, he supposed—answered. She kept crying—blubbering, really—so that Dooley couldn't believe that whoever she was talking to could actually make out what she was saying. Finally she hung up.

"Is she going to come?" Dooley said.

Teresa nodded.

"That's good." He wanted to get out of there, but: "I'll stay until she gets here, okay?" No response. "Is there anyone else you want to call, Teresa?"

She was sobbing now, her whole body wracked with loss and memories and probably the sight of Jeffie four days gone. Dooley didn't know what to do.

"You want me to make you some tea or something?" he said.

She shook her head. She didn't want tea. She didn't want anything except Jeffie. Finally the buzzer sounded. Dooley got up and pressed the intercom button.

"It's Sienna," said a smoke-filled voice from the sidewalk below.

Dooley buzzed her up. Sienna turned out to be a bottle blonde in tight jeans, an even tighter sweater, and raccoon eye makeup. She smelled of cigarettes and was carrying a giant container of Tim Horton's coffee. She looked vaguely familiar.

"Dooley, right?" she said.

He nodded.

"Wow, it's been a while," she said. "You remember me? I used to go with Jeffie."

Teresa hadn't mentioned that. Maybe Jeffie hadn't told her.

"Is it true?" she said. "Is he really dead?" She didn't look at all broken up.

When he said yes, she wanted to know how. Dooley told her what he knew, which wasn't much.

"Shit. Poor Jeffie," she said. "Do they know who did it?"

"No. Do you?"

"Me?" She looked surprised. "He used to come by sometimes, you know"—she dropped her voice a little—"when he needed a change of pace. But we didn't spend much time talking, if you know what I mean." She swallowed some coffee and nodded to the interior of the apartment. "So how come she called me? I barely know her."

"She needs someone to stay with her for a while."

Sienna looked at her watch.

"I have to be at work at three," she said.

◾ ◾ ◾

Dooley was surprised to find his uncle at home, mostly because his uncle's car wasn't in the driveway or in the garage, which was standing open. He was even more surprised to find Annette Girondin, a lawyer friend of his uncle, sitting in the living room with him.

"Where's the car?" Dooley said.

His uncle didn't say anything. Annette glanced at him and then turned to Dooley.

"The police got a search warrant. They seized it."

"What for?"

"They want to examine it."

148

Again: "What for?"

"It's related to your mother," Annette said.

Dooley looked at his uncle, who said, "Where the hell have you been?"

"I went out. I left you a note. How come the cops took your car?"

"They have someone who says they saw Lorraine get into a car the night she died," Annette said.

"*Your* car?" Dooley said to his uncle.

"A *burgundy* car," Annette said—Dooley's uncle's car was burgundy—"that the witness is *pretty sure* is the same make as your uncle's car. The witness is also *pretty sure* a man was driving the car. He didn't catch the license number, though." She sounded disgusted.

wo days later, second period English, Dooley was called down to the school office. Mr. Rektor, the A-L vice-principal, was standing at the counter. The way his eyes clicked in on Dooley told Dooley that he was the one who had summoned him. What now, Dooley wondered.

The cops, that's what.

Detective Randall and his partner Bob Something-or-Other—Dooley decided he should find out what the guy's full name was—were waiting for him in the office.

"We'd like you to come downtown and talk to us, Ryan," Randall said.

Dooley glanced at Mr. Rektor, who wasn't smiling but who might as well have been; he had a smug look on his face. Mr. Rektor had a low opinion of Dooley and was never happier than when Dooley seemed to be confirming just how right he was. Dooley wanted to ask why the cops wanted to talk to him—was it about his uncle? Probably. About Jeffie? Could be, although wouldn't someone besides Randall have caught that one? But he didn't know what the cops had said to Mr. Rektor, and he didn't want Mr. Rektor to know anything more than he already did. So he said, "Okay. Sure." The sense he was trying to convey: *Hey, I'm a good citizen. I've got nothing to hide.* The sense that he ended up conveying (to Mr. Rektor, anyway, judging from the look on his face): *You want to play that old game again? Well, all right, let's go. Catch me if you can, boys.* Living down to Mr. Rektor's low opinion again. Dooley also said, just to be clear, "Am I under arrest?"

He knew he shouldn't have bothered when Randall said, "Not at this time."

■ ■ ■

He rode in the back seat. Neither of the two detectives said anything to him until after he was seated at a table in an interview room. The walls were bare. There was nothing on the table except an audiocassette player and a file folder that Dooley assumed had something to do with Lorraine. Randall told him that they wanted to talk to him again about Lorraine's death (he called her "your mother") but that Dooley didn't have to talk to them if he didn't want to.

"I'm already here," Dooley said.

Randall said in a bored tone that let Dooley know that they both knew it was a formality, that because he was still a youth, he could have an adult present in the room while he talked to the police—a parent (which they knew he didn't have), a guardian, even a lawyer if he wanted. Dooley thought about Annette Girondin. But she was his uncle's lawyer, so maybe that would be some kind of conflict of interest.

"No, it's okay," Dooley said. "I'm fine."

"It's your right to have a lawyer present," Randall said, making sure his ass was good and covered.

"I know," Dooley said.

Randall told Dooley that they wanted to videotape the questions and answers, if that was okay with him. Dooley thought about Annette again. Maybe she knew someone he could call. But if he called a lawyer, for sure the cops would think he had something to hide. And who knew what they already thought, bringing him in here like this and video-taping everything?

"You want to talk to me, go ahead," he said. He told himself that everything would be okay as long as he kept his head and didn't panic. They made him sign a piece of paper before they got down to it.

As soon as the video camera was rolling, Randall asked Dooley again if he wanted a parent, a guardian, or a lawyer present, and Dooley said, for the camera, that he didn't. Randall told him that he could change his mind at any time; he just had to say so. Dooley said he understood that. Randall looked at him for a moment. His first question came out of left field.

"Ryan, do you know Jeffrey Eccles?"

Jeffie?

"I thought you said this was about Lorraine," Dooley said.

"Do you know Jeffrey Eccles?"

There was no point in denying it. Teresa had already

152

talked to the cops. She had mentioned his name.

"Yeah, I know him."

"How do you know him?"

Dooley shrugged. "I just know him. From around."

"Would you say that you and Jeffrey Eccles are good friends?" Keeping it present tense, Dooley noticed.

"Good friends? Not really," Dooley said. "But friends? Yeah, for a while. We kind of lost touch, though." Mostly because Dooley had been locked up. "I ran into him once, maybe six months ago, after I started living with my uncle."

"And?"

"And what?"

"What did you talk about?"

"Nothing," Dooley said. "Stuff. You know, catching up. I saw him on the street." Actually, Jeffie had seen him. If Dooley had spotted Jeffie first, there wouldn't have been any conversation. "We talked for maybe five minutes. I didn't have a lot of time. I was on my way to an appointment."

Randall perked up. "An appointment?"

"With this psychologist I was seeing." He didn't want to get into that, so he hurried it along. "We talked, I left, and I never heard from him again until he called me a couple of weeks ago."

"Do you know he's dead?"

"Yeah," Dooley said. "His girlfriend told me. But what does Jeffie have to do with—"

"His *girlfriend* told you?"

"Yeah. She called me."

"Are you good friends with her, too?"

153

"No," Dooley said. "I hardly know her."

"But she called you? Why did she do that, Ryan?"

"To tell me about Jeffie. To tell me he was dead."

"So a girl you hardly know calls you to tell you a guy you're not really friends with is dead," Randall said, making an effort to sound as perplexed as he was trying to look. "I don't get it. Why would she do that?"

Dooley thought about the video camera that was running. He wondered if maybe now was a good time to say he wanted a lawyer. Randall would love that. He'd think he was onto something.

"Like I said, Jeffie called me a couple of weeks ago. He asked me to meet him."

"Meet you?"

"Yeah."

"Are you aware that Jeffrey Eccles was in the drug trade, Ryan?"

"Don't you mean, *allegedly* in the drug trade?" Dooley said. As far as he knew, Jeffie hadn't been arrested again since that last time, and that hadn't been for drugs.

"Did you know?"

"I heard what some people said, if that's what you mean."

Randall was quiet for a few moments. Dooley had to fight the urge to fill up that silence, to explain himself so that Randall wouldn't suspect him of anything. It sounded easy—just sit there and say nothing—but it never was.

"Why did Jeffrey want to meet you?" Randall said finally.

"He wanted to borrow some money," Dooley said, feeling more confident now that he was on solid ground. He even

154

told the detective how much Jeffie had borrowed. Randall whistled softly.

"That's a fair-sized chunk of change," he said. "What did you say?"

"I said okay."

"You said okay?"

"Yeah."

"Why would you agree to lend that much money to a guy you weren't really friends with?"

"Like I said, we used to be friends. I owed him one."

"Yeah? You want to tell us about that?"

"No," Dooley said. There were some things that were none of their business.

Randall studied Dooley for a few moments.

"Where does a guy like you lay hands on that kind of money, Ryan?"

"At the bank. I have a job."

"So after Jeffrey called you a couple of weeks ago—when exactly was that, Ryan?"

Dooley told him.

"So after Jeffrey called you—two days before your mother died—what happened?"

Wait a minute. What was going on? Were they trying to connect Jeffie's death with Lorraine's? Because if they were, the only connector Dooley could see was himself.

"I went to the bank and took out the money," Dooley said. "Then I met up with him and gave it to him, and he promised to pay me back."

"Where did you meet him?" he said.

Dooley told him.

"When exactly was that?"

Dooley told him.

"So you went into the ravine at ten o'clock at night to meet Jeffrey, is that what you're saying?"

"Yes."

"I understand your uncle keeps you on a short leash, Ryan. Did you tell him where you were going that night?"

"No."

"Did he know you were out?"

"Yeah."

"Where did he think you were?"

Shit.

"I told him I was taking a walk," Dooley said.

"A walk?" Randall said. "That's it?"

"Yeah."

"You didn't mention that you were meeting Jeffrey Eccles?"

"No."

"You sure?"

"Yes."

"Why is that, Ryan?"

"My uncle didn't like me hanging around with people from ... before."

"People from before." Randall seemed to like that. He even smiled. "So you didn't tell him you were *lending money* to a guy who was in the drug trade?"

Cops. They thought they were so smart.

"No," Dooley said.

"In other words, you lied to your uncle. Is that what

156

you're telling me, Ryan?"

"Yeah, I guess," Dooley said. He hated being caught out by the cops because once they had you telling one lie, they started playing that game—if you were lying then, how do we know you're not lying now?

"You guess?" Detective Randall seemed to like that, too. He leaned back in his chair. "So you went to meet Jeffrey, and then what?"

"I gave him the money. We arranged to meet up again so he could pay me back. Then I went home."

"Did he say what he wanted the money for?"

"He said he owed someone."

"You loaned him money so that he could pay off someone he owed?" Randall said.

"Yes."

"Sounds like a bad risk, Ryan, wouldn't you say?"

"He said he'd pay me back."

There was a long pause before Randall said, "If he was borrowing money to pay off a debt, where was he going to get the money to pay you back?"

Dooley looked at the detective. He couldn't possibly be that stupid.

"I guess he was going to earn it," Dooley said.

"If he could earn money that easily, why did he need to borrow from you?"

Dooley wished he knew where Randall was going with his questions.

"He said the guy he owed wanted his money right away. He wouldn't wait. I was willing to give him a week."

"Did you meet Jeffrey Eccles in that ravine to buy drugs from him, Ryan?"

What?

"No. I don't do drugs."

Detective Randall looked evenly at him.

"I don't do drugs *anymore,*" Dooley said.

"Did you tell your uncle where you were going?"

"I already told you—no."

"Did you and your uncle discuss Jeffrey Eccles?"

Dooley stared at the detective.

"No."

"When was the last time you saw Jeffrey?"

Dooley tried to keep his face neutral and his breathing normal. He forced himself to keep meeting Randall's eyes even though what he really wanted was to look away. He knew that whoever was investigating Jeffie's murder—was it Randall and his partner, or was it some other cops?—had talked to Teresa, and he knew what Teresa had told them.

"He was supposed to meet me a few days ago to pay me back," he said. "He never showed up."

"When and where was this?"

Dooley told him. He added, "But like I said, he never showed up. If you don't believe me, you can check at the restaurant."

"Don't worry, we will," Randall said. "Jeffrey's girlfriend said he seemed happy about going to see you. Why do you suppose a guy like Jeffrey would be happy about paying back the money he owed you? Does that make any sense to you?"

"Maybe he didn't like to be in debt," Dooley said.

"Maybe he didn't like to be in debt *to you*."

That's when Dooley slipped just a little. He said, "What's that supposed to mean?"

"Jeffrey made six calls to you in the space of less than ten minutes on Monday night—three days after your mother died. He must have really wanted to talk to you. You want to tell us what that was all about?"

Dooley wasn't sure that he did. He thought about who else the two detectives had talked to or might talk to.

"He was supposed to meet me to pay me back," Dooley said. "He was calling because he said he needed an extra day to get the money together."

"An extra day," Randall said. "So he calls you six times in fifteen minutes, he tells you he needs an extra day, and then he doesn't show up when he's supposed to. Is that what you're telling us, Ryan?"

Dooley didn't say anything.

"Did you give him an extra day?"

"Yes."

"So, what, you told him he could pay you back on Tuesday instead?"

"Yes."

Randall leaned forward and pushed the play button on the tape recorder. Dooley heard Jeffie's voice saying "Leave a message." Then he heard his own voice: "It's me. Be here, Jeffie, or else." He heard Jeffie's message again, again followed by his own voice: "Get your ass over here, Jeffie, if you know what's good for you." And again: "I told you, Jeffie. You fuck this up and you're gonna be sorry." Randall

159

pressed the stop button.

"That's Tuesday, Ryan," Randall said. "The day Jeffrey arranged to meet you to pay you back, correct?"

Dooley said nothing.

"Correct?" Randall said, an edge of irritation in his voice now.

"Yeah," Dooley said. "I was waiting for him."

"You called Jeffrey a total of ten times in the space of an hour, Ryan. You left three messages. You did not sound happy."

"I was pissed off," Dooley said. "I thought he was ducking me. He never showed up."

"I see." Randall looked at Dooley but didn't say anything, probably wanting Dooley to sweat over what the next question would be. Then: "So you're saying you didn't see him at all on Tuesday?"

"No."

"When *was* the last time you saw Jeffrey Eccles?"

"Monday."

"The day he made all those phone calls to you?"

"Yeah. He came to the store."

"The video store where you work?"

"Yeah. He called my cell, but we're not allowed to take calls at work. So he came to the store. He told me that he needed an extra day. I told him okay."

"You told him he could pay you back on Tuesday instead. But you say he didn't show up."

Was he stupid? Hadn't he just said that—*twice?*

"Yes," Dooley said.

"Where were you Tuesday night, Ryan?"

160

"You think I killed him? Is that it?"

"Where were you Tuesday from the time you left school until the morning?"

"I was at the restaurant waiting for Jeffie until four-thirty. Then I went home and I was there for a while."

"Until when?"

"Until maybe eight."

"Was anyone else home?"

"My uncle."

"You spend time with him?"

"No. He went up to his room after supper."

"What was he doing up there?"

"I don't know."

"What happened at eight?"

There it was again—the subject Dooley hadn't wanted to get into before and didn't want to get into now. But it looked like he didn't have much choice.

"I called my girlfriend and then I went over to her place."

"The girlfriend whose building you were at the night your mother died? Beth, right?"

Dooley didn't want them to drag Beth into this. What would she think, especially after everything that had already happened? What would her mother think?

"Look," he said. "She's a nice girl. She's never been in any trouble. I'll answer your questions, but you don't need to hassle her. She's not involved."

Randall's partner spoke for the first time. He said, "Not involved in what?"

"Not involved in anything," Dooley said. "She's not like that."

Randall surprised Dooley. He didn't ask anything more about Beth. Instead, he said, "Was anyone else at your girl-friend's place besides you and your girlfriend?"

"No," Dooley said. He was annoyed at the heat he felt in his cheeks when Randall's partner smirked at him.

"What time did you leave her place, Ryan?" Randall said.

Too soon. Always too soon.

"Eleven-thirty." Beth had been reluctant to let him go, even as she was pulling him by the hand to the door, worried about her mother showing up. She kept kissing him. By then she had pulled on a pair of drawstring pants and a flowery little tank top. Her hair hung down in waves over her shoulders and halfway down her back. He was fully dressed, with his jacket on, but he still felt the heat of her. She kissed him, then she told him he had to go, her mother could be home at any minute, then she kissed him again until he couldn't think straight, until he wouldn't have cared if her mother was standing right there in front of him. At least, that's what he thought at first. Then he imagined how it would play out if she actually did appear, and he kissed her one more time and let her go. It was the last time that things had been right between them. He hadn't thought about Nevin even once that night. He wished Beth hadn't come by the store the next day. He wished she hadn't talked to Linelle. He wished he'd been straight with her from the start.

"You don't have to talk to her about that, do you?" he said. "Her mother—" Shit. "She'd get into trouble, that's all," Dooley said, feeling like a pussy, begging these two cops.

"What did you do after you left your girlfriend's place?"

Randall said.

"I went home."

"Straight home?"

"Yeah."

"How long did it take you to get there?"

"Twenty, twenty-five minutes."

"Was anyone home when you got there?"

"My uncle."

"Can he verify what time you got home?"

"I don't think so. I think he was asleep."

"You think? You don't know?"

"I didn't check on him or anything. I went right to my room."

"So you didn't see your uncle after eight o'clock that night, is that what you're saying?"

"Yes, but—" He knew what they were thinking: If he hadn't seen his uncle, then his uncle hadn't seen him, which meant that there was no one who could say for sure when he got home. Which meant that no one could say for sure where he went after he left Beth's house. Which meant ...

"You didn't talk to him?"

"No."

"So how do you know he was home?"

What?

"If you didn't see your uncle and you didn't talk to him, Ryan, how do you know he was home?"

"Well—" Of course he was home, Dooley thought. Where else would he have been?

"When was the last time you saw your mother?" Randall said.

163

Dooley stared at him. Randall had started out on Jeffie, but now he was back on Lorraine. What was going on?

Randall seemed to enjoy Dooley's surprise. He repeated the question: "When was the last time you saw your mother?"

Dooley spotted the difference right away. Why was Randall asking it that way this time—not when was the last time you spoke to her, but when was the last time you saw her? Dooley thought about Beth and the newspaper clipping she had and the fact that she was mad at him.

"I may have forgotten something the last time you asked me about Lorraine," he said slowly, trying to sound like this had been bothering him for some time, like he was happy to have the opportunity to clear it up now. "You remember you asked me when the last time was that I spoke to her."

Randall waited. He didn't say a word.

"I think I may have told you that I hadn't spoken to her in years," Dooley said.

"You *may* have told me that?" Randall said. "That's exactly what you told me."

"I thought when you asked me that it was because you wanted to know if she said anything to me, you know, about what she was up to or if she was still into drugs, things like that." Like he would have cared one way or the other.

Randall was looking evenly at him.

"I told you the truth. I hadn't talked to her in years. But I saw her a few days before she died. She showed up at my school."

He couldn't tell what either of the detectives was thinking, but he had a pretty good idea they weren't buying in one hundred percent.

"Your mother came to your school?" Randall said.

"Yeah. She surprised me. I came out of school and she was standing right there on the sidewalk."

"And you're telling us you didn't talk to her?"

"Yes," Dooley said. It was God's honest truth. "But *she* spoke to *me*." Beth had seen that. Beth had seen her talking to him.

"What did she say?"

"She said she wanted to see me. She wanted to know how I was doing."

"That's it?"

"Yeah."

"You haven't seen her in nearly three years, and she suddenly shows up at your school—you weren't going to that school the last time you saw her, were you, Ryan?"

"No."

"So how did she know where to find you?"

"I don't know."

"You didn't ask her?"

"No." That was the truth, too. He hadn't. He hadn't even wanted to talk to her. He'd wanted her to go away. He'd wanted her out of his life, permanently. But, boy, he didn't tell the cops that.

"So, what, she just said something like, Hi, honey, good to see you. I'll check back with you in another couple of years? Is that it?" Randall said.

"She said I should come and see her sometime," Dooley said. "She said things were different now."

"Different? Different how?"

"She didn't say."

"You didn't ask?"

"No."

"Why not?" Randall said. "You hadn't seen your mother in a couple of years, she shows up at your school and says things are different, and you don't even ask what she means?" He sounded incredulous, like what kind of sorry excuse for a son wouldn't ask, like there was something wrong with him. *Him,* not her.

"No," Dooley said. "I didn't."

Randall shook his head: *What a lowlife.*

"Did your mother say anything else to you?"

"No."

"No?"

"No!"

"Before she showed up at your school, when was the last time you saw her?"

"Over two years ago," Dooley said. "I kind of moved out."

"Kind of?"

"I stayed with friends. Then I got into some trouble." He didn't elaborate. He was pretty sure he didn't have to. "She never visited, never called, never wrote. Not when I was inside. Not since I went to live with my uncle." So what did he have to say to her?

"You didn't think too highly of your mother, did you, Ryan?" Randall said.

"I told you. We weren't close."

"That's not what I mean. I mean, you didn't like her, did you?"

"Okay, no," Dooley said. "I didn't like her. You want to know the truth? I was embarrassed by her. But I didn't kill her, if that's what you're thinking."

"Uh-huh," Randall said.

Uh-huh? What did *that* mean? Randall leaned back in his chair.

"You want to tell us about the Friday before she died?"

What?

"The manager at the video store where you work says you went home on your break that night. He says he sent you to pick up a DVD you were supposed to have returned a week before. He says you came back without it."

Good old Kevin—always finding some way to mess him up. Always.

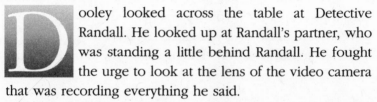

ooley looked across the table at Detective Randall. He looked up at Randall's partner, who was standing a little behind Randall. He fought the urge to look at the lens of the video camera that was recording everything he said.

"Okay," Dooley said. They had him fair and square. Denying it would only make things worse. "Okay, but it's true that I hadn't seen Lorraine for over two years until she showed up at my school that day. I didn't even know she lived in town. I thought she'd split or something."

"Why would you think that?"

Because that was pretty much what his uncle had led him to believe.

"Because she never came around. Because she always said how much she hated it here. She was always talking about moving out west. Then she shows up at my school and says she wants to see how I'm doing. She said things had changed for her. She said she wanted me to come and see her; she wanted to talk to me about something. That's all true."

Randall waited.

Dooley sucked in a deep breath. He said, "But the Friday before she died, she came to the house."

"We know that, Ryan," Randall said, sounding almost bored. "I asked you about that the first time we talked. You remember?"

"Yeah."

"You remember what you said to me?"

Dooley remembered perfectly.

"You said you weren't home."

"I wasn't."

"You said your uncle didn't tell you she'd been there."

"He didn't. He never said a word about it."

Randall watched him.

"I went home to get the DVD, like Kevin said. I was about to go into the house to get it when I heard her voice."

"Your mother's voice?"

Dooley nodded. It had hit him like a lightning bolt, which was pretty funny when you thought about it because right up until that exact moment, he'd figured that the odds of running into her were about the same as his odds of getting struck by lightning. Lorraine had done her level best to ignore him for most of his life. There were plenty of times when he believed she would have offloaded him years ago, if it weren't for the welfare checks and the extra money she got for being a single mother. Having a kid had also saved her from being evicted from the co-op they lived in when Dooley was little. A bunch of the other co-op members had complained about Lorraine; specifically, they had complained about the late-night and middle-of-the-night comings and goings at her apartment and about the chaos surrounding one of her boyfriends who tended to get rowdy when he was cranked. They wanted Lorraine gone. Lorraine had taken Dooley to the co-op board meeting where she had been summoned to answer the complaints against her. She had sat Dooley on her lap, right there in front of everyone. Afterward, she had told him, "No one wants to put a little kid out on the street." No one except Lorraine. By the time he was eight, she was telling him all the time, make yourself scarce for a couple of hours, huh, Dooley? You got some friends you can stay with, right? Suck up to one of the moms; maybe they'll invite you for supper.

Six months before his last arrest, he moved out for good. He'd made his bed on a friend's couch and, so far as he knew, Lorraine had never asked anyone about him, had never tried to find out where he was. When he finally landed in big trouble and spent eighteen months locked up, she never visited, never called, nothing. No, it was his uncle who'd showed up instead—his uncle, who he'd never heard of before. He'd kept showing up, too, even when Dooley told him to fuck off, who the hell did he think he was, Jesus, some hard-assed retired cop who dry-cleaned shirts for a living now—who wanted anything to do with that? The whole time, he hadn't heard a word from Lorraine.

Until that Friday night.

He'd come home and circled around to the side of the house, meaning to go in through the kitchen to the living room where the DVD was sitting on top of the TV. That's when he'd heard her voice and had frozen up right there in the driveway.

"She was talking to my uncle," Dooley told Randall. Except, really, it had sounded more like a fight than a conversation.

"Well, when *is* he going to be here?" Lorraine had said. For a moment there, it seemed to Dooley like she was actually interested in the answer, like she really cared, like—and maybe he was pushing it with this one—like she *wanted* to see him.

"What's it to you?" Dooley's uncle had said. He sounded angry. Harsh. At the time, Dooley hadn't known all the reasons, but it had always been clear to him that his uncle didn't hold Lorraine in high regard.

"Do you always have to be such an asshole, Gary?" She sounded like the same old Lorraine when she said that. Dooley wondered, did she look the same, or did she look worse? What if she saw him? What did she expect him to look like or to be like? What if she was disappointed? He thought about that for a moment and decided, fuck it. Who was she to be disappointed in him?

"Do us all a favor," Dooley's uncle said to her. "Get out of here."

"You can't tell me what to do," Lorraine said. "He's *my* son."

"And a great job you did raising him." The sarcasm in his uncle's voice was so sharp it could have drawn blood.

"Yeah? And what about you?" Lorraine said. "You going to tell me you were all concerned about him? You never came around even once. And now you think you can tell me I

171

can't see my own son?"

Boy, for a brother and sister, they sure knew how to go at it. Then Dooley had thought about what Lorraine had said. He thought, *Wait a minute*. But he didn't tell Randall that. He didn't tell him any of what he'd heard. All he said was: "She was talking to my uncle."

"What were they talking about?"

"I don't know. I just heard her voice and I knew it was her, that's all."

"Then what happened?"

"I took off. I went back to work. I didn't want to see her." It didn't put him in the best light, but there it was. And it happened to be true. Well, it happened to be true that he had eventually walked away. But he'd stuck around and listened for a few more minutes. "By the time I got home again after work, she was gone. And my uncle … he didn't say anything."

"What do you mean?"

He didn't say, *Guess who was here, Ryan? Guess who dropped in for a visit?*

"I mean," Dooley said, "he didn't tell me that she'd been there."

"And you didn't ask?"

"I didn't want to know."

Randall considered this in silence.

"Then what?" he said.

"Then nothing, until she showed up at my school and asked me to come and see her sometime."

"And?"

"And that's it. I never went. I never spoke to her. Then

she died. That's it."

But he wished that wasn't it. He wished she were still alive. If she were, things would be a lot less complicated. Boy, trust Lorraine to mess everyone up.

But she'd looked good, probably because she'd been straight. He should have gone to see her. He should have heard what she had to say. Maybe if he had, things would be different.

Should have, would have, could have.

Regret words.

Words from the past.

Can't-change-anything words.

He looked across the table at Randall.

The detective reached for the file folder that was sitting on the table. He opened it. There was a photograph inside. He showed it to Dooley.

"Do you know this man, Ryan?"

Dooley stared at the small, piggish eyes, the slender nose, the thin lips.

"Do you know him, Ryan?"

"Yeah," Dooley said. He never thought he'd see that face again. It made him sick to look at it.

"How do you know him?"

"He worked at a group home where I was for a while."

"For five months, four years ago, correct?"

"Yeah."

"What happened to him?"

Dooley had dreamed up dozens of things that could have happened to him, none of them pleasant.

"He quit," he said.

"Do you know why?"

Dooley shrugged, trying not to care, trying to hide the nausea he felt. "No." At least, he didn't know all the details. He'd never wanted to know. The important thing was that he had disappeared from Dooley's life.

"In fact," Randall said, "he left because he said he was suffering from stress. He specifically mentioned you by name when he handed in his resignation. Why do you think he did that, Ryan?"

"I don't know. Maybe he thought I was a pain in the ass."

"Were you?"

"What?"

"A pain in the ass?"

Dooley shrugged again. No doubt he was.

"Jeffrey Eccles was in that same group home, wasn't he? He left before you, didn't he?"

Dooley nodded. Where was this going?

"We thought that was interesting, you know, the two of you in the same group home. So we went and talked to them to see if they could give us any insight. When we heard about your old friend here"—he tapped the photograph—"and why he left, we decided to talk to him, too."

Dooley held his breath.

"Funny thing," Randall said. "He didn't seem to remember you very well. But Jeffrey? Jeffrey made a big impression."

Dooley waited. Jeffie had said he'd take care of it, and he had. The guy had left, hadn't he? Who cared what excuse he'd given—he'd gone. Dooley owed Jeffie big time for that.

Jeffie had started to tell him about it one time, but Dooley had cut him off. Just thinking about the guy made him sick to his stomach.

"Apparently, Jeffrey made certain allegations," Randall said. "And certain threats. He also extorted money. Did you know about that, Ryan?"

Dooley was pretty sure he managed to look sincere when he shook his head. But, Jesus, Jeffie had been *blackmailing* the guy? Dooley thought he'd been spinning a yarn about those pictures.

"The guy says the allegations were unfounded. Were they, Ryan?"

"I don't know what you're talking about," Dooley said.

Randall stared at him for a moment. Dooley kept his mouth shut.

"An allegation like that, coupled with a piece of work like Jeffrey Eccles," Randall said, "the guy said he didn't need the grief. He went into a different line of work, one that pays better and has a better clientele. You know what I'm saying, Ryan?"

Dooley believed this was what his English teacher would call a rhetorical question.

"Someone else made a complaint about Jeffrey a little over a year ago," Randall said. "He claimed Jeffrey was trying to extort money from him. Funny thing, though. The man dropped the complaint. We talked to him, too, Ryan. He was pretty nervous, tried to tell us it was all a misunderstanding. But he finally admitted he'd bought some marijuana from Jeffrey and when he and Jeffrey got into a dispute about

175

money owing, Jeffrey threatened to go to the man's employer—he was a teacher at a very exclusive private school. The guy would have been fired. He paid up."

Dooley shook his head. What he didn't know about Jeffie.

"Extortion seemed to be a habit with Jeffrey," Randall said. "Did you buy drugs from him, Ryan?"

The question came at him out of nowhere.

"No," he said.

"Did you buy drugs from Jeffrey to give to your uncle?"

"No!" He didn't like the way this was going.

"Did Jeffrey put two and two together after your mother died? Did he try to blackmail you, Ryan?"

Jesus H. Christ.

"No."

"Did he try to blackmail your uncle?"

What the fuck?

"Did you kill Jeffrey Eccles?"

"No."

"Did your uncle kill him?"

"My uncle doesn't know Jeffie."

"Are you sure about that, Ryan?"

"Yeah, I'm sure," Dooley said. His uncle didn't know anyone from Dooley's past.

"Suppose I tell you you're wrong?" Randall said. "Your uncle used to be a cop. He knows a lot of scumbags." He flipped over some more photographs. The top one showed Jeffie the way he had looked when they found him. His body and his face were all bloated and parts looked like they had been eaten away. He was lying face up, but his hands were behind his back, like they had been tied there. "Four days exposed to the elements," Randall said.

Dooley felt like he was going to throw up. Randall picked up the top picture so that Dooley could see the one underneath. It was a close-up, this one not showing Jeffie's face, thank God, but his neck and his chest. There was a wound a little to left of center, up under his ribs.

"The pathologist says the knife went right through his heart. He probably died instantly," Randall said. He tapped Jeffie's upper chest with one finger. Dooley looked and saw small circles cutting into Jeffie's skin. He couldn't help himself.

"What are those?" he said.

Randall stared at him and took another sip of coffee.

Dooley waited.

"Up until last week, I didn't know your uncle," Randall said. "But I talked to a lot of people who do. People who knew him before he retired. People who worked with him. People who know him now. All kinds of people. Everybody says the same thing—the guy can be a real hard-ass, but he's fair and he's solid. And I hear he's one hell of a dry-cleaner."

Dooley couldn't tell if Randall was kidding or not.

"He ever hit you, Ryan?"

"What?" What did that have to do with anything? "No!"

"You and your uncle never went at it, you know, when he yanked your leash too tight?"

"No."

"He ever get into it with the neighbors? Ever lose it when he's driving—you know, road rage?"

"No."

Randall tapped the photograph again. "Those marks on Jeffrey's chest, they're burns. From a cigarette. You smoke, Ryan?"

Dooley shook his head.

"Your uncle smoke?"

"Cigars sometimes." But Randall probably already knew that.

"The pathologist says Jeffie was burned while he was still alive. You understand what I'm saying?"

Dooley understood. He was saying that Jeffie had been tortured. But why?

"Why would anyone do that?" he said.

"That is the jackpot question," Randall said. "And here's another one. Why would a guy who's as solid as everyone says your uncle is torture a guy like Jeffie before stabbing him in the heart?"

"You think my uncle did that?" Dooley said.

"I know you and your mother didn't have an ideal relationship, Ryan."

No kidding.

"If you had nothing to do with what happened to your mother"—he kept using that word—mother—a word that Dooley rarely used—"then you should help us out. Where was your uncle when you got home from your girlfriend's place on Tuesday night? Was he home or not?"

Dooley stood up.

"Sit down," Randall said.

Dooley stayed standing.

"Sit *down,* Ryan."

Someone knocked on the door to the interview room. The

same person, another cop, stuck his head inside, and Randall went to the door. The first cop whispered something in Detective Randall's ear, and Detective Randall whispered something back. He closed the door and came and sat down again.

"Is there anything else you want to tell me about that night, Ryan?"

"No," Dooley said.

"Okay," Randall said. "Detective Myers will show you the way out."

Randall's partner stepped forward. He opened the door and nodded impatiently for Dooley to get up and get out.

Dooley stood. Were they playing him? Were they going to wait until he got to the door and then slap some handcuffs on him and tell him he was under arrest for Jeffie's murder?

He watched Randall out of the corner of his eye as he edged to the door and slipped through it. Myers stayed right beside him, walking him through a large room toward another door. It looked like he was really on his way out. Dooley started to get an itchy bounce in his legs, a mixture of impatience and excitement. He was out of there. He was really out of there.

Then both his heart and his legs came to an abrupt stop.

Walking toward him, but on the other side of the room, guided by a uniformed police officer and headed, he knew, for an interview room, was Beth, followed by her mother. Beth looked over at him. Her expression was somber. Jesus, Dooley thought, now what?

ooley should have gone back to school after the two detectives finished with him, but he didn't. Instead, he decided to give Rektor a thrill. Let him think the cops had him on something. Let him think Dooley was out of his life. Let him think Dooley had finally got whatever Rektor thought he deserved.

He should have gone to work, too, when it was time. But he didn't do that, either. Instead, he called Linelle, coughed unconvincingly, and said, "Do me a favor; tell Kevin I'm sick."

"Coward," Linelle said. Then she said, "I'm always doing you favors, Dooley. When are you going to pay me back?"

"Anytime," he said. "You name it."

Then he went over to Beth's apartment building and hung around outside the front door to wait for Beth (and her mother) to come home. It took forever.

When he started to tremble from prolonged exposure to the November air, which had turned cold and damp and which got worse when the sun started to sink in the sky, he paced to keep warm. How long were the cops going to keep her? What were they talking about? What was she saying?

A midnight blue Jag swung onto the street, glided toward the building's main entrance, slowed, then stopped altogether.

Dooley stared at it.

Behind the wheel: Nevin.

In the front passenger seat: Beth.

In the back: Beth's mother.

Nevin got out first and trotted around the front of the car to grab hold of the passenger-side door. But it was already opening and Beth was getting out. Nevin said something to her. Beth didn't even look at him. Her eyes were on Dooley. She came toward him, leaving Nevin to extricate her mother from the back seat.

Beth stopped a few paces from Dooley.

"What are you doing here?" she said.

"I need to talk to you."

Beth's mother had struggled out of the back seat and was busy trying to disengage herself from Nevin, who had taken her by the arm and was guiding her up the front walk as if she were in her nineties instead of, Dooley guessed, in her forties.

"Please, Beth," Dooley said. He felt like he was begging her all the time now when he'd never had to beg her before, not for anything.

Beth's mother shook off Nevin and raced to Beth's side. She scowled at Dooley.

"Come inside, Beth," she said.

"In a minute," Beth said.

"Now," Beth's mother said.

"Beth," Nevin said, his voice deep and smooth, brimming

with natural self-confidence. "You should do what your mother says."

"Thank you for the ride, Nevin," Beth said and, boy, Dooley knew that tone. She didn't like people telling her what she should and shouldn't do. "I'll call you, okay?"

Nevin glanced at Dooley. Then he stepped forward and kissed Beth on the cheek, like a dog marking his territory, Dooley thought. Beth, he noticed, looked more surprised than anything.

Nevin went back to his Jag. It took a few moments and a sharp, pointed look from Beth before he engaged the engine and, a little after that, drove away. Beth turned to her mother.

"I'll be up in a few minutes," she said.

Beth's mother stood her ground.

Beth took Dooley by the hand and pulled him down the walk.

"Beth," her mother called, her voice shrill. She's afraid of me, Dooley thought, afraid of what I might do. God knows what she said to the cops. "Beth, you come back here."

But Beth kept walking, dragging Dooley along with her for the first few steps until, finally, Dooley fell into step with her. She walked briskly down the street and around the corner, looking straight ahead, until finally they came to a small park. She found a bench and sat down. Dooley sat beside her. A wind had come up; it was scattering dead leaves across the spiky brown grass.

"The police came to my school," she said. Her voice was shaking, but Dooley couldn't tell if that was because she was angry or cold. She was shivering all over. He wanted to put his arm around her and hold her close to warm her, but he didn't dare. "They said they wanted to ask me some questions. My principal said I shouldn't say anything until I called my mother. I shouldn't have listened to him. I wished I'd talked to them all by myself. I'm sorry, Dooley."

Sorry? Did she just say she was sorry?

She turned to look at him, and he read a deep sadness in her dark brown eyes. What did that mean?

"The two detectives I talked to said that your mother was murdered. Is that true?"

Dooley nodded. "At first they thought it was an overdose. Then they said it was suspicious."

"You didn't tell me." What could he say? She hadn't given him the chance. "They asked me a million questions. I didn't know what to do."

"The best thing," Dooley said, "is to answer them." Especially when, like Beth, you had nothing to hide.

"I'm sorry about your mother," Beth said. "And I'm sorry I got so mad at you. You said you'd told me everything, but you didn't tell me about her. I couldn't understand why not. She's your mother—*was* your mother." She looked up at Dooley. God, she was beautiful. Every single time he looked at her, even when he was lucky enough to be with her for hours and had already glanced at her a hundred times, every single time without exception, she took his breath away.

"I should have told you," he said. "But—"

She straightened up and got a look in her face that Dooley recognized. It was her serious look, the one he saw when they were at the library together and she was working on math problems that were due the next day, the one that told him she was thinking about a difficult assignment, the one that signaled that she wasn't fooling around.

"I don't know how it works," she said.

"How what works?"

"I don't know if they tell you what they asked me or what I said." They? She had to mean the cops. "If they do ... I think I should be the one to tell you, not them."

Dooley caught his breath again. The cops had already sprung a few nasty surprises on him. Now it looked like Beth was about to do the same.

"Tell me what?" he said.

"They asked me about Tuesday night." A tiny smile pulled at her lips and she blushed slightly, which Dooley took as a good sign. "My mother was mad when I told them you were at the apartment."

"I'm sorry."

He peered into her eyes. What was that he read in them? Embarrassment? Regret? Something else?

"They also asked me about the night your mother died. They asked me if you called me that night. I told them yes. I said you asked me to go to the library with you but that I couldn't. Then they asked me where I was that night. I don't know why they asked me that, do you?"

"That's what they do, Beth," he said. "They ask questions."

"I told them I didn't know your mother," she said. "I told them I didn't even know you had a mother." She was getting worked up again.

"I should have told you," Dooley said quietly.

She took one of his hands in hers and held it for a moment. Then, just when Dooley was starting to think it was all good between them again, she let go. She folded her hands in her lap and looked up at him.

"They asked me where I was that night," she said. "They asked me who I was with."

"It's okay, Beth," he said. What was she so upset about? Oh.

"Are you afraid the girls on your history team will find out?" he said. He didn't know any of them, but he had a picture in his head of bitchy, gossipy private school girls.

Her eyes filled with tears.

"Dooley, I'm so sorry."

Why did she keep saying that?

"I—I was with Nevin."

She cried, but that didn't clarify things for Dooley. He didn't have a lot of experience with girls, but one thing he knew was that when they cried, it could be for any one of an infinite number of reasons. They cried because they were sad. They cried because they were angry. They cried because they were happy. They cried because they were disappointed, because they felt guilty, because they were tired, because they had PMS, because they were embarrassed, because they were afraid, because they were hurt (physically or mentally), because they were touched, because they were grieving, because they'd just won something, because they'd just lost something, because they were ahead, because they were behind. He couldn't think of a single occasion when a girl wouldn't cry. Not that there was anything wrong with crying.

185

At least, that's what his uncle said. What his uncle also said: Some people think that's why women live longer. They don't keep their emotions bottled up.

Dooley looked out over the dried-up grass. The sun had dropped below the tree line. Another couple of minutes and it would be dark.

"What do you mean, you were *with* him?" he said. "With him where?" It could make all the difference, the where of it. If she said, I was with him at a school debate, that wouldn't be too bad; they were both debaters; you could call it a professional interest. If she said, I was with him at the library, he might be able to live with that. After all, they were both private school kids, both high achievers and, besides, the library was a public place. If she said, I was with him at his house or at my house—well, that depended on who else was there. The worst would be: I was with him. Just that, the *with* carrying all the meaning.

"At my place," Beth said. "He stopped by. I wasn't expecting him. My mother invited him to stay for supper. She likes him."

"Your mother was there?" That was good. That limited the range of possibilities.

"She was at first," Beth said. "She had to go out."

That was bad.

"He was there when you called and asked me if I wanted to go to the library—"

Dooley's heart slammed to a halt.

"Why didn't you just tell me that?" Dooley said, the words coming out slowly because he could hardly believe it. Beth

186

had lied to him.

"I was afraid to."

"Afraid?" Jesus. "Of what? Of me?"

"I was afraid if I told you Nevin was there, you'd take it the wrong way. I was afraid you'd get mad."

"So you lied to me instead?" He shook his head. All that grief she'd been giving him, and look what she had done. "Was he standing right there when you said it?"

"No," she said, flashing with indignation, then—terrific— sagging a little. Even in the gloom he could see her cheeks turn pink. "He was in the kitchen with my mother. I think he overheard. I'm sorry. I just didn't want you to get mad."

"What about your mother?"

"What about her?"

"When did she go out?"

Her eyes slipped away from him again.

"About an hour after you called."

"And Nevin? Did he leave when she did?"

She shook her head.

"He stayed for a while."

"How long?" He pictured the two of them alone together. Her mother would never have left her alone with Dooley, not even for one second.

"Maybe an hour. But it was nothing. We were just fooling around."

"Fooling around?"

"You know, talking, watching TV."

"While your mother was gone?"

"Yes," she said. Her eyes flashed again. "I didn't ask him .

to come by, and I didn't ask him to stay. My mom did. What was I supposed to do—throw him out?"

Yes, you bet your ass. Turf the guy.

"His parents are friends of my mom's. Besides, we didn't *do* anything, Dooley. We were just talking, that's all. I'm telling you because I don't want you to find out from the cops."

"You didn't want me to find out that you lied to me, you mean?" Dooley said. "Maybe you also didn't want me to find out that he drove you home from the police station."

"I was in a debate when the police came to talk to me," Beth said. "Nevin offered to pick up my mother. He waited for us while I talked to the police and then he drove us home. He was just being nice."

"I bet," Dooley said.

Beth stood up.

"You see?" she said. "That's why I didn't tell you. I knew you'd get the wrong idea."

"Not telling you about my mother, that's one thing," Dooley said. "My mother didn't mean anything to me. She wasn't part of my life. But not telling me about Nevin?" He stood up, angry, hurt, and, yeah, jealous. Jesus, private school kids. He hated them. And kids with Jags? He hated them worse.

Then it happened, the kind of miracle that turns people religious.

Beth stepped forward, so close that he could smell her hair. When she was that close, she had to crane her neck just a little if she wanted to look him in the eye, which she did. She said, "Nevin doesn't mean anything to me, Dooley. You do. I should have told you the truth. I'm sorry I didn't. I'm sorry about your mother, too, even though I don't understand it—I mean, whatever else she was, she was your mother. But it doesn't change the way I feel about you. It doesn't."

Then she was in his arms, her hands up under his jacket around his waist, and he was holding her, pulling her as close to him as he could. She was just the right height for her head to tuck in under his chin. He held her until he felt her heat.

"You want to know about my mother?" he said.

Her head bobbed up and down, taking his head along for the ride.

"Okay," he said. "I'll tell you."

Twelve

They sat down on the cold bench again, and Beth listened. She didn't interrupt him, not even once. Her eyes never left his. Her expression, one of rapt concentration, never changed. He kept talking, even though there were plenty of times when he wanted to stop, when the voice in his head whispered, *What will she think if you tell her that?* He said, "I'm pretty sure she didn't plan on getting pregnant." He said, "She was really young—our age." He said, "She was the kind of person who got antsy unless she was out having fun." He said, "She liked to be the center of attention, you now?" He'd already told her about the drugs—that Lorraine had used them and so had he—so that part wasn't as hard to talk about. But the men … they came and they went and there were times—he told her because he'd promised to tell her everything—there were times when there would be a steady stream of men in and out of the apartment, at all hours of the night, some of them drunk, some of them ripped, some of them mean, some of them so noisy that one or some of the neighbors would call the cops. A couple of the guys she went with ended up in jail—for assault, for drunk and disorderly, for drug trafficking—and Dooley would think, thank God. But who did those guys come and check in on again the minute they were out? "That's the way she was," he said to Beth. He talked until it was completely dark and she was shivering, but still she listened, her eyes on his, never once interrupting.

And then he ran out of words.

He'd said it all.

It was all out there. She knew everything there was to know about him. Well, almost everything.

She was still looking into his eyes. She was still quiet.

"Pretty fucked up, huh?" Dooley said. He'd felt it stronger and stronger as he talked, as he laid it all out. He even caught himself thinking, well, no wonder I turned out the way I did. Look at my role models. Then he heard Dr. Calvin's voice in his ear: *Up to a certain point, Dooley* (Dr. Calvin was one of the few adult authority figures in his life who was relaxed about calling him Dooley), *you are well within your rights to lay part of the blame on your parents. But after that ...* After that, you had to play the hand you were dealt. You couldn't stack the deck; you couldn't take someone else's cards; you couldn't deal from the bottom; you couldn't palm cards; you couldn't resort to that kind of bullshit and then try to lay the blame off on someone else when you got caught. Dooley knew that. He was out of that now. He was clean, wasn't he? He was going to school, wasn't he? He was holding down a job, wasn't he? But he wasn't driving a Jag. He wasn't going to private school. He was never going to be welcomed by

Beth's mother. Maybe he wasn't even going to be welcomed by Beth—not after everything she knew about him.

Beth slid closer to him and put her arms around him again. They sat like that for a few minutes, Dooley clinging to her as if she were the only thing keeping him afloat. A lot of days—that was exactly how he felt.

"Are you in trouble?" Beth said, her voice muffled by the collar of his jacket.

"I didn't do anything," he said, which wasn't strictly speaking an answer to her question.

"Why did they ask me about Tuesday night?"

Dooley told her.

"What about the night your mother died? Why did they ask me about that?"

"It's their job. And they're Homicide cops, so they're naturally suspicious. At least half the people who are murdered are killed by someone they know. So they have to check that stuff out."

"I told them I saw her at your school that day."

"Well, you did," Dooley said. "So it's right you told them."

"They don't think you had anything to do with it, do they, Dooley?"

He pulled back from her so that he could look her in the eyes.

"I don't know what they think," he said. "But I don't think they think I killed her." The timing was off. Lorraine had been alive at ten—she'd left a message for Gloria Thomas. Her body had been found all the way across town. They had Dooley at Beth's apartment building. They also had him home at eleven. There was no way they could think he'd done it, not directly, anyway. "I'm not so sure about Jeffie, though. They asked me a lot of questions about him. They're going to double-check everything I said. But they haven't arrested me, so I guess that's something." At least, it was so far. "Come on, I'd better get you home before your mom calls the cops and they pick me up for kidnapping or something."

She was reluctant to let go of him, reluctant to get up, reluctant to go home—and he loved her for that.

Beth's mother was waiting for her in the lobby of the apartment building. She scowled at Dooley. Beth saw it, too. She looked directly at her mother before pulling Dooley close to her. She went up on tiptoes and pressed her lips against his. Then, with her mother watching, she wrapped her arms around his neck and opened her mouth. At first Dooley didn't know what to do—but only at first.

■ ■ ■

Annette Girondin was coming down the porch steps when Dooley got home.

"Is everything okay?" Dooley asked her.

"You should talk to your uncle," she said.

Dooley went inside. His uncle and Jeannie were sitting at the dining room table. There were a couple of cardboard bankers' boxes with the lids off in front of them. His uncle had his reading glasses on and was talking to Jeannie as he thumbed through a stack of paper. It sounded like he was explaining them to her. He didn't look up when Dooley entered the room.

"What's going on?" Dooley said after a few moments.

"I'm just filling Jeannie in on some things," Dooley's uncle said. He still didn't look at Dooley.

Dooley approached the table so that he could get a better look at the papers.

"What kind of things?" he said.

"Things that don't concern you," his uncle grouched. Jeannie laid a hand on his arm.

"Gary," she said in a soft voice—a caution.

Dooley's uncle put down the papers he was holding and took off his reading glasses. He glanced at her. She stood up.

"I'm going to pick up some groceries," she said. "I'm going to make you something special tonight." She bent down and kissed Dooley's uncle on the cheek. One of her hands lingered for a moment on his shoulder. The expression on her face was one that Dooley had never seen there before; she was worried. Dooley's uncle followed her with his eyes as she crossed into the hall, slipped on her coat, picked up her purse, rummaged for her car keys. Just before she turned for the door, she looked at him. They held each other's eyes for so long that it seemed to Dooley that they were trying to memorize each other's faces, as if they were afraid that something might happen that would make them forget. "I'll be back as soon as I can," she said.

The door closed behind her. Dooley's uncle turned to him and said, "Sit down, Ryan." Something in his tone chilled Dooley. He pulled out a chair.

"I saw Annette leaving," he said.

His uncle nodded.

"What's going on?" Dooley said for the second time.

His uncle leaned back in his chair. "I'm showing Jeannie the ropes. She's got a good head for business. She's going to keep an eye on things for me."

"Keep an eye on things?"

"On the stores." He meant his two dry-cleaning stores. "Wilf can do the books and Tessie"—Tessie Abramowicz, who managed the old store while his uncle built up the business at the second, newer store—"can probably run both places, but someone has to keep an eye on them for me. Jeannie's going to see if she can manage, at least for the short term."

For the short term?

"What about you?" Dooley said.

"What about me?"

"They're *your* stores. Why can't you keep an eye on them?"

"Jeannie has also agreed to take you on until we know how it's going to go. Annette is going to talk to probation services—"

"Whoa!" Dooley said. "What the hell are you talking about? Where are you going to be?"

"Lorraine has one of those relatively rare blood types, which they matched right off the bat to a blood stain they found in my car," his uncle said. "I don't have the same blood type. As soon as they found that out, they put a rush on DNA. Bumped it right to the top of the list."

Dooley felt his stomach churn. "So?" he said.

"So what they're going to find out is it's her blood. And when they do, they're probably going to arrest me."

here was blood in your car that came from Lorraine?" Dooley said, incredulous.

"That's right," his uncle said. It was all he said. Okay.

"How did it get there?"

His uncle stiffened a little in his chair. "She was in my car."

"When?"

"That night."

"The night you were supposed to be at the poker game?" Dooley said.

"Yes."

"What was Lorraine doing in your car?"

"We were talking."

His uncle answered questions like a cop in the witness box. Don't volunteer any information, don't ramble, don't embellish, just answer the question you've been asked as simply and as directly as possible. Well, okay, here's one:

"How did her blood get in your car?"

"She had a cut on her hand."

"A cut?"

"She said from peeling vegetables."

"Vegetables?" The whole time Dooley had known Lorraine, vegetables had meant French fries, but she'd never had to peel them because they came ready-peeled and cut. Most of the time they also came ready-cooked, too, in little red cardboard containers with a big golden M on them.

"Yeah, that's what *I* said," his uncle said. "She said she was into that now. She said she was trying to eat right. She also said she was learning to cook. Maybe it had something to do with the medication she was taking."

"She was taking medication?"

"I saw a pill bottle in her purse. Anti-depressants."

"She was depressed?"

"That's why people take anti-depressants, Ryan."

"Did you ask her about it?"

"No, I didn't."

"What did you talk to her about? Why was she in your car?"

"That's none of your business."

"Lorraine's in your car, bleeding all over the seat, then she turns up dead, and it's none of my business?" Dooley tried to fight back the rage he was feeling. "Why didn't you tell me you'd seen her?"

His uncle looked him in the eye but didn't answer. Did he think it was none of Dooley's business? Or was he hiding something?

"So she told you she'd cut her hand peeling vegetables?"

"That's what she said."

It occurred to Dooley for the first time that, for all he

knew, his uncle could be lying to him. Up until recently, Dooley had believed every word that came out of his uncle's mouth. Up until recently, he'd had no reason to doubt him about anything. But now … He looked at his uncle and wondered how much effort he was making. Everyone who lies makes some kind of effort. For example, when Dooley told a lie, he made sure to look directly at the person he was lying to and to keep it up until that person finally broke eye contact. Sometimes he was so conscious of doing it that he was sure it must be obvious. He wondered if his uncle felt the same way.

"If that's what she said and if there was a cut on her hand, there should be no problem, right?" Dooley said.

"It depends," his uncle said.

"On what?"

"On what they found in her apartment."

"What do you mean?"

"I mean, did they find anything that would corroborate that she cut her hand peeling vegetables? Maybe a towel with some blood on it. Better would be some vegetable peelings with traces of blood. Something like that."

Oh.

"It also depends on what they're thinking about the other cuts and abrasions they found on her body."

"*Other* cuts?"

"If they're thinking those were caused by some kind of struggle," his uncle said, "then they might not be inclined to believe that the cut on her hand was from peeling vegetables."

He spoke calmly, matter-of-factly, like he was explaining an old case to Dooley, one that involved a complete stranger.

"What are you saying?" Dooley said.

"I'm saying that I'm getting things organized so that if they arrest me, my business won't go under and you won't end up as a ward of the state. If they charge me with first-degree murder, they're not likely to let me out while I wait for trial. They almost never give bail on a murder charge. And you know how backed up the system is. I could end up in there for a year, maybe more."

"You were a cop," Dooley said.

"Yeah," his uncle said grimly.

"Maybe on account of that, they won't lock you up. Maybe they'll give you some consideration, you know, for safety reasons."

"When they arrest someone for murder, it doesn't matter if it's a cop or an ex-cop; that's not what they do. I have to get all of this in order. And Jeannie wants to cook me a special dinner. I think she's afraid this is it, that the next time she sees me, it's going to be in a visiting room. She'd never say so, but—"

Dooley stood up. "If you guys want some privacy, I can go out and get pizza or something."

His uncle shook his head. "She wants you here, too. The two of you are probably going to have to work things out, for a while at least. If I end up going to prison for this, we'll have to re-think. But in the meantime, Jeannie is ready to step up. She wants you here tonight, Ryan. She wants to get to know you better. Do me a favor, huh? She's a lady. The genuine article. I want you to promise me you'll treat her like one at all times."

"Sure," Dooley said. It wouldn't be hard. "She's nice," he said. "I like her."

His uncle seemed to relax a little, which made Dooley hesitate. But his uncle didn't miss a thing.

"You got something on your mind, Ryan?"

Only a million and one things. Like:

"Did you know Jeffrey Eccles?"

The look his uncle gave him was like a kick in the belly.

"Why are you asking?"

"Did you?"

"What's Jeffrey Eccles to you?"

"I used to know him," Dooley said. "The cops asked me about him." He could see his uncle's reaction as he absorbed this piece of information. It was like watching a poison ivy eruption. "So you *did* know him?"

"I had a few dealings with him," his uncle said.

Dooley winced. Of all the ways he could have put it …

"You arrested him, you mean?"

"A couple of times, right before I retired. It never stuck. Why?"

"Did they ask you about him?"

"Who?"

Who?

"The cops," Dooley said.

He uncle didn't answer. The two of them looked at each other. Dooley wished he knew his uncle better. Maybe if he did, he could have been able to chip away at that exterior, get to the real deal underneath. He decided on a different approach.

"She could really get under people's skin," Dooley said finally. "Lorraine, I mean. There were plenty of guys she was with, they'd smack her around because of the way she could get to them. I felt like doing it myself a few times." He ignored the sharp look his uncle gave him. "She gave as good as she got," Dooley said. "She could draw blood. I saw her do it." His uncle was still giving him that look. "All I'm saying is, maybe she said something. Maybe she acted the way she always did, and it got to you. And then she got into it and started dishing it out, too, and, you know, things got out of hand."

His uncle's eyes drilled into Dooley's skull. "You mean, maybe it was self-defense?" he said.

"You wouldn't believe the number of guys who hit her who said she drove them to it," Dooley said.

His uncle never moved a muscle; his eyes never wavered.

"She died with a needle in her arm, Ryan. It's pretty hard to claim you stuck a needle in someone's arm in self-defense, don't you think?"

"I'm just saying," Dooley said.

"Because you think maybe I did it," his uncle said.

All right. So now it was out there.

"If you did, I wouldn't blame you," Dooley said. And it was the truth.

His uncle laughed.

"Okay, Jesus, I'm sorry," Dooley said.

His uncle wiped his eyes, he'd been laughing that hard.

"I didn't kill her, Ryan," he said. "But I have to admit, when I heard they were treating her death as suspicious, I wondered if you were involved."

"Me?"

"Well," his uncle said. "I found that slip of paper in your pocket. I recognized her handwriting. I knew you'd seen her. I knew you knew where she lived." The taut smile vanished from his uncle's lips. "If I'd called you on your cell phone that night, Ryan, and if you'd answered, how would I have known you were at the library? How would I have known where you were?"

■ ■ ■

Jeannie made lamb chops. She made roasted potatoes. She made asparagus. She made a green salad with vinaigrette dressing. She made white chocolate mousse. She made it all right there in Dooley's uncle's kitchen, but she wouldn't let Dooley or his uncle help her, even though they both offered. Dooley's uncle sat at the kitchen table the whole time and watched her. She had on a skirt and blouse. She'd had on high heels when she came to the house, but she kicked those off and had pulled on the pair of slippers—strappy, red, barely-there slippers that looked to Dooley like sandals—that his uncle brought down from the bedroom. She tied on a black apron that his uncle wore when he cooked and cinched it tightly around her waist. She didn't talk much while she worked. She didn't even have to ask where things were. She knew. Every now and then she looked over at Dooley's uncle and smiled, but it wasn't her usual great big Jeannie smile. These smiles were sad. Wistful.

Like she was looking at something for the very last time.

She wouldn't let Dooley set the table, even though he offered. She did it herself, taking a white linen tablecloth out of his uncle's credenza and using his uncle's good china (Dooley still couldn't figure how his uncle even had good china; he tried to picture him going to the store to pick it out, but the picture always came out wrong—his tough, gruff uncle looking at plates and bowls, cups and saucers) and a silver service he knew (because his uncle had told him) used to belong to his grandparents—well, to his uncle's parents. She set out linen napkins, folded into triangles under the forks. She set out crystal glasses into which she poured wine for herself and Dooley's uncle, and ginger ale for Dooley.

They sat down—Dooley's uncle at one end of the dining room table, Jeannie at the other, Dooley on one side. They ate the dinner that Jeannie had made—it was the best meal Dooley had ever had, and he said so to Jeannie—and they talked about stuff that didn't matter, like the municipal election that was coming up and what was happening with property taxes and whether the city should start incinerating garbage again because what choice did it have, no one wanted a garbage dump in their backyard. The whole time, Jeannie and Dooley's uncle either looked at each other or avoided looking at each other. Dooley knew that his uncle liked Jeannie a lot. She usually came over a couple of times a week, and he even took her to the ballet and the opera if that was what she wanted. Jeannie liked to laugh—although you wouldn't know it tonight—and, even better, she made Dooley's uncle laugh. Now, seeing his uncle staring across the table at Jeannie, it occurred to Dooley that maybe his uncle had more feelings for Jeannie than he had let on to Dooley.

"I'll clean up," Dooley said after dessert and coffee.

This time Jeannie said, "That would be nice."

Dooley's uncle got up and walked to the other end of the table. He pulled out Jeannie's chair for her and supported her elbow as she stood up. He hooked the wine bottle that was on the table and took it with him when he and Jeannie went into the living room. They settled on the couch, Jeannie with her legs curled under her, nestled right in there next to Dooley's uncle, Dooley's uncle with his arm around her. As Dooley went back and forth between the kitchen and the dining room, he glanced at them. They just sat there together, holding each other. Dooley wondered what his uncle had told Jeannie and what Jeannie had asked him, if she had asked him anything at all. They were still sitting there together when Dooley finished cleaning up the kitchen.

"I'm going upstairs," he said. They both looked at him, both nodded, both in silence.

■ ■ ■

Annette Girondin was parked in the no-parking zone outside Dooley's school the next day. She got out of her car and waved him over.

"Get in," she said.

Dooley climbed in the passenger side.

"They arrested your uncle a couple of hours ago," Annette said. "He asked me to give you this." She handed him an envelope.

"What is it?" Dooley said.

"Five hundred dollars. For groceries and whatever else you need. He said to tell you the bills are being taken care of; you don't have to worry about anything."

Right. Not a thing.

"He told me he doesn't think he's going to be able to make bail," Dooley said.

"I'll give it my best shot," Annette said. "But he's probably right."

"You think he did it?"

"The way it works, Ryan, the Crown has to prove beyond a reasonable doubt that he did. My job is to mount a vigorous defense. I intend to do just that."

Which told him exactly nothing.

"So he told you he didn't do it?" Dooley said.

"Come on, Dooley," Annette said. "You know how it goes between a lawyer and a client."

Yeah, Dooley knew. He got out of the car and watched Annette zip away from the curb.

■ ■ ■

Jeannie called while Dooley was changing for work.

"I just wanted to give you a heads-up," she said. "I'm going to be at the house when you get off work. I know you'd probably rather have the place to yourself, but Gary and I talked to your youth worker and—"

"It's okay," Dooley said. "I appreciate what you're doing."

"See you then," Jeannie said, sounding as breezy and cheery as she always did, but after last night, Dooley wondered about that, just like he wondered about how much truth his uncle had told him versus how many lies. Jeannie had been snuggled up tight against his uncle, her head on his shoulder, her hand on his chest. Now his uncle had been arrested for murder, and he was supposed to believe it was no big deal to Jeannie? Dooley doubted that was true. It seemed more likely that she was acting the way she thought a grown-up should act under the circumstances. It seemed even more likely she was putting on a brave front for Dooley.

He went to work and put up with Kevin's asking him, "Would it kill you to smile once in a while?" When Linelle opened her mouth to say something, Dooley shook his head. Linelle closed her mouth again. When it was time for his break, Dooley stepped out onto the sidewalk, turned on his cell phone, and punched in Beth's number.

She answered right away.

"I've been trying to call you," she said. "Did you see the news?"

"I'm at work," Dooley said. "The only thing I've seen is the latest Robin Williams release." They played DVDs non-stop on the monitors in the store, but only stuff that the littlest kids could watch without some pickle-up-her-ass mommy complaining to management, which meant, essentially, that they only played crap, and that described every Robin Williams movie Dooley had ever been subjected to, although Beth insisted there was at least one good one and that old Robin had even been nominated for an Academy Award one time, saying it like it was a big deal.

Dooley heard a voice in the background—a female voice.

"Just a minute," Beth said. He heard muffled voices. Beth probably had her thumb over the mouthpiece on her phone. "Sorry," she said when she came back on. "My mother is freaking out. She saw the news, too. She saw your uncle was arrested for murder."

Terrific. Beth's mother already treated Dooley like he was some kind of criminal. She already didn't want Beth to have anything to do with him. Now Dooley's uncle was in lockup. Dooley could only imagine how that was going down.

"He didn't do it, did he?" Beth said. "It's all a mistake, right?"

"Yeah," Dooley said. He tried to muster some conviction.

"I mean, he wouldn't kill his own sister, would he?"

"I don't think so," Dooley said.

"You don't *think* so?"

That was the thing. He *didn't* think so, but he wasn't sure. He knew Lorraine. He knew what she could be like. He knew how his uncle felt about her. He knew his uncle had lied to him about her.

"I mean, no," Dooley said. "Of course I don't think he did it. He used to be a cop. He's Mr. Law and Order." Mr. Law and Order who had never said a good word about Lorraine that Dooley could remember and who'd said plenty of not-so-good things. Mr. Law and Order who, it looked like, had fudged it the first time the cops had asked him where he'd been when she was killed. Why had he even bothered? Did he think the cops weren't going to check? Or had he done it for the same reason Dooley had—because nobody had said murder, everyone had been talking drug overdose, so, really, what did it matter where he was, and if it didn't matter, why get into it? Everything to do with Lorraine just got messy sooner or later. But there was that other thing that kept niggling at Dooley—his uncle also hadn't mentioned to Dooley that Lorraine had been at the house the week before she'd been killed. And something else, the kicker, the thing Dooley would never have figured, not in a million years: His uncle had known Jeffie, which meant he probably knew what Jeffie was into.

"I have to get back to work," Dooley said. "I just wanted to hear your voice." That wasn't the whole truth, either. He wanted more. He wanted to see her. He wanted to touch her. He wanted to smell her and taste her and lie next to her. When he was with Beth, he didn't think about Lorraine, ever. He didn't think about drugs and booze. He didn't think about what had happened so far in his life. He didn't think about all the crap he'd done and how he wished he could undo it. When he was with Beth, he was one hundred percent there and so full of her that there wasn't room for anything or anyone else. "I wish your mom was out of town or something," he said.

"Me, too," Beth said softly.

And there he had it—the best high he could ever hope for, that floaty up-there feeling of rightness.

"I'll talk to you tomorrow," he said.

"I'll dream about you tonight," she said.

The minute he ended the call, Lorraine filled his thoughts

again. Someone had killed her. There'd been a time when he didn't think he would care, but here he was, thinking about her, unable to stop himself, and not just because his uncle seemed to be the best suspect the cops had. He'd known for a long time how messed up she was. He'd never known, until his uncle told him, how far back that went and why it might have been. He still didn't really know the why of it.

Before he went back into the store, he made another quick call, this one to Warren.

■ ■ ■

By ten o'clock that night, Dooley was restless and fed up. His uncle was in jail, and what was Dooley doing? Putting up with what seemed like an endless stream of customers who were looking for, "You know, that movie, the one with that guy in it from that TV show," but when you pressed them, they couldn't recall anything about the movie, the guy, or the TV show, not that that stopped them from giving him attitude when he had to confess (politely) that he had no idea what they were talking about. And people thought video-store clerks were brain-dead.

Dooley tried to put himself on automatic pilot—scan the product bar code, check to make sure that the correct DVD or game was in the case, demagnetize the product, take the money, print the receipt, bag the product, "Please call again"—taking on every customer in the store because Linelle, who was supposed to be up on cash with him, was making nice with a male customer in the action-adventure aisle, Linelle laughing a lot, which tipped Dooley that she was interested in the guy because most of the time—hell, *all* of the time—she had as little patience with the customers as Dooley did.

Linelle came up to the cash, still with the guy, who Dooley could see was a sharp dresser, but in a flash way, not in the money way of someone like, say, Nevin with the midnight blue Jag. The guy was buying, not renting, and Linelle rang up the sale. When she gave him his change and his receipt, he flipped the receipt over and scrawled his number on it.

"Really," he said. "Call me."

Linelle smiled at him so sweetly that Dooley wondered if she had fallen on her head on the way to work and sustained a serious head injury. The guy had obviously made some kind of impression. But what kind, exactly, Dooley wasn't sure, because the minute the guy cleared the store, Linelle was on the computer, sweetness replaced by a look of intense concentration.

"I knew it," she said with disgust a few moments later. "I fucking knew it."

Kevin's head popped up in the family section where he had been shelving new product.

"Language," he said.

Linelle flipped him the bad finger.

"The guy tells me he lives in some big-deal condo," she says. "Bullshit. He lives in a crap neighborhood. Asshole. That's why I don't give out my number, Dooley. It's why I always get guys to give me their numbers. They want to give me their cell number, okay, I'll take that. But I always insist on a landline, too. A guy tells me he doesn't have a land-line, he'll never hear from me."

"What's the big deal?" Dooley said. "A number is a number."

Linelle rolled her eyes. "Are you for real? A cell number is a number that could be anywhere." That was why Dooley's uncle had insisted on a pager at first. It was also the reason Dooley was suspicious of cell phones—well, of Beth's cell phone. "A guy gives you a cell number and tells you he's a movie producer based in L.A., how can you check? You call the number, and there the guy is. But where's there? There's no way to know. You can't check it with the phone company. You do a search on the number, and all you get is that it's not a published listing. In other words, no information. Are you with me, Dooley? But a landline? A landline is somewhere, and you can check exactly where. When a guy tells you he lives in an exclusive neigh-borhood, but the landline is registered to some dump in public housing, you know you're being snowed. Or maybe it's registered to another name—maybe the guy lives with his girlfriend. Worse, his mommy. You want me, you gotta have a landline. You gotta be 411-checkable."

Dooley gave her a blank look.

"You're kidding, right?" Linelle said. "Don't you know anything?"

"I know 411," Dooley said.

Linelle shook her head. "Come here."

He went over to the computer she was at and saw that she was on the Internet.

211

"Here," she said. "You can type in an address and it tells you who the place belongs to and the phone number—perfect for checking out that adorable hunk of man who just moved in up the block. Or you can put in a phone number and, bingo, you get the name the phone is registered to and the address. Jesus, Dooley, where have you been?"

Dooley caught movement out of the corner of his eye. Kevin was coming up the aisle toward them, a suspicious look on his face.

"You better not be gambling on-line again, Linelle," he said.

Dooley looked at her with new interest. Linelle was full of surprises.

"It was dead in here the other night," she said to Dooley. "I was bored."

"But on-line gambling?" he said.

"Hey, I was up a hundred bucks by the time Kevin busted me." She clicked off the 411 site and was back in the IMDB site that they used to check movies for customers.

Fourteen

You didn't have to wait up for me," Dooley said when he let himself into the house and Jeannie got up off the couch in the living room. He felt bad. If he'd known she was waiting for him like that, he would have come straight home. He wouldn't have stopped at Warren's place. He saw that there was a wineglass on the coffee table and a bottle of wine, half gone, on the floor beside the table.

"I never had kids," she said. "It occurred to me that you might be embarrassed if I sat up to wait for you, but then it occurred to me that you might be even more embarrassed if you came home and found out that I was asleep in Gary's bed ..." She said all that out straight, with no problem. But when she said, "Gary explained the conditions of your supervision order," she blushed. Dooley didn't know if it was because of the wine or because she was self-conscious about having to talk about him and his past, if she was one of those people who found things like that harder to talk about than the regular awkward stuff like, say, sex. "He said

213

one of the things that was important was ongoing adult supervision, which includes curfews." Her face turned even redder, which told him it wasn't the wine. "I promised ..."

"It's okay," Dooley said. "I appreciate it. Really." He looked at the half-gone bottle of wine and wondered if she'd been plowing through it because she was nervous about being here with him. "If it's okay with you, I'm going to bed," he said.

She nodded. He heard her footsteps soft on the stairs maybe twenty minutes after he crawled in under the covers. He waited until he was pretty sure she was settled in. Then he got out of bed, turned on the lights, opened his backpack, and pulled out the thick envelope he had picked up at Warren's. He opened it. Inside was a small, square photo album, the cheap kind that you can buy at any dollar store. Dooley had never seen it before. The pages were clear plastic sleeves you could slip photos into, back to back. The photos inside were mainly of Dooley, mainly from school—individual shots and group shots of his entire kindergarten class, his entire grade one class, his entire grade two class, right up to grade six. He remembered the pictures being taken, but he hadn't seen them in ages. Lorraine had never framed them or displayed them around whatever piece of-shit apartment they happened to be living in. He figured she had thrown them out or left them behind as she moved from place to place. But, no, here they were, six years' worth of school pictures of Dooley, alone and with all the kids in his class. After grade six, though, there was only one school photo. Dooley thought it must be from grade seven or eight.

He'd started skipping pretty regularly once he hit junior high and almost always dodged picture day.

Besides the school pictures, there were some snapshots taken by someone else, not Lorraine—Lorraine had never owned a camera—and a bunch of pictures taken in those little photo booths you see at amusement parks and in train and bus stations, four pictures for a toonie. He remembered that whenever they passed one of those booths, Lorraine, especially if she was in a good mood, having what she called a good-hair day, would want to duck in and get her picture taken, and Dooley would do what he could to ruin the experience by pulling faces, the goal being to crack Lorraine up so that she'd look goofy in spite of her good hair. At least, that had been his goal at first. Later he just plain acted up and made faces, anything he could think of to be uncooperative, especially if they were a threesome, Dooley, Lorraine, and whatever guy Lorraine was seeing at the time. But he hadn't seen any of those pictures in a long time. He was surprised she had kept them, let alone put them in an album. Dooley leafed through the pages, trying to remember who the guys were, most of them hard-faced or bleary-eyed. Jesus, why did Gloria Thomas think he'd want to look at the past like this? All those things he'd done to himself, that was so he could forget. After a while, the pages were blank, all the way to the last page where there was one more picture.

He stared at it for a few minutes before getting up and locating and looking at the picture Detective Randall and his partner—what was that guy's name again?—had given him.

He held the two side by side. They were the same. The same, but different.

He pulled the last photograph out of its sleeve and dumped the album into the wastepaper basket in his room. He stared at it down in there, then went to his desk and picked up the book he had brought back with him from Lorraine's apartment. He opened it and inhaled her scent one last time, and then dropped that in on top of the photograph album. He was sorry now that he'd retrieved the package from Warren. Looking at Lorraine didn't do any good. It only made him remember, and remembering made him angry. If the cops didn't think she'd been murdered, he was pretty sure he would have put her out of his mind by now.

Or would he? No matter how he looked at it, Beth was right. She was his mother. That should mean something.

He stared at the one photo he hadn't dumped. He held it over the wastepaper basket, too, but he couldn't make his fingers release it.

She was his mother, and it did mean something.

■ ■ ■

The way Dooley had figured it: He would drop by the cemetery after school; he'd walk up and down the rows; he'd use the picture Randall had given him as a guide for finding what he was looking for; and then he'd compare that to the second picture he had found at the back of the album that Gloria Thomas had thrust into his hands.

The way it turned out: He wandered around helplessly

216

for at least an hour before the sun started to drop to the horizon and he knew that (a) he'd never find what he was looking for without help because the cemetery was too freaking big; it was like the Energizer bunny; it kept going and going, down this path, over along that one, across this busy thoroughfare into another expanse of headstone after headstone after headstone, mausoleums, too, and crypts; and (b) Jeannie would unlock the front door any minute now and wonder where he was. She would also probably wonder if she should be worrying, if she should be calling his youth worker.

Shit.

He dug in his pocket for his cell phone and Jeannie's business card, which she had given him at breakfast—scrambled eggs and toast, juice, coffee, a couple of slices of melon on the side of his plate, just like at a restaurant—and on which she had written her cell phone number. Call me anytime, she had said. He punched in her number, told her he was sorry, he was still at the library, he'd be home in an hour, he promised.

"No problem," Jeannie said, which made Dooley wish she was the one who was responsible for him, not Uncle Third Degree.

He meandered through the cemetery checking gravestones until a guy on a golf cart—that was a sight, a golf cart in a cemetery—pulled even with him and said, "You look lost, son."

Dooley showed the man the picture the cops had given him. The man studied it for all of ten seconds and said, "Hop on. I'll give you a lift." He drove Dooley down a paved road, took a right, then a left, then another left, and kept going. "Relatives?" he said.

"Grandparents," Dooley said.

The man took a final right and slowed the golf cart.

"Here we are," he said, pointing at three headstones inside a small square area marked off by a chain that ran through wrought-iron pinions. Dooley stepped off the golf cart and read the names and dates—his uncle's mother, his uncle's father, his uncle's sister.

"We close the place up at dusk," the man with the golf cart said. "If you need a lift back to the gate—"

Dooley pulled the other picture from his pocket, the one from the back of Lorraine's album, and held it out to the man. "When would you say this was taken?" he said.

The man squinted at it. He got out of the golf cart, tramped up and down for a few moments. Then he said, "I'd say twenty years ago, maybe more. See? Those aren't in the picture." He pointed to some nearby stones. "Nor are those." He swept his hand off in another direction. He studied the picture again. "Definitely more than twenty years." He left the main path and examined a few neighboring headstones, comparing what he was looking at to the photo Dooley had given him. "My mistake," he said at last. He tapped a headstone. "This one clinches it. This picture here was taken twenty-two or twenty-three years ago. Here. You can see for yourself."

Dooley joined him and looked at everything the man had pointed to.

Twenty-two or twenty-three years ago.

Dooley did the math.

Either his uncle had been wrong, or he'd been lying. Again.

■ ■ ■

There were voices in the kitchen—two of them, Jeannie's and Annette Girondin's.

"—looking for?" Jeannie was saying.

"They didn't say." That was Annette. "All I know is they subpoenaed his bank records."

"Tessie said they went through his computer at work. What does that have to do with anything?"

"I don't know, Jeannie," Annette said wearily. It sounded to Dooley like it wasn't the first time she'd said it. It also sounded like Jeannie was worried. "If I find out anything, I'll let you know."

Dooley heard a sigh. Jeannie.

"Okay," she said. "Okay. I'm sorry. It's just that—"

"It's unnerving, I know," Annette said. "You just have to hang in there. We'll get this all sorted out. It just takes time."

There was a moment's silence, and then Jeannie asked Annette if she wanted to stay for supper. Annette declined. Dooley tiptoed out onto the porch. He was standing there, doing his best to look like he was just getting home, when Annette came through the front door a minute later.

"Ryan," she said, catching her breath. "You startled me."

"Sorry." He offered her an apologetic smile. "How's my uncle? What's going on?"

"There's nothing new to report," Annette said. Jesus, a lie. Why? Because his uncle didn't want him to know anything? Or was it that attorney-client privilege thing?

"The cops got anything else on him?" Dooley said.

"I'm afraid I'm not at liberty—"

"I heard they've been asking about him and Lorraine when they were kids. About something that went down between the two of them. You know what that's about?"

She wasn't surprised by the question. Dooley bet anything that she'd spoken to Jerry Panelli. Maybe she'd talked to Lorraine's friends, too.

"I have to go," she said.

"I just want to know—"

"Goodnight, Ryan."

And that was that. Her high heels clickety-clicked down the front walk and around the front of her car. A moment later, she was gone.

Dooley went inside.

■ ■ ■

Jeannie had supper waiting for him—grilled salmon and a green salad. Dooley cleaned his plate in three minutes flat. He got up, opened the fridge, and rooted around inside, but it looked like groceries hadn't been on his uncle's mind when he'd been putting his affairs in order. He remembered the envelope of money that Annette Girondin had given him and wondered how Jeannie would react if he ordered himself a pizza.

"Can I get you something else?" Jeannie said, not so breezy now. Dooley heard doubt in her voice. He pulled out a container of milk and poured himself a glass.

"I'm fine," he said.

Jeannie picked at her salmon. "Not enough food for a teenaged boy, huh?" she said. "Are you still hungry, Dooley?"

"No, really, I'm fine."

She studied him for a moment and then reached for the phone.

"What do you like on yours?" she said, boy, like she was reading his mind.

"Onions, pepperoni, and extra cheese." It was what he always ordered, unless he knew he was going to be seeing Beth. Then he skipped the onions.

Jeannie smiled and placed the order. It was no mystery what his uncle saw in her. She finished her own meal, accepted when Dooley offered to clean up, then said she had some work to do, if that was okay with him.

It was fine. Dooley spread out on the dining room table— homework and pizza. Well, homework and pizza and Lorraine, twenty-two or twenty-three years ago.

Had she had that photo from the album back then? Or had she found it later? If so, when? Had someone given it to her? Who?

He remembered what his uncle had said: *She was one of those girls, they hit puberty and all hell breaks loose.*

Was that it? Was it puberty? Twenty-two years ago, Lorraine was thirteen. Or was it something else?

To the best of my knowledge, his uncle had said, *they*

(They? Who the hell were they? His grandparents?) *never told her.*

Then how to explain that picture? And what about his uncle's arrest?

I don't like her because she killed my mother.

Now Dooley wondered: Who had killed whom?

Lorraine, from the outside: a party girl. Always laughing. Always wanting to be the center of attention. Always looking for some guy to be the one. Drinking, snorting, smoking, shooting up, getting that party high. Dooley knew what that was all about. Get out of your head, out of your skin, out of yourself, out of your life. Kill the emptiness; kill the uncertainty; kill that lurking, aching, sucking feeling, the one that's always whispering in your ear, *You're not the one.* Not the one they want. Not the one to succeed. Not the one to win. Not the one to be happy. Not the one I carry in my heart. Not the one I see when I close my eyes. It's not you. It's not you. It's not you.

Worse.

It's someone else.

He thought back.

He had come home that Friday night and had circled around to the side of the house, meaning to go in through the kitchen to get that DVD, then maybe stop in the kitchen again on the way out and check the fridge in the hope that his uncle, who was a good cook, had some leftovers stashed in there. But when he'd got to the door, he'd heard Lorraine's voice, and it had frozen him to the spot. He'd stood there and listened. Now he replayed every word he had heard.

222

"You never came around even once," Lorraine had said to his uncle.

He remembered the day his uncle showed up that first time when Dooley was in detention. Right after Dooley had got it clear in his head just who it was who was sitting opposite him at the visiting table—and that had taken some time because he was still detoxing—he had asked his new uncle about Lorraine. His uncle had snorted.

"Who knows where the hell she's at?" he'd said.

Dooley used to think about her from time to time. He'd been pretty sure that if she had died, someone would have told him. So what he decided was that she must have taken off. But that Friday, there she was in his uncle's kitchen saying, "You never came around."

You never came around.

His uncle had said something else, too. Dooley tried hard to recall the exact words. He couldn't. But it was something that had led him to believe that his uncle had been surprised to discover that he had a nephew. He remembered thinking that it was just like Lorraine not to have bothered to mention to her own brother, the only living relative she had, that she had a son. She also hadn't bothered to mention to Dooley that he had an uncle. No, she had left it to Dooley to find out on his own, which he did when he was well and truly fucked and locked up on account of it. And then who had showed up to see him then? Not Lorraine. No, it was some stick-up-his-ass, used-to-be-cop-turned-dry cleaner who was all of a sudden in his face, giving him a thorough once-over before breaking the news: I'm your uncle. And there

223

was Dooley, trying to look like he didn't give a shit while he processed what this surly guy had just told him. *Uncle?* He had an *uncle?*

It turned out his uncle was as hard a case as Dooley. He was always busting Dooley's balls about something—was he cooperating in his group sessions; was he doing what he was told and keeping his nose clean; was he doing in his schoolwork; what the hell was he doing with his spare time; was he pissing it away playing stupid games; why didn't he try reading a book, for Christ's sake; his uncle had never met a nonreader who knew squat about anything important, whereas people who read were people who were curious, people who wanted to find out about the world, people who had a life, not an *existence,* but a real honest-to-God worth-living *life.* The guy never let up. But the whole time, underlying it all, it was like he was sending a message and was hoping that Dooley would get it. And Dooley was pretty sure he did get it. He was pretty sure the message went like this: If I'd known, things would have been different, *you* would have been different, your *life* would have been different. But it's never too late. You can turn your life around, Ryan. You can make good. You can *do* good.

And then Lorraine had showed up in his uncle's kitchen, telling his uncle, *You never came around,* like the choice to get to know Dooley had been there the whole time, like it had been up to his uncle to make a move in that direction, and his uncle had declined the opportunity.

Dooley picked up the phone and called Annette Girondin. To his surprise, she answered, even though it was late. When he said, "I want to see him," she didn't hesitate. She said she would get back to him.

■ ■ ■

He lay awake until he heard Jeannie close the door to his uncle's bedroom. He waited another half hour, just to be safe. Then he tiptoed out into the hall. His uncle's bedroom was completely dark. No light seeped out from under the door. Dooley crept down the hall and listened. Nothing.

He slipped into his uncle's office and closed the door. He flicked on the small desk lamp, turned on the computer, and waited for it to boot up. He probably wouldn't be able to get into it. Knowing his uncle, everything would be password protected.

But no. A couple of minutes later, he was double-clicking on the spreadsheet icon on the desktop and watching in amazement as the program opened. He poked around the listing of files inside until he found one that looked like it might be the one he wanted. He double-clicked on it and, just like that, there it was, his uncle's financial life right there on the screen for everyone—well, for Dooley—to see. At first Dooley couldn't figure out why his uncle didn't protect it. Maybe he didn't think he had to. His uncle had lived alone for most of his life. Usually there was no one around to look into his stuff. Not until recently.

He wasn't surprised to see how detailed the accounts were. Everything was recorded, every bill payment, every purchase made on Dooley's behalf, every psychologist's bill itemized. And then that one line. It looked innocuous at first, like it was a payment for a utility bill. But it was different from all the other amounts entered into Expenses. Instead of odd amounts that varied from month to month, this was a nice round number—one thousand dollars—paid on the last day of every month. The heading on the entry was different, too. Instead of Gas or Hydro or Property Tax, this one read L.M.

L.M.

One thousand dollars on the last of every month.

Dooley stared at it and thought about what Lorraine's neighbor had said.

He pulled up the previous year's file and the one before that—for at least a couple of years now. Maybe more. He wanted to check back further, but there were only two years' worth of records that he could find. He went back to the first file and stared at the entry again.

One thousand dollars.

Lorraine's party money.

■ ■ ■

The next afternoon, Dooley had had enough. He'd barely slept. He couldn't concentrate, either. He kept thinking about everything he knew and everything he didn't. He left math class at the sound of the bell, just like the rest of his class, went to his locker to ditch his math text and grab his copy of *1984*, which was what they were reading in English, and started for the stairs because his locker was on the second floor and his English class was on the first floor. But instead of making a left at the bottom of the stairs to go down the east corridor where his English class was, he made a right and headed for the front door. He had to get out of there, now. He had to breathe. He had to think—and school was the last place to do that.

He spotted Mr. Rektor standing outside the auditorium, which was directly across from the school's main doors, and saw Warren emerging from the west corridor. Warren was in the same English class as Dooley. Warren raised a hand in greeting. "Hey, Dooley," he called. Dooley was aware of Mr. Rektor turning to look at him. So what did he do? He tossed his copy of *1984* to Warren who, being Warren, got flustered and, in an effort to catch it, which, of course, he didn't, dropped his binder and a couple of other books he was holding. Then Dooley went right out the front door and kept on going. For the first time since he'd been released, he flat out didn't care that Rektor would get on the phone to his uncle—well, to Jeannie—or that he was also perfectly within his rights to report him to Al Szabo, Dooley's youth worker. He didn't care that, technically, ditching class was a violation of his supervision order. He walked until he was out of sight of the school and then he caught the bus that ran north. He was standing outside Beth's school ten minutes before it let out.

Beth had toured him around the school grounds one weekend, but this was the first time he'd been there on a weekday, mostly because it took forty minutes and two buses to get to, and his school let out only twenty-five minutes before hers. He stood on the sidewalk looking at the ivy that covered the whole front of the place, and the lawns and playing fields that surrounded it, all of it in a nice, peaceful neighborhood filled with big houses set back from tree-lined streets. Beth told him one time how much tuition cost. Dooley couldn't believe it. Only rich people could afford to send their daughters to a place like that. Beth's mother was financing Beth's tuition from the insurance payout she'd got after Beth's father died. Beth felt bad about that, which is why she took school so seriously. She was even more serious now that her brother was gone. It was like she felt that all of her mother's hopes were riding on her and that she owed it to her mother to make good. Dooley didn't get it, but that was probably because he couldn't imagine Lorraine having any hopes for him, much less himself giving a shit if she did.

He heard a bell, and girls in uniforms—white blouses, some of them with V-neck navy sweaters under their navy blazers, and plaid skirts, some of them hiked up so high all you could see was thigh, all under open coats—started to pour out the main door. He scanned faces and legs and was surprised to see how good-looking all the girls were. There wasn't a dog in the bunch. Most of the older girls sauntered to a parking lot on one side of the school, laughing and talking, hips swaying, car keys in their hands. A lot of the younger ones walked in pairs or groups or alone to the line of mostly SUVs, mostly driven by women whose skin color didn't match whatever girls got into their vehicles.

And then there was Beth, swinging out of school, one of five girls, all laughing about something. Dooley was about to raise his hand to wave at her when a car horn tooted somewhere off to his right and Beth's eyes and the eyes of the girls with her all went there. So did Dooley's. And don't you know it, there it was again, the midnight blue Jag.

Dooley tracked back to Beth and saw that all the girls around her were giggling and nudging her toward the Jag. But Beth's focus was somewhere else. She was looking at Dooley, and she was smiling. She said something to her friends, and then she skipped down the wide stone steps and ran along the flagstone walk over to where Dooley was standing. Dooley looked back at her friends. They were talking to each other, but they were watching Beth. Mostly they looked baffled.

Beth reached him and looped one of her arms through his and started to walk him away from the school.

"What a surprise," she said. She smiled up at him. She looked happy enough, but if that were true, how come he was sensing that he'd done something wrong, that the surprise wasn't a pleasant one?

"I'm not messing up your plans, am I?" he said.

"No."

"I mean, if you were going somewhere with your friends—"

She shook her head.

"Or maybe with Nevin." He couldn't stop himself from saying it, but now that it was out there, he wished he'd kept his mouth shut. He came off sounding like a jealous kid.

"I didn't have any plans," Beth said. She nuzzled in close to him. She didn't mention Nevin—why he was there, why

229

he had honked his car horn like that, why the girls with her had all giggled when he did it, why they all seemed to be nudging her in his direction. He glanced back over his shoulder. Nevin was standing beside his Jag now, surrounded by girls, but he was looking at Beth, at the back of her walking away. His eyes met Dooley's. He smiled, his lips like ice. He said something to the girls, and they all turned to look at him, too. They weren't giggling anymore.

■ ■ ■

They went to Beth's house where Beth made tea for herself and a sandwich for Dooley. They didn't talk much. There were a lot of times when they didn't talk much. That was one of the things Dooley liked about Beth. She didn't mind when things were quiet. She didn't mind that he just sat there and watched while she put the kettle on and put a tea bag in a mug, while she got out the bread and peanut butter, moving so gracefully even when all she was doing was pouring milk into her mug, her legs long and slim under her skirt, which was short but not hiked up as high as some of the girls who went to her school. She didn't mind that he watched every move she made, and when she caught him at it, she smiled. She put the sandwich down in front of him and sat across the table from him with her tea. She didn't ask him why, for the first time since they'd known each other, he had showed up unexpectedly at her school. He wondered about that. He wondered what she really thought. He got a hint when she looked down at the sandwich on his plate. He hadn't

230

touched it. He wasn't hungry. She got up then and took his hand and led him down the hallway to her bedroom.

In her arms, he forgot about Lorraine. In her arms, he forgot about his uncle and Jeffie. In her arms, there was only softness and sweet smells and acceptance. In her arms, he was in a magical place where there was no Mr. Rektor, no school, no Kevin, no video store, no minimum-wage monkey-shit job, no twitchy reminders of how high it was possible to go, no crash-out-aw-shit-now-what moments at the come-down. In her arms, he could forget.

When he opened his eyes again, she was smiling up at him. She raised a hand and pushed the hair back off his forehead. Then she put both hands on his face and pulled him down and kissed him.

He said, "You make all the bullshit go away."

She was still smiling, but he saw a tightness between her eyebrows. "Thanks," she said. "I think."

"What I meant was—"

A cell phone trilled.

His. Names flashed in his mind: Jeannie. Al Szabo. Annette Girondin.

"I better—"

"It's okay," she said.

He groped for his jeans and pulled out the phone.

For a moment, he just stared at the display. This time he recognized the number.

It was Teresa.

She was hysterical.

"I don't have any money," she said. "I didn't know anything

about what he was doing. You have to believe me, Dooley."

"What are you talking about?" he said.

"I don't have any money," she said again. "I—Oh my god, I think something's wrong."

"What do you mean? What's wrong?"

"I'm bleeding. Something's wrong." She was screaming now. He had to hold the phone away from his ear.

"Teresa, calm down."

Beth sat up when he said Teresa's name. She looked at him.

"I think it's the baby, Dooley. Oh, shit."

Jesus, why had she called him of all people? What was he supposed to do?

"Hang up the phone, Teresa. Call 9-1-1."

"I think it's the baby," she said. "I think I'm losing the baby."

"Teresa, listen to me. Hang up the phone. Call 9-1-1."

She was sobbing now. It was all he could hear.

"Teresa, where are you?" He recognized the number but didn't know if it was a cell phone or the cordless he had seen at the apartment. "Teresa?"

She was at home. Dooley could picture the place. What he couldn't remember was the street number. He had to coax it out of her while she sobbed.

"Hang up the phone, Teresa," he said. "I'm going to call someone, okay? I'm going to call an ambulance. Just hang up the phone."

She let out one last wail and then, just like that, Dooley was listening to dead air.

He punched in 9-1-1, gave her address, and described what he thought the problem was. When he'd finished, he reached for his clothes.

"Who's Teresa?" Beth said.

"She's this girl I know. I have to go."

There it was again, that tightness between her eyebrows.

"Know her how?" Beth said. "What did you just say about a baby?"

"Beth—"

It was probably the phone call. No, it was probably a combination of the phone call and stealth. Maybe it was completely innocent. Maybe she had got off early. Or maybe it was planned. Maybe she was checking up on Beth, which, for sure, would explain why neither he nor Beth heard anything. Dooley was standing beside the bed in nothing but his underpants, holding his jeans out in front of him, getting ready to step into them. Beth was sitting up in the bed, her bare shoulders resting against a white pillow, her breasts covered by a white sheet, watching him. Then, boom, the door to Beth's bedroom opened and there was Beth's mother, looking at Dooley with cold, unwelcoming eyes. Yeah, Dooley thought later, she must have been checking up on Beth because, you know what, she didn't look the least bit surprised to see him there.

Fifteen

Much later that night, Dooley was downtown thinking how much had changed and how much was the same. He wished Jeffie was still around because that would make things easier. For one thing, he had always been able to trust Jeffie one hundred percent, not just on the fact of the sale but on the quality of the goods. Jeffie never screwed around with him. Jeffie always delivered. Some of the other guys he knew—okay, so they were guys he *used* to know—he wasn't as sure about. Yeah, they'd make the sale. No, they wouldn't set him up. But you had to be careful. You had to wonder what they were really selling. Back before, Dooley had never cared. Back before, it was, whatever, bring it on, the more the better, and there was no such thing as too much. But the fact that Jeffie wasn't there anymore, the fact that there was nobody he could trust the way he'd been able to trust Jeffie, didn't stop him from standing on the corner, eyes shifting this way and that, searching for a familiar face, his foot thrumming like Fred Astaire warming up. He was there because of everything that had happened after he had taken Teresa's call.

The first thing that had happened: Beth's mother had opened the bedroom door wide and had stood there and stared at him, and what else could he do? He pulled on his jeans and reached for his T-shirt. The whole time he was getting dressed, Beth was yelling at her mother to get out, *get the hell out*. When her mother didn't leave, Beth got out of bed, her naked body wrapped in that white sheet, ran to the door, and tried to push her mother out, which her mother didn't like. So then her mother started yelling, going on about how she had trusted Beth but that she should have known better; what kind of self-respecting girl would take up with a criminal? "For God's sake," she said, "his uncle just murdered his mother." Dooley had his jeans zipped up by that time—he kept thinking what would have happened if she'd showed up a couple of seconds earlier, while he was completely naked. Jesus, what a thought that was, Beth's mother seeing him that way. Or a couple of minutes before that, when he and Beth … He pulled on his T-shirt while Beth and her mother screamed at each other, Beth saying she was seventeen now, she was legal for sex, Beth's mother reacting to that word as if Beth had slapped her across the face, and Dooley, socks on now, sliding into his boots, realizing just how much he didn't know about girls and women.

He was dressed and in a hurry to get out of there, both for the original reason—Teresa—and for a new reason—Beth's mother. But they were blocking the door, mother and daughter. They were really going at it, and Dooley understood that although his presence had precipitated the fight, it had escalated way beyond him or anything to do with him. The mother had a litany of complaints: Beth's general lack of communication, her lack of gratitude (after all, there were plenty of other things her mother could be doing with the money she was spending, giving Beth the best education she could buy *and* her mother didn't insist she get a job and help with some of the expenses the way a lot of parents did), the fact that Beth didn't help out around the place, the fact that lately—and here Dooley was part of the grievance again, the mother throwing a dagger of a look his way—she had become insolent and talked back to her mother. Beth had a few grievances of her own: Her mother was controlling; her mother was over-protective; her mother disapproved of things she knew nothing about; her mother …

Dooley put a hand on Beth's hip—he loved that hip—to nudge her away from the door so that he could leave. She stepped aside without even looking at him; she was still ripping into her mother. But the mother noticed. She stiffened when she saw Dooley's hand on the sheet covering her daughter's hip, and Dooley knew with certainty that if the mother had had a cleaver handy, or an axe, any sharp edge, she would have hacked that hand off.

"I'll call you," he whispered in Beth's ear. Then he'd had to squeeze by the mother, who at first didn't budge. She looked up at him, menace in her eyes. But Dooley was a lot taller than her and, to be honest, he was a little pissed with her, too, for barging in on them like that, for standing there and watching him dress, and then tearing into Beth, so, yeah, maybe he'd put a little menace on his face, too. He saw a startled look in the mother's eyes. She shrank back and let him pass.

The second thing that had happened: Half an hour after leaving Beth's, he was at the hospital closest to where Jeffie used to live and was asking at the information desk in the Emergency department if Teresa was there. He was directed to a screened-in cubicle. Teresa was lying on a bed. She looked like shit. Her face was pale, there were black smudges under her eyes from where her makeup had run, and her eyes were red from crying. One of her cheeks was swollen. Her lower lip was split open and in the process of scabbing over. There were bruises on her arms and tubes running out of them. Tears dribbled down her face. But when she saw him, she sat up and put her arms out, and, even though he didn't know her all that well, he let her hug him. She was bony with tiny little breasts that he could feel pressing against him.

"I'm sorry," she said. "I'm sorry. I don't have any money, Dooley. He didn't leave anything."

"Jesus, Teresa, what happened?" he said.

The curtain around her bed opened and—uh-oh—in stepped a uniformed police officer. She was shorter than Dooley, a slight-looking woman, but with cop eyes and a don't-fuck-with-me cop expression on her face.

"And you are?" she said to Dooley.

Dooley identified himself.

"Step outside, please," the woman cop said.

Dooley released Teresa gently and helped her lie back on the bed. "I'll be back," he said.

Once he was outside the cubicle, the woman cop asked him to move out into the hall away from everyone.

"Name?" she said.

He told her.

"What's your relationship to the victim?"

"Victim?" Dooley said. "What happened to her?"

"I asked you a question," the woman cop said in the same tone used by every cop Dooley had ever met—I'm doing the asking, I'm in charge here, and don't even think about trying to snow me. It was easier to go along and completely counter-productive to resist.

"I knew her boyfriend. She called me. She said she was afraid she was losing the baby. I'm the one who called 9-1-1. What happened to her?"

"She called you?" the woman cop said. "When?"

Dooley told her.

"What exactly did she tell you?"

"She said something was wrong. She said she thought she was losing the baby."

Another uniform, a male cop, approached them. The woman cop filled him in and he walked away again, going to check on him, Dooley knew. He stood there with the woman cop and waited. A few minutes later the male cop came back. The woman stepped aside to listen to what he had to say. When she returned to Dooley, her partner had her back.

"What is your relationship with Teresa Delorme?" she said.

"I told you. I knew her boyfriend."

"Jeffrey Eccles?"

"Yes."

"Did you know that he was murdered recently?" she said.

"Yeah, I knew. Look, what happened to her?"

"What did she say happened to her?" the woman cop said.

Fucking cops. He hated their games.

"Did someone hit her?" Dooley said.

"Why do you think someone hit her?"

"Because that's what it looks like to me," Dooley said. "Is that what happened?"

"She says she fell down the stairs," the woman cop said, her tone and the way she was looking at Dooley making it clear she thought that was a crock.

Dooley supposed it was possible that was what had happened. Or maybe Teresa had thrown herself down the stairs. After all, the only person she could think of to call after Jeffie died was a waitress who used to go with Jeffie. And look who she'd called just now: Dooley—a guy she barely knew.

"Her boyfriend just died."

"Was murdered," the female cop said.

Dooley ignored her.

"She's alone. She's pregnant—"

"She lost the baby," the woman cop said.

Shit.

"Show me your hands," the woman cop said.

Dooley stiffened. It was always the same thing. He thought about telling her flat out, I'm seventeen; in other words, I have rights, and you have obligations. You have to caution me. You have to tell me I can call a lawyer and have an adult present. You have to tell me that I don't even have to give you the time of day if I don't want to. But he hadn't done

239

anything except answer his phone when Teresa had called. He held out his hands, palms up, even though he knew that wasn't what the cop meant when she'd asked to see them.

"Turn them over," she said.

He complied. He also told her, because she asked, exactly where he had been all afternoon. He kind of liked the idea that when the cops checked, Beth would back him up and, at the same time, Beth's mother would freak out that the cops were investigating him—again. He answered all of the cops' questions, and when they finally ran out of them, he went back to see Teresa.

"What happened?" he said.

She couldn't even look him in the eye when she said, "I tripped on the stairs."

She'd lost Jeffie. She'd lost her baby. She was all alone. She was covered in bruises.

"Come on, Teresa," he said. "Who hit you?"

"No one." She still wouldn't look at him. "I didn't say anything. Honest."

"What are you talking about? Jesus, look at me, will you?"

She stared wide-eyed at him, like a terrified child.

"Tell me exactly what happened," he said.

She blinked at him as if she was having trouble processing what he was saying.

"Those guys came to the apartment," she said. "At first they said they were friends of Jeffie's. Then they said Jeffie owed them money. If I'd had any, I would have given it to them, Dooley. Honest I would."

"Guys Jeffie owed did this to you?"

Tears started to dribble down her face again. He passed her a tissue. She peeked up at him while she dabbed at her cheeks.

"I'm sorry," she said.

"For what?"

"I don't have any money. If I did, I would have given it to them. Just don't let them hurt me anymore."

What?

"You think *I'm* responsible?" He was glad now that she'd told the cops she'd fallen down the stairs.

It must have been his tone. She looked directly at him for the first time.

"You said Jeffie owed you money. Those guys came to get the money he owed. You sent them, didn't you?"

"Jeffie is—was—my friend, Teresa." He couldn't believe that she thought he would send guys over to muscle her under any circumstances, let alone when she was pregnant. "The money he borrowed, I wrote that off."

"So who were those guys?"

"I don't know. But if I were you, Teresa, I'd tell the cops."

She was shaking her head even before he finished speaking.

"No way," she said. "If I tell them about those guys, whoever sent them might come back at me. No way."

He couldn't blame her. She was all alone.

"What did the doctor say? Are they going to keep you here?"

"I don't know."

"You want me to find out?"

She was so grateful for just that one thing, it made Dooley wonder what kind of life she'd had and whether Jeffie had made it better or worse. It took a few minutes, but he finally tracked down a harried young doctor who told him, no, her X-rays had checked out, there was nothing broken, there was no reason to keep her, but she needed bed rest, plenty of liquids, and she should check in with her family doctor the next day. When Dooley told Teresa that, she said she didn't have a family doctor.

"Weren't you seeing someone?" Dooley said. "You know, for the baby?"

"There's a walk-in clinic a couple of blocks from the apartment," she said. "I've been going there."

Dooley guessed that would have to do.

"You want me to take you home, Teresa?"

She started to cry again. "What if those guys come back?"

Boy, he wished Jeffie was still alive.

"You want to come home with me, just for tonight?" Dooley said. He couldn't think of any other plan. "You can rest, and we can figure something out tomorrow." Maybe Jeannie would have some ideas.

Teresa started to cry again, with gratitude this time.

"You get dressed," Dooley said. She looked pretty rough. He didn't think she would be able to manage the bus and the walk from the bus to his uncle's place. "There's a cash machine across the street. I'm going to get some money for a taxi, okay? I'll be right back."

The third thing that had happened: He'd walked through the front door of his uncle's house, Teresa leaning heavily on him—groggy, it turned out, from some painkiller they had given her at the hospital—and directly into a shit-storm, only he didn't realize it right away. No, right away all he saw

242

was Jeannie, who came out of the kitchen when she heard the front door.

"This is Teresa," Dooley said. "She's going to stay here tonight, if it's okay with you."

Jeannie's expression was tense and confused. Dooley couldn't blame her.

"Teresa, this is Jeannie."

Teresa nodded weakly.

"Come on," Dooley said. "You can sit down in here." He helped Teresa into the living room and eased her down onto the couch. He even slipped her shoes off and helped her put her feet up. Then he pulled Jeannie toward the kitchen. "She was pregnant," he said. "She just lost her baby and she doesn't have any place to stay. I was—"

Jeannie squeezed Dooley's arm hard but too late. Someone else came out of the kitchen. Beth's mother. She glowered at Dooley and then at Teresa, who was so out of it that she smiled back. Then she said, "I'll see myself out."

Dooley glanced at Jeannie, who shook her head and waited until after the front door had closed behind Beth's mother before she said, "You've had some day, Dooley."

"I can explain," Dooley said.

"I'm sure you can," she said. "But we have company."

Jeannie took charge. She sent Dooley into the kitchen to put water on for tea. Then she dispatched him to get clean sheets out of the linen closet and put them on his uncle's bed. When he had done that, she helped Teresa upstairs and sent Dooley back down to make the tea. "And toast," she said. "Lightly buttered."

Dooley did as he was told and then was stumped by what to put in the tea. Should he ask? Should he guess? He decided on one teaspoon of sugar and a little milk and carried the mug of tea and the plate of toast on a tray up to his uncle's room. By then Teresa was in bed. She was wearing what Dooley recognized as one of his uncle's pajama tops and was propped up against the pillows. Jeannie took the tray from him and arranged it on Teresa's lap.

"The tea will warm you up," Jeannie said, which Dooley couldn't figure. It was nice and cozy in the house. But then he noticed that Jeannie had put an extra blanket on the bed and that Teresa's hands were shaking when she raised the mug of tea to her mouth using both hands. Jeannie turned to Dooley and said, "Take your time, but when you're done here, we need to talk." She left them alone.

"She's nice," Teresa said, her eyes lingering on the doorway long after Jeannie had disappeared. "Is she your mother?"

"She's my uncle's friend," Dooley said. "I have to go downstairs, Teresa. If you need anything, just yell, okay?"

"Thanks, Dooley."

"And drink your tea, okay?"

■　■　■

Jeannie was in the kitchen. The coffeemaker was on and Dooley could see that there was maybe a cup of coffee left in it, but Jeannie had taken a glass out of the cupboard and was pouring vodka into it.

"Sorry," she said, "but it's been quite a day." She knocked

back what she had put in the glass, poured herself another, and sat down at the table. "Annette called. She says you can see Gary tomorrow. She'll pick you up and take you there."

"How's he doing?" Dooley said.

Jeannie let out a long sigh. It was the closest she had ever come to looking defeated. "I talked to him for a few minutes on the phone. He says he's fine. He wanted me to check on the new presser he hired. You know."

Yeah, Dooley knew.

"Then the vice-principal at your school called. He said you skipped some classes today."

"One class," Dooley said. "English. *1984*."

"According to Gary, one of the conditions of—"

"I know," Dooley said. "I know and if you want to report me, I don't blame you. But, Jesus, Jeannie. All the stuff that's been going on, and I'm supposed to sit there and analyze some futuristic society that isn't even futuristic anymore; 1984 came and went before I was even born. And, yeah, I know about all that totalitarian bullshit, but, I mean, what the fuck?" He took in the slightly stunned look on Jeannie's face and remembered what his uncle had said about treating her like a lady. "Excuse my language," he said.

He and Jeannie looked at each other—two strangers, feeling their way, bumping up against each other, assessing each other, trying to decide. Then Jeannie laughed.

"It's okay. And I take your point," she said. It was no mystery what his uncle saw in her. She sighed again. "I gather, from what Gary told me, that there is room for accommodation, *provided*"—the heavy emphasis she put on the word made her

245

sound, just for that one second, exactly like his uncle—"you go about it the right way. You know what I mean, Dooley?"

"Yeah."

"I told Mr. Rector—unfortunate name, don't you think? I'd bet dollars to doughnuts that he was teased mercilessly when he was a kid—that it was all my fault, that you had an appointment in conjunction with your uncle's circumstances and that I, acting as guardian in his stead, had neglected to either write you a note or call the school and alert them." She took a sip of her drink. "I get the impression that he didn't quite believe me. But he didn't push the point, either, so I think we're okay."

"Thanks, Jeannie."

"And then Mrs. Manson showed up."

Beth's mother.

"She was looking for you and was surprised—gob-smacked, in fact—to find a woman in the house. She had quite a tale to tell." Dooley caught the flicker of a smile, and his cheeks suddenly felt like they were on fire. He bet Jeannie was picturing him standing there, caught practically in the act. "You care about this girl, Dooley?"

Dooley sank down onto the chair opposite her and tried not to look at the vodka in her glass.

"Yeah," he said. "I do."

"And when you and she—" Jeannie took another sip of vodka. "I don't have children, Dooley. I have nieces, but no nephews. God help me. You take precautions when you're with this girl, right?"

"Her name is Beth," Dooley said.

"Beth." Jeannie nodded, and Dooley could tell that she liked the name.

"Yeah, I take precautions." It was bad enough his uncle asking him about this. But Jeannie? "What did her mother say? Why was she here?"

"What did she *say?*" Jeannie shook her head. "I think you can imagine what she said."

"And?"

"Well, when you get right down to it, you're both seventeen. In less than a year, it's out of anyone's hands." She took another sip of vodka, and apologized for it. "But I get the feeling she's not the type to let go easily."

"Her husband was murdered. Her son, too," Dooley said. "Mark Everley. You remember."

"I do," Jeannie said.

"Did she tell you she didn't want me anywhere near Beth again?"

"She did."

Well, that was no surprise.

"I told her I couldn't imagine why not. I told her I know you as well as anyone does. I told her exactly what I think about you, Dooley."

Dooley held his breath.

"I told her you're a sweet, responsible young man who's caught a lot of bad breaks but who is working very hard to put all that behind him."

Dooley wanted to hug her.

"I won't flatter myself that I was making much progress with her, but I was holding my own—until you showed up with that girl. This baby she lost—it wasn't by any chance—"

"It was her boyfriend's," Dooley said. "He was sort of a friend of mine."

"Was?"

"He was killed."

"Killed?"

"Murdered."

"Good lord," Jeannie said. She finished the vodka in her glass and set the glass aside. "I'm going to check on that girl."

"Teresa," Dooley said.

"I'm going to check on Teresa and then I'm going to make up the pull-out bed in Gary's study and I'm going to get some sleep."

Dooley glanced at the clock above the stove. It was ten o'clock.

After Jeannie went upstairs, Dooley dialed Beth's cell phone number. Voice mail. He hated voice mail. Still: "Hi, it's me. Call me."

By eleven, she still hadn't called. Dooley imagined the scene at her house. He imagined Beth's mother telling Beth, "He brought a girl home. She's staying there." Knowing Beth's mother, she'd jumped to all the wrong conclusions. He wished now that he'd had the chance to explain about Teresa. It ran around and around in his brain: Her mother telling Beth, *He brought a girl home, a girl who had just lost her baby*. What would Beth think? Why would someone bring home a girl who had just lost a baby unless the lost baby was his? He tried her cell phone again. Still no answer. He left another message: "It's not the way it looks." He wondered where she was. With Nevin, maybe. Good old solid Nevin, whose only interaction with the cops, Dooley was willing to bet, was *maybe* some traffic cop giving him a speeding ticket.

He tried her again. And again. And again. He knew she wasn't going to pick up. He told himself maybe her mother had confiscated the phone. It was possible, maybe even probable, knowing Beth's mother. Or—this was also possible—Beth had jumped to her own conclusions, the wrong ones, and she was mad at him because he was supposed to have told her everything and here he was holding back again.

He tried her one more time.

Nothing.

He got up and opened the cupboard in the kitchen where his uncle kept a bottle of vodka for Jeannie and one of scotch for himself. He listened. It was quiet in the house. But quiet enough? He crept up the stairs—it was easy to do, they were carpeted and one hundred percent squeak-free—and peeked in at Teresa. She was sound asleep. The door to his uncle's study was closed. The lights were off. He pressed his ear to the door—and what do you know? Jeannie was snoring. It was a soft sound, more like a dentist's drill than a buzz-saw, which is what his uncle's snoring sounded like. He went back down the stairs, out the door, and started walking. He told himself he needed the air. He told himself the exercise would do him good—all that tension, walk it off, Dooley; it was the least destructive way to deal with it.

And now here he was on the corner, eyes shifting this way and that, searching for a familiar face.

And there it was, the face belonging to a guy he knew named Luz, who did a double take when he saw Dooley and then broke into a grin.

"Dooley, shit, man, it's been a while."

"Yeah," Dooley said.

Luz looked around. "You here by yourself, man? Can I do something for you? You need something?"

Dooley nodded. Yeah, he needed something all right.

Sixteen

This was a bad idea. A very bad idea. There was a dog across the street somewhere, a big one, from the sound of it, that wouldn't shut up. Lights were going on in houses up and down the street, and a few heads peered out of windows to see what the dog was barking about. Dooley pressed on, trying to give the impression that he belonged in the neighborhood and that he knew exactly where he was going until, finally, he found the number he was looking for. It was a stuccoed house, nice and tidy, surprising Dooley by not surprising him at all. It was exactly the kind of house he figured a guy like Dr. Calvin would live in. There was even a light on, which told Dooley that maybe it wasn't too late after all, even though it was five minutes to midnight.

He hesitated on the sidewalk. Who was he kidding? You don't ring a person's doorbell at midnight, especially when you haven't seen that person in a couple of months and, before that, maybe six months.

He glanced around. A police car was sliding down the street toward him. That decided it.

He turned up the walk, climbed the porch steps, and pressed the doorbell. Out of the corner of his eye, he saw the police car slow to a crawl.

The porch light came on.

A face appeared in the glass and then vanished again.

The inner door opened, then the outer door.

"Dooley," Dr. Calvin said, frowning.

"I'm sorry," Dooley said. The minute he heard the words, he wanted to kick something. He was tired of being sorry for everything, tired of apologizing to everyone. "I just—"

"I heard about your mother," Dr. Calvin said. "Your uncle, too. How are you holding up?"

A wave of self-pity washed over Dooley. No one had asked him that. Bullshit was piling up around him, and no one had asked him how he was coping. Dr. Calvin's eyes shifted from Dooley to the street.

"I think you'd better come in," he said. He stepped aside to let Dooley pass and then looked out into the street again for a moment before closing the door behind him.

■ ■ ■

"Charlie?"

A woman appeared. An extremely pretty woman with long blonde hair pulled back in a ponytail, creamy clear skin, and nice, full lips. She was wearing a long silky robe over a long silky nightgown.

"My wife," Dr. Calvin said. "Jenny, this is Dooley. Dooley, Jenny."

Dooley nodded and felt bad now that he had come here.

"Can I get you something?" Dr. Calvin's wife said.

"Tea would be wonderful," Dr. Calvin said.

Dr. Calvin's wife smiled at her husband—Dooley never would have guessed by looking at him that Dr. Calvin could score such a babe—and disappeared.

"Sit," Dr. Calvin said. "And tell me what brings you to my door."

Dooley hesitated. He shouldn't have come. Dr. Calvin wasn't his therapist anymore. He hadn't been since Dooley was released. But Dooley liked him. He wasn't distant, like some of the other therapists Dooley had seen. He seemed more like a regular guy.

"Please," Dr. Calvin said. "Sit down."

Dooley dropped down onto one end of the sofa.

"So, what's up?" Dr. Calvin said.

Boy, where to start? Who to start with?

It came out in a jumble. Lorraine's sudden reappearance in his life. Her just-as-sudden death. What he had found out about her.

"Except he's not really my uncle," he said. There it was, the part that had been eating at him, the part that he hadn't said out loud yet. "And he wasn't really Lorraine's brother, either. You think maybe that's why she was so fucked up?"

"Because she was adopted, you mean?" Dr. Calvin said.

"Because she was a replacement," Dooley said. "They even called her by the same name."

"That could have been a burden on her," Dr. Calvin said. "Especially if she thought she had to live up to her namesake.

253

And it is true that some adopted children feel a certain alien-
ation, a sense of not belonging, that can cause identity problems, which, in turn, can lead to, say, certain sometimes
destructive behaviors ..."

"You think that's why she got into drugs?"

"I really can't say, Dooley. She wasn't a patient of mine."

"But based on what you know," Dooley said. "Based on
your experience."

Dr. Calvin leaned back in his chair and studied Dooley for
a moment.

"Well," he said finally, "theoretically, it's a possibility. I'm
saying this as someone who never met her, you understand,
Dooley?"

Dooley nodded.

"Someone in your mother's situation *might have* had
conflicted feelings, such as the feeling that she had been
abandoned by her birth parents. She may also have felt
directioned—pushed into—a role and possibly a persona that
was not her own. As a result, she *might* have developed
certain feelings that may have been so uncomfortable or so
painful to her that she may have attempted to dull them by
resorting to self-medication."

So, basically, yes.

"Every time I think about her, I mean *every* time, I see her
as fucked up," Dooley said. "She was high, or she was
coming down and was in a bitch of a mood because of it,
or some guy was giving her a hard time, or she was giving
some guy a hard time, or she was trying to get some money
together so she could get high again. Even times when she

was supposedly trying to do the right thing, like Christmas. Do you have any idea how many Christmases she ruined, either because she was high or drunk or because she was seeing some asshole guy and they'd get into it?" He shook his head. He couldn't remember a Christmas that resembled anything like a picture on a Christmas card.

Dr. Calvin waited. When Dooley didn't go on, he said, "What's the real question, Dooley?"

"The real question?"

"Why are you here? What is it you want to know?"

The jackpot question.

"What I want to know," Dooley said, "is why I even give a shit."

Dr. Calvin's wife appeared just then.

"Sorry," Dooley mumbled.

She smiled at him as she set a tray down onto the table. On it were two mugs of steaming tea, a couple of spoons, a sugar bowl, and a small pitcher of milk.

"I'm going upstairs," she said to Dr. Calvin. She bent and kissed him lightly on the cheek.

Dr. Calvin watched her go before stirring a teaspoon of sugar into his tea.

"Go on," he said.

"Why do I even care about her?" Dooley said. "She never wasted much time thinking about me. She didn't even make my court date."

When he'd gone to court that last time, he'd believed, given the seriousness of the charges, that she would be there and was surprised at the disappointment he'd felt when she didn't show. Then he got mad at himself for being such an idiot—of course she wouldn't show. He got mad at her, too, when the judge had wondered where "the mother" was and was told by Dooley's lawyer that she had been notified and was expected but that the lawyer had no idea why she was a no-show. She never visited while he was in detention, either, not even once. Never wrote. Never called. Didn't send a card on his birthday, didn't send a gift at Christmas. Nothing.

"Are you angry with her for that?" Dr. Calvin said.

"I don't care," Dooley said.

"Your question is why do you care, and now you're telling me you *don't* care? It sounds to me as if *you're* conflicted."

"For nearly three years I didn't see her or hear from her," Dooley said. "Then she shows up all of a sudden and tells me things are different and she wants me to come and see her. I find out later"—too late—"that she got herself cleaned up. She'd been going to meetings, she had a sponsor, the whole deal. My whole life I never knew her anyway except fucked up and then, just like that, there she is, clean. How did that even happen?"

"You're clean," Dr. Calvin said. "At least, I assume you are."

An hour ago, he'd been on the edge. *Can I do something for you? You need something?*

"Yeah, I'm clean."

"Well, how did *that* happen?"

Dooley gave him a look. "They locked me up," he said. "They cut off access."

"Nice try," Dr. Calvin said.

Nice try. Dooley couldn't help it; he smiled. He used to

256

want to punch Dr. Calvin's face in when he said stuff like that. Dooley used to hate having to meet with him. Dr. Calvin would sit there, all preppy and dorky looking, and he'd ask some dumb-ass question like, *Why do you think you hit that boy, Dooley?* And when Dooley answered him—*Because he was an irritating little asshole who wouldn't lay off*—he'd look at Dooley with that I'm-not-going-to-let-you-know-what-I'm-thinking expression of his and say, *Nice try.* Then he'd sit and look at Dooley some more until Dooley came up with something else or until his time was up, one or the other. But that was then. Now Dooley was willing— well, some of the time—to think things over.

"You mean after that, right?"

Dr. Calvin didn't say anything.

"You mean how come I'm still clean," Dooley said. "I guess because I'm tired of being fucked up. I don't want to be like her—like she was." He thought maybe Beth was a reason, too. And his uncle. But mostly it was because he was tired of being fucked up and of everyone expecting nothing from him except attitude and trouble. "You think maybe Lorraine was trying to change?"

"She was *your* mother. What do you think?"

Lorraine and change—in Dooley's experience, the two didn't go together. He'd felt like he'd been sucker-punched when he'd come out of school and seen her standing there on the sidewalk. His knees had gone weak; he'd almost crumpled. She hadn't look anything like he remembered. She was thin, but not all sallow skin and sharp bones like she used to be. She had a nice shape to her. Her hair was nice—short but perky, with some color in it to lighten it up, and a real shine to it, not brittle and dull the way it had been when she was at her worst. Her face looked good. She didn't look dragged out; she didn't have dark circles under her eyes. No, she looked pinkish and healthy. Well rested. Her teeth were whiter than he remembered and she'd ditched the red lipstick she usually wore, the stuff that always made Dooley think of blood. If she was wearing anything, it was light and natural, like the kind Beth wore. He hated to admit it, but she'd looked great, even if she was his mother.

"But why all of a sudden?" Dooley said. "I mean, she was the way she was for maybe twenty years."

"Well, that *is* the question, Dooley," Dr. Calvin said. He finished his tea and stretched.

Dooley set down his own mug, untouched.

"There's probably no way to know, huh?" he said. "And even if I did find out, it's too late. Right?"

"That depends on what you're after," Dr. Calvin said. "If what you want is to establish or re-establish a relationship with your mother, then, yes, it's a little late. If, on the other hand, you want to understand something about the woman who gave birth to you, then I'd say, no, it's not too late."

Why had she shown up all of a sudden? Why had she decided to seek him out after all those years? Why had she invited him to come to her place? Why had she told him that she wanted to talk to him? What did they even have to talk about?

Dooley glanced at the clock on the mantelpiece and was shocked at the time.

"I'm sorry for keeping you up," he said. "I should go." He stood. Dr. Calvin stood. Dooley realized that's what he liked about Dr. Calvin; it was why he was here: Dr. Calvin didn't bullshit. The fact that he wasn't objecting meant that he was agreeing—yes, it was late. But he wasn't bitching about it. You came to my house, I let you in, I listened, and, yes, it's late.

Dr. Calvin walked him to the door.

"I'm sorry about your mother," he said.

■ ■ ■

It was quiet in the house when Dooley got home. He looked in on Teresa. She was sound asleep. He hesitated as he passed the door to his uncle's study. What if Jeannie had woken up? What if she had checked on him? He felt the urge to confess everything to her. Then he looked at his watch. It was nearly two. Jeannie had a job. She had her own stores to look after in addition to his uncle's business. She needed her sleep. He went down the hall to his own room and crawled into bed.

Seventeen

J eannie was putting a plate of scrambled eggs on a tray together with a glass of orange juice, a mug of tea, and a couple of slices of toast.

"How's Teresa?" Dooley said.

"She says she's hungry, so I guess that's good," Jeannie said. "I'm going to take this up to her. After she eats, I'm taking her to my G.P., who also happens to be a close personal friend."

"Thanks, Jeannie," Dooley said. She was doing far more than she should. She didn't even know Teresa.

"After that, I'm taking her home. I don't mind looking in on her, Dooley, but I don't feel comfortable having her stay here. It's your uncle's house."

"It's okay," Dooley said. "I'll check on her. I promise."

"I'll have to lend her something for now. But she wants to know if you can go and get her some clean clothes to go home in." She put a key and a piece of paper on the table in front of him. "You know where she lives?"

Dooley nodded.

"She wrote down what she wanted."

"I'll go now," he said.

"Also, Annette called," Jeannie said. "She says she'll pick you up here at three."

Dooley did a rough calculation. He'd already got someone to cover the early part of his shift. Alicia's party was at one. He didn't have to be at work until six. Yeah, he could handle it.

After Jeannie went upstairs, Dooley gulped down some coffee and headed for the door. He made a quick call and ended up having to leave a message. Then he headed to Jeffie's.

■ ■ ■

He let himself in with the key Teresa had given Jeannie and went straight to the bedroom to go through the closet and the dresser with all the makeup and framed pictures on it, which he figured—it was a no-brainer—belonged to Teresa. He found everything she wanted—even underwear. He was surprised it didn't bother her, the thought of a guy she hardly knew going through that particular drawer. He dug a bag out from under the sink in the kitchen and put the stuff in it. Then he went back into the bedroom and looked at the other dresser, this one taller, not so long, with a bottle of men's cologne on it and a package of disposable razors. Jeffie's dresser. The cops had probably been here already. They'd probably gone through Jeffie's things and had removed anything they thought might help them nail whoever had killed him. But Dooley opened the top drawer anyway. It was crammed with stuff—packages of rubbers, handfuls of change, pennies and nickels and dimes, old bills that had been paid (at least, Dooley assumed they had), underwear, socks that looked to Dooley like they didn't match, a couple of pairs of sunglasses, a pair of black leather gloves, a couple of packs of cigarettes, a crumpled scrap of paper torn from the newspaper—Dooley smoothed it out—with four numbers scrawled on it, a bunch of cheap ballpoint pens, a couple of disposable lighters, a dozen or so matchbooks with some or most of the matches gone.

Junk.

On the bright side: There was nothing to indicate that Jeffie had been in touch with Dooley's uncle. On the not-so-bright side: If there had been anything like that, the cops had already found it. He hadn't been surprised when Randall had asked: *Did you kill Jeffrey Eccles?* He'd been expecting that. But he hadn't been expecting the next question: *Did your uncle kill him?* It had shaken him.

His uncle knew Jeffie. He'd said he'd busted him a couple of times. And Lorraine had died of an overdose. There were bruises. Maybe someone had forced her. Someone with drugs and the whole kit. Maybe his uncle. He couldn't see it. No way. But it was what Randall was kicking around. That and the blood in his car were why his uncle had been arrested.

Dooley wished now that he'd said more down there in that ravine when Jeffie had mentioned his cop uncle. Maybe if he had said his uncle's name, Jeffie would have reacted—*that's* your uncle? No shit. He could have pushed Jeffie on it—what did he mean, did he know his uncle? It could have led somewhere. As it was, back when they'd hung out together, Jeffie had been no wiser about the existence of an uncle than Dooley himself had been—forget knowing his uncle's name. Hell, Jeffie had never even met Lorraine.

In the rest of Jeffie's drawers, clothes: T-shirts and sweaters, jeans and chinos, socks and more underwear. None of it special.

He poked around the rest of the apartment, but most of the stuff looked like it was Teresa's, not Jeffie's. Besides the furniture, there were a lot of photographs in frames, almost all of them showing Teresa and Jeffie together. There was a pile of stuffed animals in the window seat of the window that overlooked the street, some dried flowers in a vase on one of the end tables, a bunch of celebrity magazines on the coffee table, and hundreds of CDs—Dooley scanned them. Half looked like they might be Jeffie's, the other half definitely did not. He also saw half a dozen word search puzzle books, most of them with the puzzles all done. That had to be Teresa. Jeffie had enough trouble reading words when the letters were going in the right direction. There was only one real book in the whole place—no surprise there; Dooley couldn't recall ever seeing Jeffie read. It was a book of baby names. Dooley thought about throwing it out, sparing Teresa's having to look at it. Then he thought, maybe she'd still want it, maybe it meant something to her, so he left it where it was, on top of the big-screen TV.

He locked up and took the bag of Teresa's clothes and toiletries back to his uncle's house. Teresa wasn't there. Neither was Jeannie. He left the bag on the table in the front hall and headed for the coffee shop a couple of blocks away to wait.

Randall was alone, thank God. He got out of his car, glanced around, then trotted across the street and into the coffee shop. He didn't even glance at Dooley. Instead, he went straight to the counter and placed an order. Then he stood there, looking everywhere but at Dooley, until the girl behind the counter handed him his coffee. Randall chatted with her while she made change. Only then did he come over to Dooley's table. He dropped down opposite Dooley, blew on his coffee, took a sip, and said, "What's on your mind, Ryan?"

"You've been asking people about my uncle and Lorraine."

Randall took another sip of his coffee.

"I want to know why," Dooley said.

Randall shook his head. "You have some information for me, Ryan, I'm all ears," he said. "You think I'm going to sit here and give you the lowdown on my investigation, you're out of luck."

He started to get up.

"She was my mother," Dooley said.

"Your mother who you weren't close to," Randall reminded him.

Dooley hesitated. He wasn't about to tell Randall anything he might not already know. But he needed to get a fix on what was going on.

"You asked about rumors, about why she left home, about my uncle."

Randall settled back down in his chair and studied Dooley for a moment.

"She never talked about him?"

Dooley shook his head.

"Never mentioned him?"

"I told you, I didn't even know I had an uncle. I didn't know anything. Then you showed me that picture."

"You talk to your uncle about that?"

"Yeah."

"And?"

"He told me some stuff."

Randall waited.

"He told me she was adopted. He told me about his other sister—and about how his mother died. He said that's why he and Lorraine weren't ... why they never talked."

"I see."

He *saw?* Dooley watched him take another sip of coffee. What did he mean, he saw?

"Is that what you meant? Is that the weird shit you've been asking about?"

Randall stared at him for another full minute. Dooley hated that. He hated the way cops always acted like they were holding all the cards. He especially hated it when they were.

"Here's a mystery for you, Ryan," Randall said at last. "A seventeen-year-old adopted girl gets pregnant, leaves home, severs all ties with her family. There's no contact between her and her big brother—who isn't really her brother—for, what, fourteen, fifteen years? Then the kid, her *son,* drops himself in the crapper and, all of a sudden, out of the blue, this respectable retired cop and all-round good citizen big brother steps up to the plate and takes responsibility for the kid." And pays her a thousand dollars a month each and every month, Dooley thought. He bet Randall knew about that. He bet that's what the subpoena for the bank records had been all about. "What do you suppose that's all about, Ryan? Why would your uncle all of a sudden step into your life?" And pay for the privilege, Dooley thought. Jesus, had Lorraine been blackmailing him? Did she have some kind of leverage? But what? What could she possibly …

Jesus. No way.

He stared at Randall. Randall looked blandly back at him.

"Are you saying …? You don't think …?"

Randall seemed to soften in that instant. Or maybe it was all an act. Maybe he wanted to see how Dooley would react.

"We talked to some of your grandparents' old neighbors. One of them remembers overhearing a fight at your grand-parents' house one night. She says your mother … well, she made certain accusations."

Accusations?

"This neighbor called the police, who asked your mother about it. She refused to talk to them. She said she'd been angry at your uncle. He never mentioned that?"

"No. What are you—"

"Did your mother ever tell you who your father was, Ryan?"

What? Where did that question come from?

"Some guy," Dooley said. "Some guy named Dooley."

"You know him?"

Dooley shook his head. He remembered Lorraine used to

talk about the guy sometimes. Half the time she'd be crying over him: *He was the best guy, ever, Dooley. He was so fine, you would have liked him.* The other half the time she was throwing stuff, saying what a jerk he was, how he'd left her like that with a baby on her hands, what an asshole, and, big surprise, the way Dooley acted half the time, he was just like his father, *and that's no compliment, Dooley, just so you know.*

"You don't remember him? You don't remember anything about him?"

"She said he took off when I was a baby."

"He took off?"

Dooley looked at Randall. What was he getting at?

"Did you know that she didn't list a father on your birth registration?"

No, he didn't know that.

"Why do you think she left his name off?"

"I don't know."

Randall contemplated him again.

"You could ask your uncle," he said finally. "And there are tests. DNA tests. You can find out for sure."

Find out what?

"It would explain a lot," Randall said.

"I don't know what you're talking about," Dooley said.

"That's the other mystery, Ryan," Randall said. "Either you know exactly what I'm talking about, or you don't. If you don't, then think about it. Think about why your uncle suddenly dropped into your life after all those years. Or maybe you know exactly what I'm talking about, in which case ... well, your uncle isn't the only one who knew Jeffie

267

and what he did for a living."

They were fishing on that one, Dooley thought. They already know where he was that night. If they had anything to connect him with what had happened to either Jeffie or Lorraine, he'd be sweating it out in an interview room. He stood up.

"Thanks for meeting with me," he said.

Randall sat with his coffee while Dooley left. He went straight to Warren's house where he smiled through chocolate ice-cream cake with Alicia, her mother, Warren, and some of the kids Alicia went to school with. She was thrilled with the DVDs Dooley gave her—some new stuff, all of them about animals, that he'd special-ordered for her. At ten to three, he hugged her and wished her many happy returns.

"Thanks for coming," Warren said. "She talked about you all morning."

"No problem," Dooley said.

Warren peered at him.

"Are you okay?" he said.

"Yeah. See you Monday, okay, Warren?"

He got home just as Annette Girondin's car pulled up at the curb.

■ ■ ■

An hour later, Dooley found himself talking to his uncle under conditions he never could have imagined. His uncle looked tense; his skin was gray; his eyes were tight and watchful.

"You okay?" Dooley said.

"I'll live," his uncle said.

"I just wanted to tell you," Dooley said. "I didn't tell them anything."

His uncle didn't say anything.

"All that stuff you told me that night," Dooley said. "I kept it to myself."

His uncle didn't react the way he had expected. Instead, he leaned forward a little and said, "If they subpoena you and make you testify, do everyone a favor, Ryan. Tell the truth. Okay?"

"If they subpoena me?" Dooley said. "You're going to get off, right?"

"I sure as hell hope so," his uncle said. "But it's complicated."

One-thousand-dollars-a-month complicated. Not-brother-and-sister complicated.

"What do you mean?" Dooley said.

"This isn't a good place to go into it, Ryan. You got something else you want to talk about, go for it. Otherwise—"

Dooley couldn't believe it—his uncle actually stood up, making it clear what he would discuss and what he wouldn't, still assuming the in-charge position.

"Okay," Dooley said. "Can I ask you something?"

His uncle, wary, dropped back into his chair.

"How did she seem when she came by the house?" Dooley said.

"Who?"

"Lorraine. I know she came by. How did she seem? Was she clean? Was she high? What?"

He hadn't told his uncle he knew about the visit, so he

was expecting his uncle to be at least a little taken back or, possibly, embarrassed. He was neither.

"She was a pain in the ass," his uncle said. "She was all smiles until she found out you weren't home, and then she got pissy."

Dooley sincerely hoped that his uncle hadn't taken that attitude with the cops.

"Besides that," he said.

"To tell you the truth, she looked pretty good." His uncle sounded surprised as he said it, like he still couldn't believe it. "Not her usual trashy self, you know what I mean? She told me she was clean, and she looked it."

"Did she tell you why she did it?"

"Did what?"

"Cleaned up her act."

"No. She said she wanted to see you. That's all."

"You didn't tell me."

"Turns out I didn't have to," his uncle said. "You had her address and her number."

Dooley dropped his voice a little. "What about the money?"

His uncle's eyes narrowed.

"You know what I mean, right?" Dooley said.

His uncle didn't answer. Dooley knew what it felt like to be in his position, so he didn't push it. But, boy, he had a million questions about all that cash and about what Randall had told him—and about why Randall had told him. Did he feel sorry for Dooley? Or had he agreed to the meeting and told him what he had for some other reason? Dooley ached to get into it with his uncle, but there were some things he

270

couldn't ask, not here. Still, he couldn't help wondering, as he watched his uncle, do I look anything like him? Is it true what Randall had insinuated? Is that why his uncle had had Lorraine cremated, why he had never even suggested that she be put to rest in the family plot? Is that why, after all those years …

"You remember that first time you came to see me?" he said.

"Yeah," his uncle said. "I'd be amazed if you remembered it, though. You were in bad shape."

But Dooley did remember.

"I was surprised," he said. "You remember that? I was surprised because I didn't even know I had an uncle."

"I didn't think you were able to concentrate enough to be surprised about anything. I thought you were still focused on how you were going to score in there."

"Yeah, well, that, too. But I was also surprised. Lorraine never mentioned you. Why do you think that was?"

"How the hell would I know?" his uncle said, irritable now. Well, why not? He was in here, wasn't he?

"My whole life I never knew about you, and then you showed up out of the blue. You said something like, you didn't know about me. Something like that."

"I believe what I said," his uncle said, his eyes hard on Dooley's, "was that if I'd known, maybe I could have done something sooner."

Dooley nodded. Yeah, that was it. That was what he'd said—*If I'd known,* which, of course, Dooley had taken to mean, if I'd known about you. He looked at his uncle now. Since he'd gone to live with him, Dooley had never had to guess what his uncle was thinking. If he was angry with Dooley, if he was worried, if, God forbid, he was proud of something Dooley had done, he put it all right out there for Dooley to read. But for the past couple of weeks, it had been different. For the past couple of weeks, he hadn't been able to read his uncle. It had taken a while for him to get it. His uncle had been a cop most of his adult life. Cops, in Dooley's experience, were good at hiding what they were thinking. They were good at bluffing when they knew you'd done something but they couldn't prove it and when, therefore, they were trying to trip you up so you would hang yourself and save them the trouble. They were good at telling you that they understood exactly how it could have happened: The guy pissed you off, right, Ryan, and you got mad, right, and so you swung at him; you didn't mean to, and you wouldn't have done it if he hadn't acted like such a jerk, right, Ryan? Telling you they understood when the truth was that they were probably disgusted with you for being such a lowlife; they were stringing you along so you'd finally come clean and say, yeah, I did it and here's why, and then, there you were, hanging yourself again. Dooley couldn't see why his uncle would have been any different when he was a cop, which meant that, if he wanted to, he could probably hide what was really going on in his head just the same as every other cop Dooley had ever known.

"What exactly did you mean when you said that?" Dooley said.

"What do you think I meant?"

"I thought you meant that you didn't know about me.

I thought you meant that you'd just found out about me."
Dooley had been pretty messed up at the time. Maybe his
uncle was right. Maybe he hadn't been thinking straight.
"But that's not it, is it?"

No answer.

"Is it?" Dooley said. He heard Lorraine's voice in his head:
You never came around.

His uncle didn't answer.

"You knew she had a kid, didn't you?" Dooley said. There
was no other way to explain what Lorraine had said. "You
knew about me. You knew I existed." That had to be it. "You
just didn't know what things were like." Say it. Ask him: *Are
you my father?* That's where Randall had been going with his
questions. But, Jesus, did he really want to know? "Am I right?"

"I thought it would be easier if you and I started out with
a clean slate," his uncle said. "Without any baggage."

"You mean, if we started out without me wondering
where you'd been my whole life?"

It took a few moments before his uncle said, "Something
like that."

"So, what, you just didn't care?" Or maybe he hadn't wanted
to face it. Maybe he *couldn't* face it. Maybe that's what all
those cash payments were about. It sure as hell was what
Randall had been hinting.

"I told you, Ryan. Lorraine and I didn't get along."

"But you knew she had a kid."

"Yes."

"And you never came to see me?"

He searched his uncle's face but saw no emotion.

273

"No," his uncle said.

"Why not?"

"What difference does it make?"

"It makes a difference," Dooley said.

Nothing.

"The past couple of years," Dooley said, "what's that been all about?"

His uncle just sat there. Jesus, what a hard-ass.

"I know about the money," Dooley said. "I know you were paying her regularly for at least the last couple of years."

There it was, out in the open and hanging between them now, the complicated thing his uncle didn't want to talk about. And what did his uncle do? He stood up and hammered on the door, summoning a guard, that's what.

Shit.

■ ■ ■

That night: Customers looking to fry their brains with the latest in mindless entertainment. The busiest night of the week, and Dooley was stepping outside every time Kevin turned his back to try Beth's cell number again.

Thinking about Beth.

Thinking about Lorraine, too, and about the regular cash payments that she regularly transformed into a good time—until six months ago when the partying had stopped and she'd opened up a savings account. His uncle had still been giving her money then. He'd seen the spreadsheets. Had she started saving all that money? She'd cleaned up her act, too.

Were the two things related—saving instead of partying and getting herself together? And that day outside his school, she had looked good. She'd looked almost like a regular mom, not some cheap slut party girl. Why had she all of a sudden changed? Had she got religion? He couldn't see that happening. But it had to be something. If there was one thing Dooley knew, it was that someone who was that long and that far gone didn't just wake up one morning and think, hmm, why don't I try the straight life for a while? No, there had to be a reason. Everyone he'd ever met who'd made the change had come face to face with a reason—a hard-core one. Was she sick? Sometimes that happened. People with lung cancer finally stopped smoking. People who were HIV-positive gave up the needle. Some people quit because they'd had a life-altering experience; maybe they'd climbed behind the wheel while under the influence and ended up killing or maiming or paralyzing someone. When that happens, what do you do, assuming they don't lock you up for it? You either change or you get yourself more fucked up. Or maybe your doctor says, unless you make some serious lifestyle changes, you'll be dead in six months. Maybe you don't care. But if you do, if you're not ready to check out, you make some changes. You start eating right, you exercise a little, you butt out. It's always something. There's always a reason.

Something had put Lorraine straight. But what?

Who would know? Who could tell him?

A hand fell on Dooley's shoulder. He spun around.

Linelle. She said, "Kevin says to tell you if you don't get back into the store right now and do your job, he's going to write you up. He's such an asshole."

Dooley glanced through the store window and saw Kevin's pinched face looking out at him.

"Tell him I'll be there in a minute," Dooley said.

"He's an asshole, but he's a pissed-off asshole, Dooley. This could get you fired. And if that happens, I'll pretty much have to kill myself. You're the only thing that makes this job tolerable."

He looked at her. "Yeah?"

"Definitely," she said. "I would have bled out a long time ago if it wasn't for you."

Good old Linelle. She always said the right thing.

"Two minutes, I promise," he said. He punched in another number, talked fast, made an appointment, and then went inside and did something he'd never done before. He apologized to Kevin. Kevin was so stunned that all he could do was flap his gums; no words came out.

■ ■ ■

Dooley's cell phone rang at one in the morning, just as he was getting into bed. It was Beth.

"I've been calling you," Dooley said.

"My mother confiscated my phone," she said, confirming one of Dooley's theories and dispelling all the Beth-dumps-Dooley scenarios that had been plaguing him ever since her mother had marched out of his uncle's house. "She totally freaked out, Dooley." She was talking softly, as if she were afraid she might be overheard. "She told me she wants to send me down east to live with my uncle and aunt."

Anything, Dooley thought, to keep her away from me.

"I told her if she did, I'd run away. She forbids me to see you anymore."

"Beth, I—"

"I told her she can't forbid me to do anything. I told her if she tries to stop me from seeing you, I'll move out, get a job, and get my own place, and there's nothing she can do about it. She's trying to lay this trip on me, Dooley, how I'm all she has left and it's her responsibility to make sure I get the very best—the best education, the best start in life, meet the best people, stuff like that. I know you probably don't like her, but she's not really the way she comes across. It's just been hard, you know—first my father, then Mark. She worries all the time. She keeps thinking that something's going to happen to me and then she won't have anyone. She thinks we should go for counseling—her and me. I told her I would—she's my *mother*. I don't want to be fighting with her all the time. But I told her if I did it, she had to stop giving me a hard time about you. She finally said she would be prepared to do that."

Dooley let out a sigh of relief.

"When can I see you?" he said.

"We're up north," Beth said. "We left right after school yesterday."

"Up north where?"

"At a place in the country," Beth said. She said something else, but her voice faded out.

"I can hardly hear you," Dooley said.

"That's because everyone's asleep. I found my mother's cell phone and snuck out of the house. I can see stars, Dooley. You can't believe how many there are. I wish you were here." Dooley wished he was, too. "My mom wanted us to spend the weekend connecting, you know? She says she feels like she doesn't know me anymore. We went for a hike this morning and then we spent the afternoon at a spa. I won't be back until late tomorrow night. But I wanted to talk to you. I didn't want you to worry."

"I'm glad you called," Dooley said.

"So I'll see you when I get back?"

"I can't wait."

loria Thomas was working on a bowl of latte when Dooley arrived at the coffee shop the next morning. Dooley grabbed a coffee and sat down opposite her. She studied him for a moment, searching his eyes. What was she looking for? Did she see some of Lorraine in him? Or had Lorraine spilled her guts about him and was Gloria wondering what he was doing to get through the day?

"How can I help you, Dooley?" she said.

Yeah, that was probably what she was thinking.

"I want to know why she did it—why she joined a group, why she was trying to get clean."

"We really didn't talk about that."

"But you were her sponsor."

"She called me when she felt tempted or when she felt she couldn't hang on anymore. We'd get together for a coffee—just like this—and she'd talk."

"She must have said something," Dooley said.

"She said a lot. She talked a lot about you. She said she

felt that she never really knew you."

Dooley shook his head. How could you know someone you never paid any attention to?

"She said she was sorry about that," Gloria Thomas said.

"She had a funny way of showing it," Dooley said, with more acid than he'd intended.

"She said she knew she wasn't a good mother. She regretted that. She had a lot of regrets. She talked about them all the time—people she'd known, relationships she'd been in, some of the things she'd done or hadn't done."

"Did she talk about my uncle?"

"No."

"Her parents—her adopted parents, I mean?"

"No."

Dooley sighed. He'd been hoping.

"I'm not one hundred percent sure, but I felt that she was getting to a place where she felt she could move out of the past and take some steps forward—make amends, if that's what she felt she had to do, re-establish relationships, plan for the future."

"But why? Something must have made her clean up her act," he said. "Was she sick?"

"No sicker than anyone else in her situation."

"Was she in trouble with the law?"

"Not that I'm aware of."

Dooley didn't get it.

Gloria Thomas sipped her latte. "She didn't come right out and say so," she said slowly, "but I always had the feeling that she was doing it for someone besides herself."

"What do you mean?"

"She never said. But I think it involved a man."

There you go. A man. Not Dooley. Not her son. Of course not. Some things never changed.

"Did she say who it was?"

Gloria Thomas shook her head.

"She said she wanted to change her life. She said she had her reasons but that she didn't want to talk about it because she didn't want to jinx it. I don't know, there was just something about the look on her face that made me think it was a man. I could be wrong. That's all I know. I'm sorry."

"When did she start?"

Gloria Thomas frowned.

"I mean, when did she get her act together?" Dooley said.

"Six or seven months ago. Why?"

Six, seven months ago—about the time she started saving instead of spending.

■ ■ ■

Dooley stopped by Teresa's place to ask her if she needed anything. He buzzed and buzzed. No answer. He put his mouth up to the letterbox and called her name.

"It's me," he said. "It's Dooley."

He stepped back on the sidewalk, almost to the curb, and looked up. A curtain fluttered. He went back to the door and peered in again. This time he was buzzed through and saw Teresa standing at the top of the stairs, a frying pan in her hand.

"I just wanted to see how you're doing," he said.

She nodded, a signal for him to come up.

She was wearing a T-shirt and jeans, and Dooley saw that the bruises on her arms had darkened to black and purple. She was still holding the frying pan. It was one of those heavy cast-iron ones, the kind that could inflict serious brain or spinal cord damage if you hit the right spot with the right amount of force. Her knuckles were white around its black handle.

"You expecting someone besides me?" Dooley said.

She lowered the frying pan onto the stove top.

"I've been thinking—what if those guys come back?"

"Why would they?" Dooley said. "You already told them you don't have the money, right?"

She nodded. "But maybe they'll want to take some of my stuff instead."

Dooley looked around. Besides the big-screen TV, he didn't see anything worth taking, nor could he picture anyone wrestling that TV down those stairs. Besides, it wasn't even new.

"Those guys who were here," he said. "You said they wanted money that Jeffie owed them, right?"

She nodded.

"The thing is, Teresa, Jeffie borrowed money from me to pay off someone else he owed. He said he needed it right away because the guy wouldn't wait. Then, the day before he died, he came by the store where I work. He said he needed another day before he could pay me back, which I figure means he'd already used my money to pay whoever he owed and he was having a little problem getting the money together to pay me." This had been bothering him. "So the thing is, if he took my money and paid the guy he owed, who were the guys who were here giving you a hard time?"

Teresa's eyes filled with tears.

"I don't know," she said. "They didn't tell me their names. I thought they were friends of yours, you know, because you told me Jeffie owed you money."

"Yeah, but they weren't. You don't have any idea who they were?"

She looked down at the floor. "I guess maybe it could have something to do with the gambling."

"Gambling?" Dooley shook his head. "He got back into that?"

"When he won, he said it was the biggest rush. But he didn't always win." She looked at him again. "He told me he was going to stop. He said if he could get it together, maybe we could go down east, you know, where he was from. He said it was nice and quiet down there; maybe he could get a job in a garage, maybe get a little place on the ocean. Jeffie was crazy about the ocean."

Jeffie was just plain crazy, if you asked Dooley, gambling with owed money. Boy, now Dooley could see it. Jeffie had promised to pay him back. Maybe he'd even made that money he'd been hoping to from that downtown party guy he'd told Dooley about the first time, the one he'd said reminded him of Dooley. But then he'd pissed it away gambling on … well, whatever he gambled on. It looked like maybe he had lost more than he could afford so that he didn't just owe Dooley, he owed someone else, too. Maybe that's how he ended up dead.

"Did you tell the police that, Teresa?"

She shook her head.

"I think you should. It'll give them something to go on." Something besides Dooley and his uncle. "You want them to find out who killed him, don't you, Teresa?"

She looked reluctant. She was probably scared. But Dooley thought maybe he could talk her into it.

"You've been so nice to me," she said. "Jeannie, too. I'm sorry Jeffie never paid you back."

"You told the cops he was looking forward to seeing me."

"He was," she said. "He'd been in a bad mood for a couple of days. I could tell something was bothering him. He was on edge, you know? He spent a couple of days sitting there"— she nodded at the couch—"looking at the TV and flipping through the channels. That used to drive me crazy. You never had a chance to figure out what show he was on before he'd flip to the next one. I used to want to kill him." Her eyes got all watery again. "If he was here now, I'd let him flip through the channels all he wanted."

"Did he say what was bothering him?" Money problems, Dooley bet. Probably paying-Dooley-back problems if he'd gambled away a bundle.

She shook her head. "He was just sitting there, flipping through the channels. But he couldn't find anything he wanted to watch, and it was pissing him off. Everything was pissing him off. I went into the kitchen to microwave some popcorn. I thought maybe that would cheer him up. Jeffie liked popcorn, really salty, with extra butter. All of a sudden he came into the kitchen. He had a great big smile on his

284

face and he hugged me and said his problems were over. Then he went out to make a phone call."

"Went out? You mean, took his cell phone outside?" Maybe to have some privacy.

"No. He went out to use a pay phone."

"A pay phone?"

"Yeah."

"But he had a cell phone."

"He went out to use a pay phone, Dooley. He did that sometimes. I don't think he wanted me to know about it, though. He always said he was going out for a smoke—he never smoked in the apartment. But I watched him one time. He went across the street to the pay phone on the corner. That's what he did that night. I could see him out the window. I thought he was calling you."

Jeffie had called him Monday night, but he'd called from his cell phone. Dooley had seen the caller ID on his own phone's read-out.

"What makes you think that?"

"Because when he came back, he said everything was going to be okay with you. I asked him what he meant, but he said I shouldn't worry about it, which I didn't get because I didn't know there was anything to worry about. He said the important thing was that you were going to be happy."

"He didn't say anything else?"

She shook her head.

"He went out for a while after that. He never ate the pop-corn I made him."

To the video store, Dooley thought. Jeffie had gone out

and made a call on the pay phone. Then he must have called Dooley—a bunch of times—before finally coming down to the store to speak to Dooley in person, to ask for more time.

"He never mentioned any guy he'd met recently, some downtown guy that liked to party a lot?"

"Downtown guy?"

"Some guy he knew who worked or lived downtown?"

She shook her head again. Then, "Well, he told me one time maybe a couple of weeks ago that he was in one of those big buildings, you know, the gold one that's down there, it's all windows and all the windows are gold? He told me there's a restaurant at the top of that building, they charge twenty-five dollars for a hamburger. He said he heard two guys talking about it while he was waiting for the elevator. You think that's true, Dooley? You think someone would actually pay twenty-five dollars for a hamburger?"

Dooley bet someone like, say, Madonna, would pay even more, assuming she ate meat—hell, assuming she ate at all. He bet there were people who would eat twenty-five-dollar hamburgers just because a whole lot more people could never in a million years afford to.

"What was Jeffie doing down there, Teresa?"

"He didn't tell me. He just said he was there."

"Did he say who he went to see? Did he mention a name?"

"No."

"Are you sure?"

She was sure. "I guess I should clean out his stuff, huh?" she said. "Maybe give his clothes to Goodwill?"

Dooley said he thought it might be a good idea.

"Teresa?"

She had picked up a bunch of CDs and was flipping through them. Tears trickled down her cheeks.

"Did Jeffie ever say anything to you about a cop or an ex-cop?"

"What do you mean?"

"Did he ever mention that he was going to meet a cop or that he was doing business with a cop—or an ex-cop?" Like, say, Dooley's uncle.

Teresa shook her head. But given how little Jeffie had told her, what did that really mean?

■ ■ ■

He went to the video store to pull a half-shift for Linelle— and she said he never did her any favors. Then he went home.

The first thing he saw when he came through the door was the photograph album that Gloria Thomas had given him, the one he'd tossed into the wastepaper basket in his room. But it wasn't in the wastepaper basket anymore. It was sitting on the table in the front hall.

"Dooley, is that you?" Jeannie called. She came out of the kitchen. "I went out to see Gary this afternoon. He asked about you." She saw what he had been looking at, and she flushed with embarrassment. "I wasn't snooping," she said. "Garbage pickup is tomorrow. I was just emptying wastepaper baskets, and I saw that and … I … I understand that you and your mother … it's just … well, I guess I didn't want you to be too hasty."

"Did you look at it?"

"I did. I'm sorry. I know I shouldn't have. And after I did, I just couldn't bring myself to throw it away. I was afraid you would regret it one day."

Gloria Thomas had said the same thing about Lorraine. Dooley looked at the album. He doubted he would regret tossing it. But he wasn't mad at Jeannie. She was just trying to do the right thing.

"I'm sorry," she said. "I didn't mean to upset you."

"It's okay," he said.

"Are you hungry? Did you have any supper?" She seemed eager, as if she wanted to make it up to him.

"Some fries."

"Sit down," she said. "I'll make you something."

Dooley watched her disappear into the kitchen. He looked at the photograph album sitting there on the front hall table. He picked it up and saw the self-help book under it, the one that he'd pitched out with the album, the one that smelled like Lorraine. He left the book where it was but carried the album into the living room. He put it down on the coffee table and stared at it for a moment. Then he flipped through the first couple of pictures of himself way back when.

Jeannie was back in a couple of minutes with a sandwich—cold cuts with some lettuce in there, a side of potato salad, and a few slices of tomato and cucumber all nicely arranged—and a glass of soda water. She set the food down on the coffee table, glanced at the picture that was staring up from the photograph album, and smiled.

"You were a cute little boy," she said. "How old were you there?"

"I'm not sure," Dooley said. "I think I was in kindergarten." He took a bite of the sandwich. It was terrific, ham and Swiss cheese and spicy mustard. "Jeannie, can I ask you something?"

She sat down on the sofa beside him.

"How long have you known my uncle?"

Jeannie looked up from the photograph album. "Eight or nine months."

"That's all?" She must have still been getting to know Dooley's uncle at about the same time that Dooley was getting ready to move in.

"I took a silk dress into his store to get cleaned," she said. "It came back without the buttons. When I complained, the girl behind the counter said that happened sometimes, usually with cheap buttons." She shook her head. "It was an eight-hundred-dollar dress. When you take an eight-hundred-dollar dress to the dry cleaner, you expect it to come back with the buttons on it—at least, I do. And if it doesn't, the very least you expect is an apology. I got neither. I was pretty steamed, I can tell you." If you asked Dooley, she was getting steamed all over again just thinking about it. It must have been some dress. "I demanded to see the manager. I got the owner instead." Dooley's uncle. "I gave him an earful. I told him if he didn't make good on my dress, I was prepared to take him to court. I also told him that I would tell everyone I knew what kind of establishment he ran."

"I bet he liked that," Dooley said.

Jeannie smiled. "He said he was sorry—right away, as

289

soon as I finished talking. He said, of course I was right to be upset; he'd be upset himself if one of his suits came back without the buttons. He asked me to come back the next day and promised that the dress would be as good as new. He was so nice and polite." Dooley had trouble imagining that. "It took the wind right out of my sails. I went back the next day and there was my dress, with brand new buttons on it. He'd even managed to match the original ones. I have no idea how he did it, but he did. He also gave me a refund on my bill. He fired the girl who had been rude to me. On top of that, he insisted on taking me out to dinner. Your uncle is quite the charmer, Dooley."

Those were certainly not the words Dooley would have used to describe him.

"Did he talk about me—before I moved in, I mean?"

Jeannie nodded. "He told me the first night we had dinner together that he had a nephew who was going to come and live with him. He told me that you'd been in some trouble, but that you were a good kid."

"He said that? *Before* I started living here?"

"He did."

"Did he talk about Lorraine?"

Her face got more serious. "He never mentioned her. I got the impression your mother had died, although now that I think about it, I don't remember him actually saying that. When I saw her picture and heard her name, it never occurred to me that she was Gary's sister."

"You saw her picture?"

"On TV. I don't watch a lot of TV. But your uncle and I

were going through a bad patch a couple of weeks ago. Something was bothering him and he refused to tell me what it was. So there I was, spending more time at home than I cared to." She shook her head. "I think I spent one whole weekend in front of the TV, and I never do that. I was just telling myself that I had to snap out of it. I decided that I would go down to Gary's store first thing the next morning and force the issue—either he told me what was eating him or we were through. I was just about to turn off the TV when the news came on. They mentioned the name Lorraine McCormack and showed her picture, and I remember thinking, what a coincidence. Here I am thinking about strangling a certain Gary McCormack if he doesn't open up to me and tell me what the hell is going on—and another McCormack shows up dead on the TV." She flushed again. "I don't mean any disrespect, Dooley."

"It's okay," Dooley said.

He was thinking about what Detective Randall had said. Why hadn't his uncle shown any interest in Dooley all those years? Why had he let Dooley think that he didn't even know about him? Why did he only come around after Dooley had got himself into serious trouble? He had a few questions of his own, like: Why had he been paying Lorraine regularly, in cash? Did she have something on him? At first when Dooley had found out that his uncle wasn't really his uncle, he couldn't figure out why, in that case, he had taken responsibility for him, especially knowing what he knew now about how his uncle felt about Lorraine. Now he wondered if Lorraine had forced him into it: *Your turn, Gary.* He sure hoped that Randall was wrong.

"Your mother was very pretty," she said.

"Yeah, I guess." She had never had any trouble attracting men, that was for sure.

"You don't take after her, though, do you?"

Dooley shrugged. He'd never seen any resemblance between himself and Lorraine—any physical resemblance, that is. But then, he'd never looked.

"I have a brother," Jeannie said, smiling. "He takes after my mother and her side of the family. But you're like me, I guess."

"What do you mean?"

"You look like your father."

He stared at her. What was she talking about? She had never met his father—unless …

Her smile wavered. "I'm sorry," she said, unsure of herself again. "I thought those pictures …"

"What pictures?"

"There are some pictures in here of a man who reminded me of you. I assumed he was your father."

Dooley put down his sandwich and picked up the photograph album. He handed it to Jeannie.

"Which man?" he said.

Jeannie leafed through the pages until she came to a strip of four black-and-white pictures that had been taken in a photo booth some place, Dooley had no idea where— Lorraine and Dooley, just a tiny baby—no hair, no teeth; Dooley couldn't even believe it was really him—and a guy who looked like he might be in his early twenties with shaggy dark hair and piercing eyes.

292

"You look just like him," Jeannie said.

Dooley stared at the picture, but he didn't see the resemblance.

"In the eyes," Jeannie said. "And the mouth. And the cheekbones. Isn't that your father?"

Which put Dooley in the position of having to admit: "I don't know. My father"—the word stuck in his throat like a piece of bone—"she said he took off when I was just a baby. Who knows, maybe right after that picture was taken."

"Your mother never told you who he was or showed you what he looked like?" Jeannie said, sounding like she couldn't believe it.

"She'd cry about him sometimes," Dooley said. Usually when she was between men and had been drinking. Drinking made her weepy, right before it made her mean. "The way she talked about him, I thought maybe he was dead."

"Didn't you ask her?" Jeannie said.

Dooley looked at her. He bet she had never met anyone like Lorraine.

"What for?" he said. "It wouldn't have changed anything."

■ ■ ■

Upstairs in the bathroom, Dooley stared into the mirror. Jeannie was right. He didn't look anything like Lorraine. But he didn't look anything like his uncle, either. Not even remotely.

The guy in the photo album, though, that was another story. At least, according to Jeannie it was. Dooley held the picture up to his face and looked at it—at the eyes, the wide mouth with the full lips, the sharp, high cheekbones. Then he looked at himself. Boy, Jeannie was better at this than he was. He stared at the man in the picture until he was sure he could recognize him in a crowded room, but he didn't see himself in that face.

If Jeannie was right, then Randall was wrong—maybe about a lot of things. Okay, so his uncle had been giving Lorraine money, but maybe it wasn't for the reason Randall had insinuated. Maybe Lorraine was supposed to have used it to look after Dooley. But all her friends said she'd spent it. She'd partied with it, up until about six months ago, which, according to Gloria Thomas, was when she had decided to clean up her act.

Because of a man.

He picked up the self-help book that was sitting on the back of the toilet where he'd set it when he came into the bathroom. He opened it and inhaled Lorraine's now much fainter scent. He thumbed through it page by page until he found what he was looking for. He flipped open his cell phone and started to punch in the number she had written in pencil in a margin. He flipped the phone shut again after the first four digits. What was the point? What would it change?

Still, before he went to bed, he ripped a piece of paper out of one of his notebooks, scrawled the number down, and tucked it into his wallet.

Nineteen

There was a folded piece of paper sitting next to Dooley's coffee mug when Dooley came down to breakfast the next morning.

"A note for Mr. Rectal about your absence," Jeannie said. He couldn't tell if she was making an honest mistake or poking fun. Either way, he didn't correct her.

"I'm working tonight, six to closing," Dooley told her. "And I have some things I have to do after school, so I don't think I'll be home for supper."

Jeannie just nodded. She didn't give him the third degree the way his uncle would have.

School was torture, as usual. Well, except for the look on Mr. Rektor's face when Dooley marched into the office and handed him the note Jeannie had given him. He stood there while Mr. Rektor opened it and read it. Dooley was pretty sure he wanted to say something about it, guessed he probably couldn't think of anything because, after he'd scanned it, he put it back into the envelope. Dooley turned for the door.

"Terrible thing about your mother," Mr. Rektor said. "And

about your uncle."

Dooley didn't turn around to look at him. He could imagine any one of half a dozen expressions on Rektor's face, and every one of them would only make him want to punch him. He left the office without a word.

■ ■ ■

Dooley sat at a table alone in the back of the cafeteria, a bottle of juice and a slice of pizza in front of him. So far he hadn't touched either. He was thinking about Jeffie.

Jeffie had been watching TV and all of a sudden he'd perked up and told Teresa that his problems were over. He'd gone out right after that and had made a phone call at a pay phone. Then he'd come to the store and told Dooley that things hadn't gone according to plan—meaning, maybe, that he'd gambled and lost—but that he was coming into some big money.

From what? More gambling? A big bet? Maybe someone tipped him to something?

But he had sounded so sure. He'd looked and acted one hundred percent confident that he was going to have the money to pay Dooley what he owed.

And then he hadn't turned up.

Dooley thought about Jeffie outside the video store on Monday night, pumped, practically dancing, telling Dooley that with the money he was going to get, he would be able to go home. On a gamble? No, wait a minute. He said he'd seen someone. He'd seen a guy. No, not a guy. *That guy*. The one he had told Dooley about. The downtown guy. It had to be. He'd seen the guy, and the guy had been with someone. But who? Dooley had cut Jeffie off. He'd told him he didn't care; he didn't even want to know. All he wanted was his money. But Jeffie was jazzed, that was for sure. He was jazzed about a big payday and it had something to do with a guy he had seen and maybe, according to Teresa, something he had seen on TV.

One more thing. *He'd said, If I'd known, I would have taken a picture.*

What would he have done with a picture?

A picture of what?

He thought about what Randall had said. He thought about Edward-you-can-call-me-Ed Ralston, who had been in charge of Dooley at the group home for a couple of months until Jeffie had taken care of him. He thought about the other guy Randall said had made a complaint against Jeffie and then had dropped it.

What had Jeffie seen?

What had he been onto?

A shadow fell across his table.

Warren.

"Are you okay?" he said.

Dooley looked up at Warren's thin face and thick glasses.

"It's just, you know …" Warren said. Dooley didn't know. He waited. "I heard some kids talking about your uncle," Warren said. "And your mother." Dooley didn't doubt that there were plenty of kids in his school—teachers, too—who had heard about the whole mess by now and who had talked about it among themselves. He had caught a lot of looks in the halls and the cafeteria, in classrooms, in the can. But apart from Rektor, no one had said anything to him.

"You never mentioned them to me."

"Sorry," Dooley said.

"I just wanted to say that if there's anything I can do ..." Dooley stood up.

Warren recoiled and then, just as quickly, recovered.

"I'm sorry if I—" he began.

"It's okay, Warren," Dooley said. "I appreciate your asking. I'm okay. I just have to make a call. But thanks, okay?"

Warren blinked behind his glasses.

"Okay," he said.

■ ■ ■

Dooley went outside and walked down the sidewalk a ways. Teresa had told him that Jeffie had used a pay phone to make a call the day before he'd disappeared. He'd used it before, too, to make other calls. Dooley knew all of his uncle's numbers—home, his cell, his stores. There was no way Jeffie would remember any of those without looking them up. Or writing them down. He thought about the scraps of paper that had fallen out of Jeffie's pocket. He pulled out his phone and punched in Teresa's phone number. It took five rings before she answered, and then she sounded groggy.

"Did I wake you?" he said.

"Yeah. But it's okay." She didn't sound right, like maybe she was on something.

"Teresa, did Jeffie have a special place where he kept phone numbers?"

"In his phone, I guess."

"I mean the ones he wouldn't have kept in his phone."

"What are you talking about, Dooley?"

"He wrote the numbers down sometimes, Teresa. He kept them in his pocket. Did he put them somewhere when he got home?"

"I don't know, Dooley."

If he'd had all those numbers with him when he was killed, the cops would have them, too—unless whoever had killed him had taken them. Or unless he'd been smart for once and had left them at home.

"What about that night you told me about? You said he went out to use a pay phone. Did he take a phone number with him? Did you see if he had a piece of paper or something with him when he was dialing?"

"I don't think so. Why?"

Jeffie was terrible with phone numbers.

"So what did he do? Did he look up the number when he got down there?"

"Look it up?"

"In the phone book?"

"Have you used a pay phone lately, Dooley? They don't have phone books in there anymore. They've all been ripped off."

"Did you tell the cops about the pay phone, Teresa?"

"No." There was a pause. "You think I should?"

"No," Dooley said. "No, it's okay."

He wondered if he should tell the cops. Would they be able to find out what calls had been made from that phone that night? He bet they could. But did he want them to find out? What if Jeffie had gone out there to call Dooley's uncle?

"That night Jeffie saw something on TV—you don't have any idea what it was?"

"He was flipping channels. And then I was in the kitchen. I'm pretty sure he was watching the news—I heard the theme they play, you know? But I didn't see it."

"But you said it was Monday night, right?" Whatever he'd seen on TV, he'd seen it right before he'd started calling Dooley. Before he showed up at the store. He'd come up with some way to get the money he owed Dooley and he'd come down to the store to tell Dooley in person that he needed another day to pull it off.

"No," Teresa said. "It was Sunday night, late."

What?

"Are you sure, Teresa?"

"I'm positive. When he came back from making the call, he was smiling. He went out for a while, and when he came back, he was in an even better mood. We had a great time that night, Dooley. A really great time." She started to cry.

■ ■ ■

Dooley felt his insides go cold when he came down the steps after school and saw Annette Girondin standing beside her car at the curb. Had something happened to his uncle? Had someone—maybe some guy who knew his uncle when he was a cop—attacked him in lockup? Or had the cops finally come up with something that would nail him good?

"What's wrong?" he said.

"The police are going after a DNA warrant for you," she said. "It's in relation to the murder of Jeffrey Eccles."

Dooley stared at her. He couldn't tell from her face whether or not she thought he might have had anything to do with that.

But wait a minute. They'd already taken a sample from his uncle for DNA after they'd found Lorraine's blood in his car. So if they were coming after Dooley now, then they must have ruled his uncle out on Jeffie's murder—right? He asked Annette.

"I don't know. They don't share those things with me," she said. She handed him a business card. "A colleague of mind has agreed to represent you. Call him before you talk to the police, Ryan. It's what your uncle wants."

Dooley glanced at the card.

"Okay," he said. He tucked it into his pocket.

"I mean it, Ryan." What she was really saying was, his uncle meant it.

"Tell him I said okay."

■ ■ ■

The cops had ruled out his uncle as Jeffrey's killer.

They had ruled out his uncle, but not Dooley.

He checked his watch.

He had some time to kill before he had to be at work.

Jeffie had told him that the downtown guy who was going to save his ass worked in one of the big towers. Teresa had said Jeffie had been inside the gold building. Dooley caught a bus and headed downtown to check it out. In the late afternoon this time of year, when the sun was sinking in the sky, it lit up the whole tower so that it looked like it was made of solid gold. Dooley wondered if the people looking out from behind all the glass saw the whole city in a tint of gold instead of in the dull gray it really was.

The building was so big that it had entrances on all four sides, which meant on four different streets. But the street address was the same, no matter which side of the building you were on. Inside there were information desks in two corners diagonally across from each other and banks of elevators in between. Some elevators only ran halfway up. Others didn't stop until they had reached the upper floors. Altogether, there were sixty-eight floors. Sixty-eight floors that could hold, who knows, thousands of people.

He strolled around the main floor until he found a building directory. There were dozens of companies on it, some of them occupying more than one floor as far as Dooley could tell. He skimmed the list. His heart slammed to a stop when he came to a company name he recognized.

Jesus.

He glanced around, looking for a pay phone and seeing an information desk instead. He headed for it and asked a surly-looking security guard for the phone number for Integra Financial Services. He repeated the number over and over until he was far enough away that the security guard wouldn't hear. Then he punched in the number and asked to speak to Larry Quayle, his uncle's financial advisor.

"It's Ryan Dooley," he said to the woman who asked if she could tell Mr. Quayle who was calling.

"Ryan, this is Larry Quayle," a briskly warm voice said. "Your uncle has told me all about you." Dooley doubted that. "What can I do for you?"

"My uncle came down to see you a couple of weeks ago—on a Tuesday afternoon," Dooley said. "The thing is, he had my mid-term report with him. He's been looking for it and he says now he thinks he may have left it in your office."

"How is your uncle?" Larry Quayle said. Dooley wasn't sure, but he got the impression that Larry knew his uncle was locked up.

"He's okay," Dooley said. "But he said I should try and track down my report."

"I see he was here a couple of· Thursdays ago," Larry Quayle said.

"And then he came back the following Tuesday."

"No, I'm afraid not," Larry Quayle said. "I don't have that in my appointment book. But, tell you what, I'll take a look around and see if I can find that report for you."

Dooley thanked him.

He was positive his uncle had said he was coming down here that Tuesday, the day before Lorraine died. Maybe his uncle hadn't killed Jeffie—maybe Jeffie's getting killed had nothing to do with what had happened to Lorraine. Maybe it had to do with the money he owed. But his uncle had lied to him about coming to see Larry Quayle that day. What if he'd arranged to meet Jeffie here so that Jeffie didn't know where he lived? What if he was Jeffie's downtown guy?

■ ■ ■

Monday night in the video store: a good night if the absolute last thing you wanted to do was slap a smile on your face and make nice with customers because, guess what, there were hardly any customers on Monday night. That invariably meant that the time dragged because, of course, Kevin insisted that Dooley *do something constructive,* which meant straightening up the shelves, putting things back where they belonged instead of where some customer had decided to drop them after he or she—usually he—had changed their mind for maybe the third time. It meant restocking the candy displays and refilling the pop coolers. It meant printing out a list of people whose late returns were about to morph into charges on their credit cards, and then it meant calling those people, which Dooley hated doing and had managed so far to avoid. But Kevin was on his case tonight and had stuck him on the phone before he went on his meal break.

"We can't always have the fun jobs," Kevin said. "We have to share the pain."

Dooley thought about the pain he would like to share with Kevin.

As soon as Kevin left the store, Dooley went to the computer and got on the Internet. He pulled out his wallet and dug out the piece of paper on which he'd written the phone number he found in Lorraine's self-help book. He went to the 411 site that Linelle had showed him and typed in the phone number—and got a message that said that the number he'd typed in wasn't a published number. What had Linelle said about that? It meant it was probably a cell phone number. Or an unlisted number. The only way he'd be able to find out who it belonged to was to call it—and he wasn't ready for that. He had no idea what he would say to whoever answered. He couldn't come right out and ask, *Excuse me, but was my mother in love with you?* Besides, what difference would it make now?

Fuck it.

He thought instead about who Jeffie had called that night before he came to the store. Suppose it was his downtown guy, the guy in the gold tower. Suppose it was someone other than Dooley's uncle …

He typed in the address from the gold building. Up popped a long list of companies, with their phone numbers. Jesus, Jeffie could have called any one of these numbers or none of them at all. But, wait a minute—what had Jeffie said the night he came to the store? The number of his downtown guy was a pizza number. What did that mean? That the guy worked for a pizza company—maybe a pizza company that had its main office downtown? Dooley scanned the list but didn't see anything like that. He shook his head in disgust. What a waste of time! All Jeffie had said about the guy was that he was downtown and he liked to party. Besides, it was a stretch to think that Jeffie had called any of these numbers. He could have called someone else altogether.

Still, he kept reading down the list.

And came to one of those phone numbers you'd have to be brain-dead to forget, the same three numbers followed by four zeros, the kind of phone number you'd hear on a commercial or in a jingle. An easy-to-remember phone number, like—was it possible?—like the number of a pizza chain. A pizza number—a number that even Jeffie couldn't forget.

Dooley reached for the phone, punched in the number, and got a recorded message telling him what company he had reached—it was a string of names that sounded like it might be a law firm or something—followed by the numbers he could punch to get their mailing and shipping addresses, the number he could punch to get the staff directory, the number he could punch to talk to an operator, and, if he knew the four-digit extension of the person he was trying to reach, he could enter that at any time. Dooley punched three to get to the staff directory, which turned out to be alphabetical. He'd listened to nearly twenty names before he got out of the A's and B's and into the C's. The company was huge. There must be hundreds of people working there. You either had to know who you wanted to talk to or you had to have an extension number.

He hung up the phone and stared at the computer screen and at the number you'd have to be a moron not to remember. After a few moments, he picked up the phone again and dialed Teresa's number.

"Did you clean out all of Jeffie's stuff yet?" he said.

"I was going to do it today," she said. "But I couldn't get started, you know?"

It sounded like she'd been crying again.

"Jeffie had a piece of paper in the top drawer of his dresser," Dooley said. "It looks like it was ripped out of a newspaper. It has four numbers written on it. Can you do me a favor, Teresa? Go and get it and read me the numbers."

"Okay." She didn't ask how he knew what was in the top drawer of Jeffie's dresser. Dooley heard her put the phone down. He heard a shuffling sound, like she was walking across a bare floor in slippers. He heard a drawer being pulled out. Then more shuffling. "Four-two-eight-one," she said. "What do they mean, Dooley?"

"I'm not sure yet, Teresa," he said. "When I find out, I'll let you know."

He ended the call and dialed the number on the screen again. This time when he got the automated voice system, he pressed four, two, eight, one.

"Hi. You've reached the voice mail for Ronald D. Malone," a voice said. "I'm sorry I can't take your call right now, but if you leave a detailed message after the beep, I'll get back to you as soon as I can."

Dooley hung up the phone.

The electronic buzzer over the door went off and Kevin came back into the store. He smiled when he saw Dooley put the phone down.

"See?" he said. "It's not so bad, is it?"

■ ■ ■

Twenty minutes later, Dooley's cell phone rang. He checked the readout. It was Beth's home phone number.

"I'm taking my break now," Dooley said. He ducked out from behind the counter and answered his phone on the way to the door.

"I missed you," Beth said. "I wish you weren't working tonight."

"Me, too," Dooley said. "When can I see you? After school tomorrow?"

"I have a debate. Don't worry, it's with another girls' school," she said. "Meet me in front of the library after supper. Seven o'clock."

"I'll be there," he said.

■ ■ ■

Dooley stopped at a phone booth on his way home. He dug a slip of paper out of his wallet and stared at the phone number he had written on it. If Lorraine had written this number in her book, she'd done it sometime in the past six or seven months. She'd drawn a heart around it, too, and Gloria Thomas had said she'd had the impression that Lorraine was cleaning up her act for a man. Dooley told himself that he didn't care, that he didn't want to know. She was dead, and his uncle had been arrested for killing her. What difference did it make who she'd been seeing?

Except that it did. It mattered.

What if whoever she'd been cleaning up for was serious about her? What if he'd seen a Lorraine that Dooley himself had never seen? What if she really had been turning her life around? What if—?

He punched in the number. He had nothing to lose. Whoever was on the other end wouldn't be able to trace him. He didn't even have to say anything if he didn't want to. He could just listen, see what the guy sounded like. He could maybe get his name, look into him a little before he decided whether or not he wanted to take it any further.

The phone rang once. Twice. Three times. Then it kicked into voice mail.

Dooley listened to the voice mail message—no name, just Hi, sorry I missed your call, leave a message and I'll be sure to get right back to you. Linelle was right about cell phones. You couldn't tell who you were calling or even where you were calling. He didn't leave a message.

■ ■ ■

He didn't sleep that night. Couldn't. There was too much noise in his head, too much stuff going on. His uncle who wasn't really his uncle was in a cell somewhere, charged with killing Lorraine. His upright, uptight uncle, who had lied to him from the get-go. He'd known about Dooley the whole time. He'd known and yet he had never come around, not once. Why was that? Was it because he hated Lorraine for all the grief she had caused, or was there some other reason, like Randall seemed to think? He'd been paying her, too. A thousand a month, for a couple of years now. What was that all about?

Lorraine.

She was dead, and for the first time ever Dooley felt some

regret with regard to her. Maybe it was because he was older. Maybe it was because he was straight. Maybe it was all that bullshit therapy that they made him sit through. But he felt—too late—that maybe he had a sliver of insight into her, not that it was going to do him any good. It was too late for that.

Because someone had killed her.

And then there was Jeffie. Also dead. After being tortured. Why? By whom?

He knew what the cops were thinking: Dooley's uncle knew Jeffie. Jeffie had drug connections. Dooley's uncle could have got the drugs from Jeffie that had ended up in Lorraine's arm. Dooley had even managed to develop his own theory on how that could have happened. Maybe his uncle had run into Jeffie down there while he was on his way to or from a meeting with Larry Quayle and Jeffie was contacting his pizza-number guy. Maybe his uncle had arranged to meet Jeffie there again that time he was supposed to have been at Larry Quayle's office but wasn't. Yeah. And he could see Jeffie assuming that this cop from his past worked there now, maybe in security. Theory: Dooley's uncle had bought drugs from Jeffie and then had offed him to get rid of any loose ends.

But then why did they want to test Dooley for DNA? That must mean that they'd eliminated his uncle as Jeffie's killer.

Or had they?

What if they'd found two specimens—his uncle's and someone else's? He thought about all the questions Randall had asked him. What if they thought that Dooley had been in on it with his uncle?

Dooley shook his head. That couldn't be right. Even assuming he could imagine his uncle killing Jeffie—or anyone else, for that matter—he couldn't imagine him doing it with someone else. Why take the risk?

Jesus, listen to yourself, Dooley.

Someone killed Jeffie.

Maybe the guys he owed money to.

Or …

What about those pictures?

The non-existent pictures—the ones Jeffie said he wished he'd taken.

Think, Dooley.

Jeffie had said he'd seen his downtown guy out behind Jay-Zee's. He'd said the guy had been with someone, but he hadn't said who. He'd said the guy hadn't seen him. He'd said he wished he'd taken pictures. And he'd been dancing around out there on the sidewalk the whole time he was telling it, jazzed, excited about getting Dooley's money back and even more—enough to move back down east. This had been on Monday—the day *after* he'd seen something on TV. According to Teresa, he'd been watching the news. The late news. What on earth had he seen on the late news to make him dance like that?

Dooley had watched the news late that Sunday night. But the only thing he remembered about it was Lorraine's face and that he'd been glad that Beth wasn't around to make the connection between that and the woman she'd seen outside Dooley's school.

Jeannie had also seen Lorraine's face that night and heard

311

her name. It had reminded her that she felt like strangling Dooley's uncle.

But what about Jeffie?

Jeffie had seen something, too, something to do with his downtown guy, his guy in the gold building. Jeffie had seen an opportunity. What?

How could a person sleep with all those questions, all those fears, running through his head?

But he did. He must have, because he woke with a jolt. It had been right there the whole time, practically staring him in the face. He spent an hour staring at his ceiling, his heart racing, trying to decide what to do. Finally he got up, pulled out a notebook, and started to write.

Twenty

D ooley was up early the next morning—too early. Offices don't open until nine o'clock. By nine o'clock, Dooley would be on his way from homeroom to the first class of the day. Either that or he'd get marked late, and Mr. Rektor would be on him about it if he did, ready to make a federal case of it. He thought about asking Jeannie for a late note, but to do that, he'd either have to tell her the truth—which was far too complicated and, anyway, he didn't want to have to explain all about Jeffie, especially since she'd helped Teresa—or he'd have to lie. Dooley didn't want to start lying to Jeannie.

He stuffed a thick envelope into his backpack and headed off to school, making one stop on the way at a doughnut shop where he fed two quarters into a pay phone and tried the number in the self-help book again—and ended up again in voice mail.

At five to ten, in the five-minute period between classes, Dooley stepped out onto the playing field behind the school and called the phone number for the company that sounded

313

like a law firm in the gold building downtown. He punched in the four-digit extension number and, shit, found himself in Ronald D. Malone's voice mail. He tried again. Voice mail again. And again. Still voice mail. Fuck, fuck, fuck. One last time.

"Ron Malone," said the same rich, smooth voice that was on the voice mail message—a voice that bothered Dooley because there was something familiar about it. "How can I help you?"

Dooley drew in a deep breath.

"Hello?" Ron Malone said.

"Yeah, hi," Dooley said.

"May I ask who this is?"

"Jeffrey Eccles," Dooley said.

There was silence on the other end of the phone, just a second or two, but enough that when Ron Malone said, "I'm sorry, but I don't know any Jeffrey Eccles," Dooley was pretty sure he was lying.

"Sure you do," Dooley said. "We did some business."

"Look, I don't know who you are or why you're calling—"

"I can give the pictures to you or I can give them to the police," Dooley said.

"Pictures?" Ron Malone said, confused or managing to sound that way. "I'm sorry, but I have no idea what you're talking about."

Jesus, did he or didn't he? Was Dooley wrong about the ridiculously easy-to-remember phone number? Had Jeffie being doing business with someone else who worked in that building? All those companies with all those offices, Dooley bet there was someone else, maybe two or more people, who worked for different companies in the building and had different phone numbers but the same four-digit extension. He could think of only one way to find out.

"You have sixty seconds," he said. "You call this number if you want to talk." He rattled off his cell phone number. "If I don't hear from you, I call the cops. I'm sure they'll be interested in what you were doing back behind Jay-Zee's. I hope you've got a good story." He pressed end and stood there, holding his cell phone, wondering if he had done the right thing.

He counted to ten.

Eleven.

Twelve.

Thirteen.

His cell phone rang. He checked the read-out.

"You know where to find me?" Ron Malone said.

"Yeah. The gold building downtown."

"There's a food court under it. Meet me there at noon, in front of the sushi counter. We can talk."

Dooley bet the food court would be jammed with office workers at noon—probably thousands of them. How would he recognize the guy? But he couldn't ask—he'd just told him he had pictures. If he had pictures, he should know what Ronald Malone looked like.

"I heard there's a restaurant at the top of that building where you can get a twenty-five-dollar hamburger. How about we meet up there? I'll even make the reservations."

"I think I can handle that," Ron Malone said. "Noon. Be there."

Dooley closed his cell phone and headed back inside. Warren was just about to go into math class when Dooley found him.

"I need to talk to you," he said.

"But the bell—"

"Warren, I need a favor."

Warren glanced over his shoulder into the math classroom. Dooley saw the math teacher—the same one Dooley had—up at the board. The teacher glanced at Warren before zeroing in on Dooley.

"I wouldn't ask if it wasn't important," Dooley said. "And there's no one else I can ask."

Warren cast a nervous glance into the classroom, but he followed Dooley down the hall to the boys' bathroom where Dooley scrawled some numbers on a piece of paper and told Warren what he wanted him to do.

"You might get Rektor up your ass for skipping—"

"I'll tell my mom I had an allergy attack," Warren said. "I'll get her to write a note."

Just like that. Without even asking what it was all about. Dooley didn't understand Warren, but he sure was glad that he knew him.

Dooley left first, taking the back stairs and cutting across the athletic field to the bus stop.

■ ■ ■

Dooley squirmed as he rode the elevator up to the top floor of the office tower. People got on and off every other floor or so, and Dooley noticed that none of them was dressed in jeans and sweatshirts. He started to worry about what it would be like at that restaurant with the twenty-five-dollar hamburgers. What if some snooty maitre d' wouldn't even let him in? He'd look like a complete idiot.

He got off the elevator on the top floor. The entrance to the restaurant was right there. He crossed to it and approached a man in a black suit who was standing behind a little podium that had a big book open on it with names written in it. The man inspected Dooley's jacket and sweatshirt and jeans before looking at Dooley. He waited for Dooley to speak.

"I'm meeting Mr. Ron Malone," Dooley said. "He has a reservation."

The man in the black suit took another look at Dooley's jacket and sweatshirt and jeans. Then he raised a hand and flagged a waiter. The man in the black suit told him Malone's name, and the waiter looked at Dooley's jacket and sweatshirt and jeans.

"Follow me," he said.

Dooley followed the waiter past the maitre d' and across a big room filled with tables and booths and with floor-to-ceiling windows on two sides. The tables weren't all jammed together like they were in most restaurants Dooley had been in. They were spaced out so that the people who were eating could talk to each other without the people at the neighboring tables hearing everything they said. They had white linen table cloths, and there were delicate little flower arrangements in the middle of each one. The waiter led Dooley toward a booth on the far side of the restaurant.

Dooley stopped and stared at its occupant—a man with wavy black hair, generous lips, and piercing blue eyes. He was wearing a charcoal gray suit with a pale blue shirt and dark-blue-patterned tie. His right hand was wrapped around a glass of water, and Dooley could see that he'd had a manicure, either that or he spent more time on his nails than most girls did. He looked up at Dooley and held him with his eyes, his lips curled into the semblance of a smile. It was obvious he was loaded, with money, with confidence, with balls. Jesus, and this was the guy Jeffie had tried to snow?

The waiter had reached the booth and turned to locate Dooley. Dooley continued on to the table. The waiter stood aside so that he could slide onto the upholstered bench across from Malone. He set a menu down in front of Dooley.

"Don't get too comfortable," Malone said as the waiter withdrew. He slid out of the booth and motioned for Dooley to do the same. "This way," he said, indicating a door off the main dining room.

Dooley hesitated.

"You come with me or you walk away," Malone said. "Your choice."

Dooley followed him. The door opened onto a corridor.

"In there," Malone said.

There was the men's room.

The place was deserted. Opposite a row of urinals were four stalls. But these were more like little rooms, with walls that went right down to the floor and right up to the ceiling.

"The one at the end," Malone said.

It was the wheelchair-accessible stall. Malone nudged

Dooley inside. He came in with him and shut the door.

"Hey," Dooley said.

"Strip," Malone said.

"What?"

"You called me and said you were Jeffrey Eccles," Malone said. "That's that kid who was found murdered. I read all about it. He was known to the police. It said in the paper he was a drug dealer."

"You said you didn't know him. If that's true, what are we—"

"Don't give me that shit," Malone said. "I'm here, aren't I? But how do I know you're not a cop? How do I know this isn't some half-assed cop sting operation?"

"Sting operation?"

"How do I know you're not trying to set me up?"

"I'm not a cop," Dooley said.

"Did the cops send you here?"

"No."

"Prove it," Malone said. "Strip. No strip, no talk."

Shit.

Dooley pulled off his jacket. He yanked his T-shirt and sweatshirt up over his head.

"Okay?" he said.

"The rest of it," Malone said.

Dooley pulled off his boots. He unbuckled his belt and then hesitated.

"Go on," Malone said. It seemed to Dooley that he was enjoying himself.

Dooley kept his eyes on Malone's as he unzipped his

jeans and lowered them. Malone went through Dooley's pockets, paying special attention to Dooley's cell phone. He seemed to know what he was looking for and he obviously didn't find it because he handed the phone back to Dooley, who stuffed it into his jeans pocket. Finally Malone said, "Let's have lunch."

He leaned against the door of the stall and watched as Dooley got dressed again. He didn't even check before he opened the door and strode out. Thank God there was no one else in the room.

Dooley followed Malone back to the booth.

Malone slid into his seat. Dooley saw that a drink had arrived for him while they were in the men's room. It looked like scotch. A double. Malone took a sip.

"So," he said, caressing the glass, "why am I talking to you? What do you want?"

Dooley looked at the amber liquid in Malone's glass. He wished he had a drink, too, to take the edge off.

"I want what Jeffie wanted," he said.

Malone looked evenly at him for a moment. Dooley wondered what kind of business he was in. A cold one, he decided, something to do with money and all the crap you had to do to make a lot of it.

"I believe you said something about pictures," Malone said.

Dooley nodded.

"Do you have them with you?"

"First we make a deal," Dooley said. "Then you get the pictures."

"In other words, you don't have them with you." Malone

smiled at Dooley. "There *are* no pictures." He said it smoothly, as if there was no question about it.

"Yeah, there are," Dooley said. "Jeffie told me he saw you back behind Jay-Zee's. He took pictures."

"Jeffrey was mistaken about seeing me," Malone said. "And since he was mistaken, there are no pictures. He admitted as much to me."

He came across like a smart guy, but there was just one thing.

"If you weren't there like Jeffie said you were, and if there are no pictures, why did you agree to meet me?"

Malone picked up his glass, swirled the liquid around in it, and took another sip.

"I was curious. I knew Jeffrey slightly. I think you know how. He knew that I have money. He knew I liked to enjoy myself. Instead of being discreet as someone in his business should be, he tried to take advantage of me. He tried to blackmail me, if you can believe it. Then I read in the paper that he died."

"He was murdered," Dooley said.

"And the next thing I know, you pop out of the wood-work. I wanted to see what you would do, how you would play it. I wondered what kind of person imagined he could squeeze money out of me with such a ridiculous bluff."

Yeah, confidence and balls.

"Well, I guess now you know, huh?" Dooley said.

"You're wasting my time," Malone said.

"I sure don't want to do that. So maybe I should be a good citizen and go have a talk with the police."

Malone laughed.

321

"You think that's funny?" Dooley said.

"Forgive me, but you don't seem the type to go running to the police."

"Yeah, well, I didn't used to be. But now I try to do the right thing."

"Like blackmailing me."

"Like telling the cops that right before he died, Jeffie went to see you—to try and blackmail you, just like you said."

"He was bluffing. He was an idiot."

"He was murdered. And I think he was murdered *because* he tried to blackmail you. Okay, so maybe he didn't have pictures. But he did see you behind Jay-Zee's. He saw who you were with."

"You think *I* killed Jeffrey?

"You have an alibi for when he was murdered?"

Dooley didn't like the way Malone kept smiling at him. Was he wrong about this guy?

"What possible motive would I have for killing Jeffrey Eccles? As I've already said, he was mistaken about what he thought he saw."

"Was he?" Dooley said. "So it won't matter to you if I tell the police what Jeffie told me? You're that sure no one else saw you that night, no one else saw who you were with? You're sure no one saw your car? You're sure that if the police start looking into it, they're not going to find anything? Because one thing I've learned about cops, they're not as dumb as some people think they are. You want to take that risk? Your alibi for that night is solid?"

A cell phone trilled—not Dooley's.

Malone dipped into his jacket pocket.

"If you'll excuse me," he said.

Dooley snuck a peek at his watch. Right on time.

"Pizza?" Malone was saying, annoyed now. "You have the wrong number." A pause. Then louder, pissed now, his sharp eyes even sharper, like knives, so that it wasn't hard to see him pressing a lit cigarette into warm flesh: "What are you—deaf? I just told you. You have the wrong number." Dooley felt his belly clench as he watched Malone flip the phone shut and drop it back into his pocket. He wished it was his hand wrapped around that glass instead of Malone's. He wished he could raise that glass and smash it right across Malone's face.

Malone turned his attention back to Dooley. "What is it that you want? Money?" He nodded as if, of course, it was. "It's always about money, isn't it?"

"You know what they say," Dooley said. "You do the crime, you have to pay—one way or another."

Malone seemed to like that. He raised his glass in a salute to Dooley, swallowed the rest of the scotch, and then he held the glass up, a signal for the waiter to bring him another one.

"How much do you want?" he said.

"Twice what Jeffie asked for."

"Twice?"

"Twice the crime, twice the price," Dooley said.

"Twice the crime?" Malone said, amused. "Correct me if I'm wrong, but no one has established that I committed any crime at all."

"That's the point, right?" Dooley said. "You don't want

anyone to establish that."

The waiter brought a fresh drink for Malone and took away the empty glass.

"You're wasting your time and mine," Malone said, swirling the ice in the amber liquid. "I'm not paying you anything. I have no reason to." He leaned back in his chair, manicured, polished, smug.

"Even if you ditch that phone," Dooley said, "there's going to be a record somewhere of the number and the fact that it belonged to you. You can count on that. They're going to find out that you knew her."

"Knew who?" Malone said.

"Lorraine," Dooley said.

"Lorraine?"

Dooley had to hand it to Malone; the guy gave away nothing. It was as if the name meant nothing to him.

"Lorraine McCormack. She had your cell phone number."

Malone smiled. "A lot of people have my number."

"And Lorraine was one of them. And someone killed her, in case you missed that on the news."

Still nothing.

"That phone call you just got," Dooley said. "That was a friend of mine. I gave him your number. Lorraine had it written in a book—she drew a little heart around it."

Malone laughed. "So?"

"She was cleaning herself up," Dooley said. "She was getting her life together. I talked to her sponsor, you know, from the meetings she used to go to. She said she thought Lorraine was doing it for a guy. She was doing it for you, right?"

"I don't know who you're talking about."

"Cut the crap," Dooley said, louder than he had intended, loud enough that a couple of suits at the next table turned in his direction. "Jeffie saw you with her." Sunday night on the late news, for the first time in his life, Jeffie had set eyes on Lorraine. He didn't know she was Dooley's mother. But he did know that he'd seen her before, back behind Jay-Zee's with his downtown guy who worked in the gold office building. "That's what this is all about—Lorraine."

Malone glanced around. Maybe to the people at the tables around them he looked calm, unruffled. But Dooley saw the tightness around his mouth when he smiled.

"You said there were no pictures," Dooley said. "But you're wrong. There's one. You give me a hard time, you try to bull-shit me, you don't tell me what I want to know, and I'll take my story and that picture to the cops and they'll be all over you, making their case and making your life miserable while they do. I can guarantee it."

"What picture?" Malone said.

"A picture of you and her"—he was going to say, *and me,* but he couldn't make his mouth form the words. "From sixteen or seventeen years ago." He waited to see if Malone would make the connection. If he did, he didn't show it. "You knew her. You dumped her. And she was trying to get her act together again so she could be with you. Am I right?"

Malone said nothing.

"Am I right?" Dooley said, raising his voice again. This time more people turned to looked at him. "You answer my questions or I walk—now."

Malone took a sip of scotch.

"I heard what happened to her," he said finally. He kept his voice low, soft, like a man trying to soothe a vicious dog before it decided to take a bite out of him. "And I'm sorry. Okay, yes, she contacted me. And, yes, I agreed to see her. But a lot of water had passed under the bridge. We were together for a few months, but that was a long time ago, and her life ..." He shook his head.

"Did you love her?"

"What?"

"Did you love her?"

"Is that important?"

Dooley surprised himself when he said, "It is to me."

Malone contemplated his glass of scotch for a moment. "She was a fun girl but, no, I didn't love her."

"She loved you."

"So she said. She was pretty intense, you know what I mean?"

He was talking to Dooley now like he knew for a fact that Dooley had known her, that she wasn't just some woman he had seen once, like Jeffie had. Dooley wondered if Lorraine had talked about him.

"My situation wasn't like hers," Malone said. "I took a year off school, had some fun, but then I had to get on with life."

"So you just split?" Dooley said, wondering if Malone would mention that there had been a child.

"Something like that."

"Then what?"

Malone shrugged. "Then nothing—much. A few teary phone calls at the beginning. A few idle threats—"

"Threats?"

"She was going to hurt herself—or so she said."

She'd managed that just fine.

"After that?"

"Nothing."

"Until maybe six or seven months ago, right?" Dooley said.

Malone didn't answer.

"Right?" Dooley said, raising his voice again.

"More like nine months ago," Malone said. "We ran into each other. She made a fool of herself. I thought that was it. Then, somehow, she found out where my office was, and she called me. She showed up at my house, for Pete's sake."

"So you killed her?"

"No."

"What was she doing with you behind Jay-Zee's?"

"I told you," Malone said, working now to stay smooth, but not doing well with it. Dooley was getting under his skin. "Jeffrey was mistaken. Lorraine had a substance abuse problem. She never did know when to stop. People like that are prone to overdose."

"She used to cry about you."

"I can't help that."

"She cleaned herself up for you."

"I never asked her to. I never asked her to do anything for me."

"It wasn't right the way she died," Dooley said. "It took the cops almost a whole day to even find out who she was."

"That doesn't surprise me," Malone said. "The way she lived—that's what it's like down there. There are people

327

who see a body lying half-naked behind a dumpster and what do they do? Do they call the police, like any normal person would do? No, they take her money, her wallet, any pills they find that they think they can sell. That's the kind of people she hung around with."

Dooley studied Malone while he thought about what he had just said.

"You know who I am, right?" he said.

"Some scumbag friend of Jeffrey Eccles," Malone said.

Right.

"Did she put up a fight?" he said.

Malone stared evenly at him.

"They said there were bruises on her arms. Did she put up a fight?"

Nothing.

"I bet Jeffie did, though," Dooley said.

"Look, you came to me for money—I'm sure we can come to some kind of agreement. You give me that picture of Lorraine and me. You forget she had my phone number. We can work it out. What do you say we get together tomorrow, somewhere a little more private, where we can do the exchange?"

"Now you want to pay me off, even though you weren't behind Jay-Zee's that night and you have nothing to do with what happened to her?"

"My clients pay me well for my advice—for my reputation. It's worth it to me to keep the police out of my life."

"So you want to meet me and pay me and maybe do me like you did Jeffie?" Dooley shook his head. He started to get up.

"Be reasonable," Malone said, soothing, very soothing. "You give me something I want, I give you something you want."

"What does the D stand for?" he said.

"What?"

"The D—Ronald D. Malone. What does it stand for?"

Malone's lips stretched into a smirk.

"David," he said.

David. Not Dooley.

"She fed you a line, huh?" Malone said.

Apparently she had, not that Dooley minded, not now that he'd met the guy.

He glanced around and was surprised to see Randall coming past the maitre d' so soon. He hadn't been sure whether Warren would be able to get hold of him. But he had. Myers was right behind him. A couple of uniformed police officers followed. Forks and glasses paused in midair as people turned to watch them march through the dining room and stand at the opening to the booth where Dooley was sitting.

"Jeffie fought back," Dooley said. "They have blood. They're going to go for DNA."

Malone sat where he was, but he wasn't smiling anymore.

"Ronald Malone," Detective Randall said. "We'd like to talk to you about Lorraine McCormack and Jeffrey Eccles."

■ ■ ■

Dooley called Beth and told her he couldn't meet her at seven o'clock after all because the police needed him to make a formal statement. He said it would help to get his uncle released.

"They found the person who did it?" Beth said.

"Yeah," Dooley said. He knew he would eventually have to tell her who that person was. But when he did, it would be in person, not over the phone. "I'll call you, okay?"

"Sure," she said. "Tell your uncle I said hi." There was a pause. "That sounds kind of lame, doesn't it?"

"I'll tell him you were asking about him. He'll like that."

■　■　■

Dooley's uncle got out the next afternoon. The first thing he wanted to do was go home, take a shower, and put on some clean clothes. The next thing he wanted to do was cook what he called a decent meal. He wouldn't let Jeannie or Dooley do a thing. He poured some wine for Jeannie and a Coke for Dooley and sat them down at the kitchen table. They could watch—in fact, he seemed to want them there, although he didn't come right out and say so. He didn't say anything about what had happened, either. He just cooked and drank wine and smiled at Jeannie, and then they all ate together. Dooley left them both in the living room while he cleaned up the kitchen. But his uncle didn't stay there. He came into the kitchen and put on an apron to help Dooley.

"It's okay," Dooley said. "You stay with Jeannie."

"Jeannie's okay on her own for a little while," his uncle said. He rinsed a couple of plates and put them in the dishwasher. He said, "Your friend Jeffrey could have saved everyone a lot of grief if he'd just come out and told you he saw Lorraine."

330

"He didn't know I knew her," Dooley said. "He never met her."

His uncle digested this. He rinsed some cutlery and put that in the dishwasher.

"About the money," he said.

Dooley had the tap running, filling the sink with hot water so he could tackle the pots and the broiler pan. He turned it off and looked at his uncle.

"I wanted you to have a chance," his uncle said. "The first time I went to see you, you were so messed up, you were practically climbing the walls. You remember that? And what you did—you were fifteen years old. When I was a kid, fifteen-year-old boys were out playing hockey or softball. They weren't doing what you were doing. Getting locked up was probably the best thing that ever happened to you."

Dooley wasn't sure he'd go that far.

"I wanted her to stay away from you, that's all," his uncle said. "She'd made a mess of her life and yours. I didn't want her to make things worse, not when it looked like you might have a chance. Maybe I shouldn't tell you this. Maybe you don't want to hear it. But she was willing, Ryan. I didn't exactly have to twist her arm to get her to take the money and stay the hell away from you."

"She knew," Dooley said. He had been chewing it over ever since he'd visited the cemetery. "You said they never told her about your sister, but she knew. I figure she found out when she was thirteen or fourteen." Dooley explained about the picture he had found. "Did you tell her?"

"No."

"You think maybe your parents did?"

"If they did, they never told me." He looked hard at Dooley. "I have something for you, Ryan," he said at last.

Dooley waited.

"It will have to wait until tomorrow, when the bank opens," his uncle said.

Twenty-One

Dooley's uncle came out of the bank with a manila envelope in his hand. Dooley watched him look both ways before darting out into a gap in the traffic and jogging over to the coffee shop where Dooley was waiting for him. He was breathing a little harder than normal when he dropped into the chair across from Dooley and eyed Dooley's coffee.

"You want one?" Dooley asked.

His uncle shook his head.

"This is for you," he said, handing Dooley the envelope.

Dooley hefted it, fingered it, but he couldn't tell what was inside.

"I got a call," his uncle said. "This goes back a couple of years. Some guy—it turned out he was a neighbor—tells me it's a miracle she hadn't done it already, the way she led her life."

Done it? Done what? Dooley thought about asking, but decided against it. His uncle would get to it. It was better to let him tell it in his own way.

"The paramedics said it looked like it was mostly for

show," his uncle said. "A nice big gash, but not deep. She was out cold, but it wasn't from blood loss. It was the booze and the pills. She didn't have enough of either in her system to do the job, though."

Some show, Dooley thought.

"The fire, though—if the neighbor hadn't smelled something, that might have done the trick," his uncle said. "She might have taken a few people with her, too."

Jesus, after everything that had happened, he still hadn't heard one good word about Lorraine. Her life was misery after misery, a real fuckup.

"Those were scattered around," his uncle said said, nodding at the envelope. He stopped talking then, and Dooley understood that he was supposed to open it.

There were more envelopes inside. Letters. Half a dozen—no—nine. Nine letters. One was addressed to Lorraine at a post office box Dooley had never heard of. The other eight were addressed to someone named Patrick Ryan Dooley. Dooley glanced up at his uncle, but his face gave nothing away.

Dooley picked up the envelope addressed to Lorraine and opened it. There was another envelope inside. Like the other eight, it was addressed to Patrick Ryan Dooley. Unlike the other eight, this one had been opened and its contents presumably read before it was put back into its envelope, sealed in a second envelope, and mailed back to Lorraine. Dooley pulled out the two sheets of paper—pink—and unfolded them. He skimmed the letter and then went back and read it again slowly. He checked the date. He'd been six months old when it had been written.

He refolded the sheets, put them back into the envelope, and laid it flat on the table. He picked up the other eight envelopes—still sealed after all these years—and lined them up according to the dates on the postmarks.

Nine envelopes in all, and what a story they told.

"She always said I had my dad's name," he said.

His uncle didn't say anything.

In fact, he had Lorraine's father's name—her birth father. Her birth mother, according to the first letter, written by Lorraine, had died right after Lorraine was born.

Lorraine had originally registered Dooley as Ryan Dooley McCormack. Then, when she finally had an address to go along with the name she'd managed to find, she'd had his name legally changed. She'd dropped the McCormack and made him Ryan Dooley. Then she'd written that first letter to her father in loopy girlish handwriting, telling him all about herself and her little boy, telling him, "I can't wait until he meets his grandpa." He pictured her waiting for the reply, checking her mail box every day, antsy and anxious, until finally she'd opened the box and found an envelope addressed to her. The envelope she had been waiting for. But when she opened it—not a word from her father. No, just her letter, returned without a word of acknowledgment.

Seven more letters had all been returned unopened, the words, "Return to Sender," scrawled across them, the pen biting into the paper of the envelope.

The final letter, also unopened, had also been returned, but this time the envelope had been stamped "Moved—Address Unknown." That was the end of the correspondence.

Dooley imagined how confused she must have felt when she found out about the first Lorraine. She'd acted out over that discovery. She'd also begun the search for her real parents—and look how that had turned out.

He stacked the letters and slipped them back into the manila envelope.

"To give her some credit, she must have really worked at finding him," his uncle said. "The records were sealed. It couldn't have been easy for her to track him down."

And there it was—the first positive thing Dooley had ever heard his uncle say about Lorraine.

"You said you found these when … you said it was a few years back," he said.

"Two years ago this past June."

"Around the time I was arrested that last time," Dooley said.

"Turns out it was the day after," his uncle said.

"Turns out?"

Dooley's uncle looked at him for a few moments, like he was trying to decide how to answer or, maybe, whether to answer.

"I asked her about you while she was still in the hospital," he said finally. "I asked where you were."

Dooley bet she had no clue.

"She was a little vague on the subject," his uncle said.

There you go.

"Anyway," his uncle went on, fiddling with a packet of sugar that Dooley hadn't used, avoiding eye contact now, "when I finally tracked you down …" He shrugged. It was a few seconds before his eyes met Dooley's. "She was right back in it. I know she was your mother. She was my sister."

Except she wasn't. Not really.

"She was a baby when we got her. Not even a year old." His uncle picked at the edges of the sugar packet, folding it and unfolding it.

"Maybe it explains something about the way she was," Dooley said. "It's hard enough sometimes, not knowing where you belong."

Dooley's uncle shook his head slowly.

"I went out there to see you the first time because I wanted to see what kind of screwed-up kid she had raised," he said. "I told myself I wasn't surprised, given how fucked up she was. I went back the second time because I felt sorry for you. After that—" He shrugged. "Fifteen is pretty young— too young to give up on a person. I thought maybe if someone took you in hand, you could turn out okay."

"But I'm not related to you. You're not really my uncle."

"Lorraine was my sister, even if she was adopted. That makes you my nephew and me your uncle. I don't have a problem with that. Do you?"

Dooley didn't know what to say.

"I gave her some incentive to stay away from you," his uncle said.

"She probably wouldn't have come to see me anyway," Dooley said, although he thought she might have, maybe once. Or maybe not.

Probably not.

Dooley thought for a moment before meeting his uncle's eyes.

"That day you said you were going downtown to see

337

your financial advisor ..." Larry Quayle had had no record of an appointment.

"I went to meet Lorraine. She was a no-show."

"And the night she died?"

"Same story. I went to talk to her. When she was at the house that time, she told me that she wanted to get involved in your life again. She tried to convince me that things would be different this time. I wanted her to stay the hell out of it. The night she died, I went to see if we could come to some kind of arrangement. Instead we got into an argument. She told me she'd already made contact with you and there was nothing I could do about it. I was pretty pissed off."

Pissed off enough to get drunk and lose track of time? Dooley couldn't believe it. Did his uncle really care that much?

"She was trying to make changes."

"But with her track record ..." He shook his head again. "Maybe I should have given her a little more credit. I'm sorry."

Dooley didn't know what to say. He hadn't felt any differently than his uncle had. If his uncle had been wrong not to give her a second chance, so had Dooley.

"If you want to make alternative living arrangements," his uncle said, "I'll understand."

"You want me to move out?" Dooley said. Where would he go?

"I want you to stay. But after what happened ... if you'd rather not live with me, I'd understand."

"I didn't give her much credit, either," Dooley said. Even now, he wasn't sure that he'd been wrong.

"You want to think it over?"

Dooley shook his head. "I already made up my mind."

■ ■ ■

Dooley looked up from the scanner when he heard the electronic bell sound over the video store door. Detective Randall walked in. He came straight to the counter where Dooley was scanning returns.

"How's it going, Ryan?" he said.

"You tell me," Dooley said.

"How about I buy you a cup of coffee?"

Kevin, who had been coming up an aisle toward the cash when Detective Randall came in, said, "Break time's not for two hours, Dooley."

Randall glanced at Kevin, pulled out his ID and said, "Official police business."

Kevin stared at the ID. He didn't say anything as Dooley came out from behind the counter, went into the back room to grab his jacket, and walked with Randall to the coffee shop a couple of doors down from the video store.

"I thought you'd like to know," Randall said after he'd put some coffee in front of Dooley. "Malone made a deal."

"What kind of deal?"

"We got him on Jeffrey. His DNA is a match for what we found under Jeffrey's fingernails. We also got him on your mother. What was stolen from her—we held that back. Your uncle said she had a purse with her when she got out of his car. He said there was a bottle of prescription medication inside." Anti-depressants, he'd told Dooley. "Malone as good as told you that the purse was gone by the time she was found. He knew there were pills in the purse, and he knew she didn't have any ID."

"He could say he was just assuming," Dooley said.

"He could try. He could also try to explain how he knew she was found behind a dumpster," Randall said. "The only thing we released was she was found in an alley."

"The person who found her might have told someone. Word gets around."

Randall gave him a look. "Which side are you on, Ryan?" he said. "Besides having him for Jeffrey, we have traces of Lorraine's blood in his car from where she cut herself. We have him unaccounted for during the time frame when she was murdered. We have traces of narcotics. And the best one—we have a usable fingerprint from the dumpster. We got him. You did good."

Good, but too late. He stood up, ready to go, then turned back to the detective.

"Jeffie told me that Malone reminded him of me, but I don't see the resemblance, do you?"

Randall studied him.

"Maybe a little," he said. "Around the eyes and the mouth. And maybe the cheekbones."

■ ■ ■

Dooley had a one-thirty dentist appointment the next day. There was no point in going back to school, so he decided to go up to Beth's school and surprise her. He was standing out on the street when the bell rang and girls came flooding out of the building. When Beth saw him, her face lit up. She broke away from the girls she was with and came running toward him.

A car horn tooted just as she arrived.

Dooley glanced over his shoulder. It was a midnight blue Jag. The driver's side window whirred down.

"Beth," a voice called. Nevin's voice. "I'm glad I caught you. Here." A hand came out the window. There was a sweater in it—a soft blue sweater that Dooley recognized. "You left it at the cottage on the weekend. My mother's been nagging me to get it back to you."

Beth looked from the sweater to Dooley. She wasn't smiling anymore. Dooley thought, I'm not the only one with secrets.

ooley was contemplating the possible consequences of putting his fist through the wall of his bedroom when his uncle called up to him.

"You've got company."

Company? What company could he possibly have?

He got up off his bed and headed downstairs.

He saw her before his foot hit the third step: Beth.

She was standing on the mat in the front hall. Usually when she dropped by, she chatted comfortably with Dooley's uncle. His uncle was standing in the front hall with her, but neither of them was talking. They both turned when they heard Dooley on the stairs. Beth looked up nervously at him. Jesus, now what?

His uncle tactfully retired to the kitchen. Beth glanced around, frowning.

"Do you think we could go outside?" she said.

The weather had turned during the night. Fall was past tense. Winter was now. And she wanted to go outside? Not a good sign. It meant she wanted to talk to him somewhere

where there was no chance his uncle would overhear. It meant she was going to dump him.

"Okay, sure," he said, trying to hide the dead feeling inside him. He grabbed his jacket from the closet and stepped out onto the porch with her. He had to hand it to her—she looked at him full on. She wasn't shying away from what she had come here to do.

"It's about Nevin," she said.

Here it comes, he thought. He had to fight the urge to pummel something—the reinforced front door, the porch railing, the brick exterior of his uncle's house—something that would bloody his fists and make physical the pain that was ripping him apart.

"I'm sorry," she said.

Right.

"My mother really likes him. She's been friends with his parents forever. They helped her a lot after my father died."

All the more reason, he supposed.

"I've known him for a long time, too."

It just got better and better.

"He never came near me when Mark was alive." Mark was her brother. "I think he was afraid to." Here she offered a faint smile. "Anyway—"

He couldn't stand it. He couldn't take the tension that was building as she prefaced what she had to say.

"Look, Beth—"

"My mother would probably think she was in heaven if I went out with Nevin," she said. "I know she would. And I know Nevin likes me, too. I'm pretty sure that's why he acts

343

the way he does."

Yeah. Chauffeuring her around in that Jag of his. Taking her on in impromptu debates. Dropping in on her and scoring eager invitations to dinner from her mother. Spending a weekend with her up at some country place that, Dooley bet, had all the conveniences of home, plus a waterfront view.

She looked down at the steel-gray paint of the front-porch floor.

"It's my fault, too," she said.

It felt like a hand had reached right into Dooley, had grabbed his stomach, and was squeezing it and twisting it all at the same time.

"I was mad when I found out about your mother," she said. Her eyes met his again. He looked deep into them but couldn't see himself reflected there. "And I was mad when I heard you'd been in the building. I thought you were checking up on me."

"I guess I was," he said. Jesus, *I guess?* Could he be more of a weasel?

"And I should have told you where my mom took me for the weekend, except ..."

Except by then she probably thought it was none of his business.

Her eyes slipped away from his again. Her fingers picked at one of the buttons on her coat.

"His parents are my mom's best friends," she said. "That makes him hard to avoid. The thing is ..." She shook her head. She looked annoyed.

Dooley closed his eyes.

"I don't know how to say this," she said. "I don't want you to think—" She took one of his hands in hers. He opened his eyes. "I was mad," she said, "because I thought I knew you."

Jesus, the best thing that ever happened to him, and he had fucked it up by fudging the truth. Fudging? There he was, being a weasel again. He had lied to her. To Beth, of all people. Okay. Time to come clean.

"I thought if I told you about my mother, you'd—"

"I love you," she said.

He stared at her.

"There, I said it. If you don't feel the same way, I'll understand. But I wanted you to know. What happened before I met you, all that stuff with your mother, that's not you. At least, it's not the you that I know. And Nevin—he's not a bad person. Actually, he's pretty nice. But he acted like a jerk when he returned my sweater. He did it on purpose. He doesn't like you."

No kidding.

"So, anyway," she said, picking at the button again, uncertain again, "I just wanted to tell you that. And, like I said, if you don't feel the same way—"

He caught hold of her other hand and pulled her to him. He didn't know what to say, so, instead, he kissed her.

About the Author

Norah McClintock is the author of more than thirty novels for young adults. She is a five-time winner of the Crime Writers of Canada's Arthur Ellis Award. Her books have been translated into more than a dozen languages. She lives in Toronto with her family.